Laughter in a . ͏od

First published in the United Kingdom in 1999 by

Dewi Lewis Publishing
8 Broomfield Road
Heaton Moor
Stockport SK4 4ND
+44 (0)161 442 9450

All rights reserved

The right of Peter Gilbert to be identified as
author of this work has been asserted
by him in accordance with the
Copyright, Designs and Patents Act 1988

Copyright ©1999
For the text: Peter Gilbert
For this edition: Dewi Lewis Publishing
Front cover photograph: Pat O'Hara, Tony Stone Images

ISBN: 1 899235 12 4

Printed and bound in Great Britain by
Biddles Ltd, Guildford and King's Lynn

2 4 6 8 9 7 5 3

Laughter in a Dark Wood
Peter Gilbert

DEWI LEWIS
PUBLISHING

The End

Bernard Steinway woke suddenly. It was still dark. He was in a cold sweat. He looked at the clock, it was five a.m. – thank God he didn't have to get up yet. Instead, he could go on suffering for as long as he liked – for a couple of hours anyway. He felt lousy, as if the bottom had fallen out of his life. He'd had another of those nightmares about Olivia. There was nothing unusual about that. For months now he had been woken up regularly by the psychic secret police; they always arrived about the same time, gathered round his bed and drove him from sleep. This was just another routine enquiry. In this dream Olivia was being attacked by lions in a room full of people so absorbed watching television, that they ignored what was going on. He had woken up at precisely the moment she had screamed and called out to him for help.

Although they had been apart for years now he still found their separation very hard to bear. Sometimes, he thought he'd never get over it. He reached his hand out across to the other side of the bed – no, she wasn't there. He stretched his other hand out for a Gitane, lit it and inhaled deeply, feeling the consolation of the nicotine spreading around inside his lungs. Every Gitane tasted just as good as every other. That at least was something you could depend on. Not like women, he'd never been able to rely on them. And anyway they didn't come in packets of twenty. He laughed, at the same time realising it wasn't much of a joke. But what was all this smoking doing in the deep darkness inside him, a region he knew so little about he found it hard to believe it really existed. In the last few years he'd noticed that his chest had seemed to change shape, becoming heavier and deeper, so something must be going on in there. Just his luck that one of his greatest pleasures in life should almost exactly equal his greatest anxiety – that of getting lung cancer in the next ten or fifteen years, or even tomorrow.

Despite a rising feeling of anxiety, Bernard carried on smoking while he listened to the wind rattling and whistling in the window frames. He remembered how it was on nights like these when his friend Maurice Hasselblad was over from Italy on one of his business trips, that he would run around the flat shouting: 'All hands on deck. Batten down the hatches. Man the mainbrace.' Yes, when the wind was as strong as this, Bernard's flat, at the top left-hand corner of the building (a position which sometimes made him add to his address the words, 'opposite the stamp') really did feel like a ship in a gale. Perhaps he should try to give up smoking, although when he'd suggested doing so in the past to his ex-therapist, Dr Lear, he'd always said: 'No, this is no time to give anything else up Bernard.' That was a long time ago but not much had changed. Perhaps he was still right.

How long had Olivia been gone now, was it four years, five, maybe it was even six? The car was B registration, so it must be five. His mother-in-law always added on a year but he never believed her. Recently their accountant had begun to talk about their getting a legal separation, but he wasn't separated – he was scrambled. There were other things he couldn't remember either. He could never remember the name of the hotel in Venice where they'd spent their honeymoon. He remembered the pale pink lamps on the tables in the restaurant overlooking the lagoon. He remembered the waiters eating from the serving trolley behind the bushes; and the one who always used to come over to ask them in his comic English, 'if anything was missing'. But he could never remember that name, not even when he was walking across San Marco. It was only as he stood looking at the launch, which took hotel guests back and forth across the lagoon twenty-four hours a day, that it came back to him. But a few seconds later, when he was no longer standing there, it had gone again.

He could hear her voice calling to him again now, 'Bernie, Bernie.' Her long thin arms outstretched towards him were like the fragile branches of a young tree. What had he done to deserve this? He crossed his legs, as if he were tying his ankles in a bow, somehow that always made him feel more secure. But the anguish went on gurgling away inside him anyway. It was the same old tune, muzak really. 'Give us this day our daily anguish and forgive those who never get any,' Bernard murmured to himself. Perhaps anguish was his natural milieu, God knows he'd experienced more of it than most people.

Now the dining-room table was going too. Of course it was trivial by comparison with having lost her. Still, he was going to miss that table. He loved the way the veneer turned a pale gold in the centre, as if the sun had risen there thousands of times. He'd always enjoyed polishing it. But there was something else as well. It was a link, a thread, that drew him back to his childhood. He remembered it standing in the dining-room under a Venetian chandelier of mustard yellow lilies, and lying on the floor at the age of six or seven, watching the French polisher bring the walnut table up to a rich oily glow. That at least was a happy memory.

Now he could see Olivia's face, it was full of love and anxiety, there was a terrace of frowns on her forehead. He couldn't blame her for leaving him when she did. He had been so depressed in that period of his life it was amazing he hadn't disappeared through the earth's crust altogether. Not that it was the only reason she'd left him. He remembered wishing, as Olivia was standing in the doorway, a packed bag in her hand, the tears streaming down her face, that he too could somehow get away from that wretched Steinway himself. But of course he'd never managed it, and they were still stumbling along together.

He sighed, as the memory of that awful afternoon rose uncontrollably within him, brushed off some ash that had fallen amongst the grey hair on his chest, then lit another cigarette. Lately, he had begun to wring his hands. He'd never been very successful with women, not really successful. Most of them had left him sooner or later. Maybe it was his fault. Perhaps he always chose the wrong ones? Instead of clever beautiful women, maybe he should have been content with a dull one who would have looked after him, at least that was what his sister always said.

Olivia might well have come back to him by now had she not become so obsessed with Gotsky and Potsky's movement for achieving higher human consciousness when she did. If only she'd felt as passionate about the sublime foolishness of Laurel and Hardy, instead of that pair of charlatans, things might have been very different. It wasn't Bernard's idea that they should part forever. He had simply thought, that since things were so difficult at the time, they were going to separate for a while and then come back together for the rest of their lives. What's more, Olivia had always said that she would never decide anything without first discussing it with him. Well, she had. She wouldn't come back. And he found it hard not to feel that she was being disloyal. He would never have deserted her. Sometimes, he felt so angry, he thought he'd turn his back on her in heaven, if there was such a place. But he knew he'd never do anything like that.

The funny thing was that when she'd first mentioned her interest in Gotsky and Potsky he'd hardly taken any notice at all. It was only that day, as he was driving her to the airport to visit her parents in Italy, when she had almost casually said that she could never contemplate coming back to him because of his total lack of interest in what she elusively referred to as 'The Work', that he first became really alarmed. All that night he'd lain awake thinking about what she'd said, unable to believe that she could think that anything was more important than their relationship. He was still in such a state the following morning, that he telephoned her hotel, but she was out and he had to conceal his agitation from her father by pretending he'd phoned to make sure she'd arrived safely, which only confirmed his father-in-law's belief that he was unbelievably extravagant.

From then on she was forever talking about 'The Work' and looking wistfully at him, as if she knew something he didn't, or had just finished talking to God on the telephone. Then there was that bizarre experience in the bank when she had suddenly started telling him how everyone was asleep, although they all looked perfectly wide awake to him. At first, he'd wondered if she'd gone completely crazy and he felt so anxious he could practically feel the blood pressure rising within him. He only calmed down when he realised that what she was referring to was their level of consciousness and not whether they were literally awake or not. But he never knew what to make of all that other stuff she said about cosmic consciousness and the presence of higher beings on earth who were secretly working for the good of mankind, although perhaps she had always been predisposed to believe that kind of thing. He remembered, for instance, how she would often wake him in the middle of the night because she was anxious about the meaning of life – as if he knew what it meant! Even now, Bernard only had to see a picture of Gotsky on the cover of one of his books – with his hypnotic eyes, enormous domed head, and the wax tips of his moustache pointing up towards heaven, for a great wave of anger to come over him. Sometimes, when he was looking at himself in the mirror, he imagined he saw Gotsky's face staring malevolently at him over his own shoulder. But perhaps he shouldn't even be thinking any of this. What if Gotsky really was the man who knew everything, as his followers believed. Bernard had certainly been very impressed by him himself, during the time he'd regularly visited his headquarters, when he thought it might help to bring about a reconciliation with Olivia. How would it be if he eventually found himself being confronted by him in heaven, no sooner than he had finished shaking hands with Abraham, Isaac and Jacob, and was sipping his first glass of celestial champagne.

Worst of all Olivia had met another man during one of those weekends at Gotsky's place. Not surprisingly, Bernard had disliked him from the first time he saw him sitting by her bedside in the hospital. Bernard's initial reaction to Christopher turned out to be confirmed by everything he subsequently learned about him. How he had gone to live at Gotsky's school, and had voluntarily donated ten per cent of his income for the cause – not to mention his enormous willingness to do everything Olivia told him to, however absurd. There was no doubt in Bernard's mind that had Olivia decided to take up knitting because she'd discovered it promoted spiritual growth, he would have done so as well. But Olivia never took any notice of anything he said about Christopher, no more than she ever listened to his negative remarks about Gotsky and his so called 'Work'. She always used to give him one of those unworldly looks of hers, which appeared to suggest that she was conversing with angels, or that it was just a case of 'for those who have eyes to see and ears to hear' – which he clearly didn't. But maybe, if their relationship worked out, Christopher would be better for her than he had been. Considering his gentleness, lightness and spiritual disposition, it wasn't hard to imagine them being happy together. Even so, he was very pleased that not long before he had finally managed to show Christopher exactly what he thought of him. Generosity of spirit was one thing, but expressing what he really felt proved far more satisfying. But what was the use in going over and over all this now, Bernard thought, shaking his head, as if by so doing he would somehow manage to shake out all the despair.

The only good thing about living apart from Olivia was not having to go for those tedious long walks in the country any more. He'd never enjoyed that sort of thing anyway; especially since, instead of sticking to the path, as he would naturally have preferred, Olivia would insist that they went cross country, with the result that on one occasion, he had sunk above his ankles in mud, in a field that appeared to be full of the bones of dead sheep. He had protested loudly at the time that his whole background prevented him from deriving any pleasure from that kind of thing, but she didn't take any notice. No, he had never enjoyed any of those trips to the country, or indeed hardly ever managed to tell one tree from another. He had only been brought up to appreciate the delights of day trips to the seaside. As a child his father would often insist he took the day off school so they could drive down to the coast. Once there they always followed the identical routine. First, they took a brisk walk along the seafront, while his father exhorted him to breathe in deeply to receive the full benefit of the ozone. This was followed by a plate of shellfish, then an enormous lunch that lasted for at least two hours, during which the waiters would be encouraged to gather round and watch Bernard demonstrate his prodigious appetite. Anyway, he'd always much preferred the countryside in Russian novels to the real thing. Not long ago he had been foolish enough to make a joke about this to Olivia, which unfortunately only made her even more convinced that she'd been right to leave him when she did.

But life was very lonely without her and now he would willingly have gone for those walks if they were together. Perhaps he'd never understood real loneliness before. It was certainly true that when Harry Rozensweig used to phone up all the time complaining of feeling lonely, shortly after his wife had left him, all Bernard had been able to think of to say to him was that loneliness was just a normal part of the human condition, and the best way to cope with it was to go for a ride on the Underground until the feeling passed. He deeply regretted that he hadn't been more sympathetic. No wonder Harry had stopped phoning. Well, he certainly knew now what loneliness was! And it looked as if it was going to be his constant companion for the rest of his life. Only last night he thought he saw it lurking in the shadows beyond the light on his desk. And that wasn't any rarer an experience than the anguish that often visited him in the morning while he was having coffee.

Towards dawn Bernard fell asleep again, exhausted by the shoals of thoughts which felt as if they'd been assailing his mind for hours.

Bernard's Schtuck

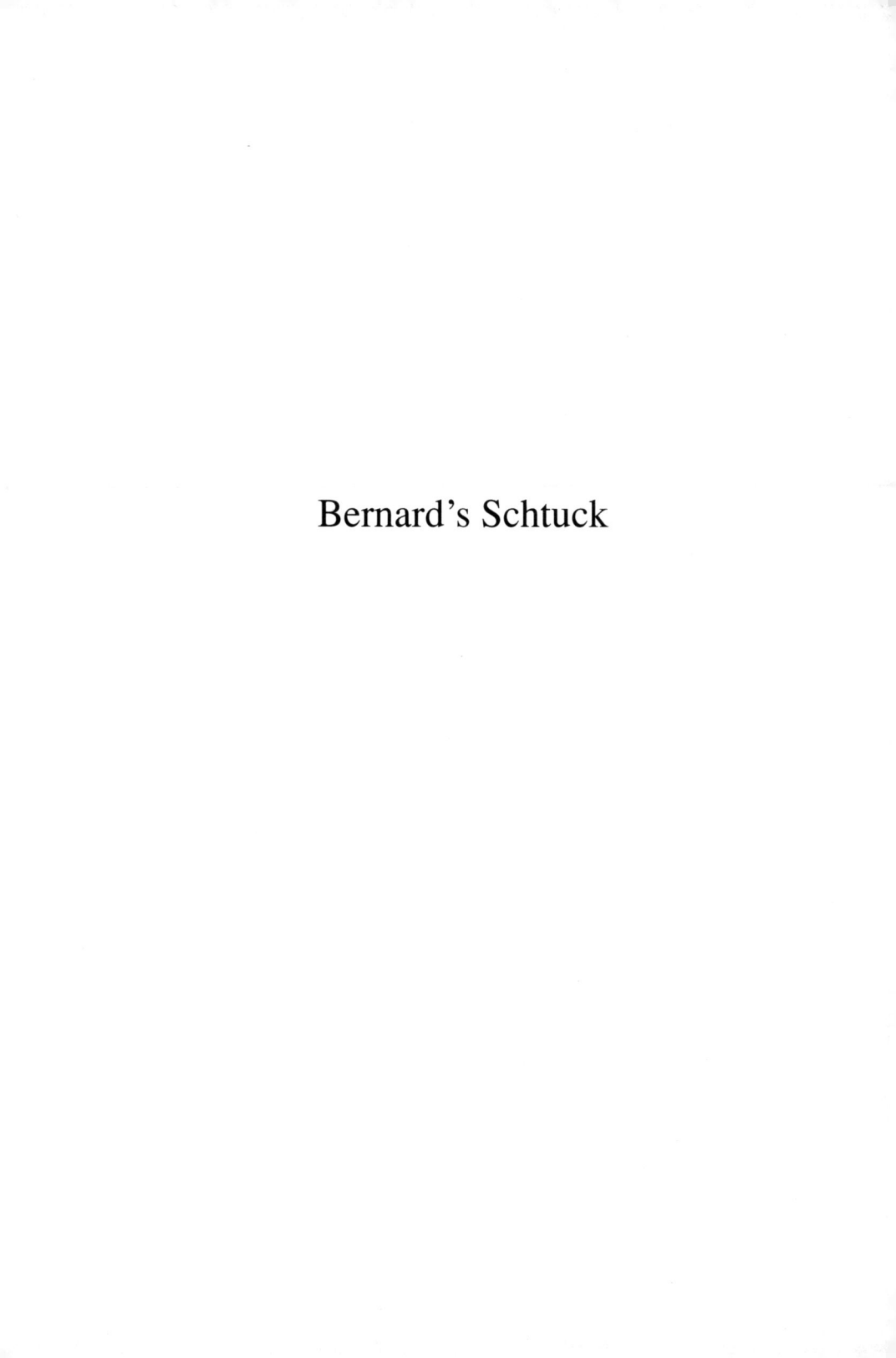

1

Of course there had been other women in Bernard's life since Olivia left him. How could it have been otherwise? He wasn't a monk or even one of life's natural bachelors, as some of his uncles had been. No, he certainly wasn't like them. He had always needed the admiring, loving and totally undivided attention of a woman for at least four hours a day just to feel he was still alive.

But to begin with – a beginning that at the time seemed to be quite without end – he was completely alone. And although outwardly he appeared to cope quite well, in reality he couldn't bear it, but did so simply because he had no choice. Within a few months of separating from Olivia he noticed that he had already begun to behave rather strangely. He talked to himself. He engaged shop assistants in long, irrelevant conversations with the result that they sometimes looked at him as if he were slightly crazy. If he was worried about anything – which was frequently the case – instead of gradually disappearing, as in the past, his worries now raced round his mind like motorcyclists on a wall of death, for hours, or even days on end. All of which made it pretty obvious that he was spending far too much time alone.

For a long time there wasn't anything Bernard could do about any of this. He was still far too much in love with Olivia to even contemplate looking at another woman. The idea of waking up in the morning with someone else in bed next to him was unthinkable (had he done so he knew perfectly well he would have felt a complete traitor to his feelings). When he did finally become aware of other women again, which must have been about a year or so after he'd started to live by himself, it was not because his love for Olivia had in anyway diminished, but because he was simply unable to repress his emotional and sexual needs any longer. Even then, on the rare occasions Bernard managed to find a woman to go out with, he almost always – however attractive she might be – spent nearly the whole evening comparing her to Olivia. Or, if by some miracle he managed to avoid doing that, he would inevitably, at some point in the evening (perhaps in answer to a simple question about what Olivia was like), ruin everything by beginning to sing her praises with such ardour and eloquence as to leave little doubt in his companion's mind that he was still deeply in love with his wife. Even Bernard realised that this was a mad way to have behaved. More than once during one of his flights of eloquence, he'd noticed the woman shifting about in her seat in the restaurant, as if she would have done anything to get up and leave him right there and then, but was simply too inhibited, or perhaps too well brought up to do so. Yes, to them Bernard must have seemed just like one of those people who, when you ask them how they are, proceed to tell you their whole life story, however long it takes, or however painful it might be to listen to. The sort of person who in those days Bernard was very close to becoming. So perhaps it was just as well – at least for the sake of any of the women he might have met – that the occasions when he took someone out were extremely rare.

Not that Bernard wasn't still a very attractive man. At the age of thirty-three he would have fitted the cliché 'tall, dark and handsome' perfectly – had it not been that he walked with the stoop of the intellectually curious and slightly perplexed, that his hair had long since turned grey, and that his undoubted good looks were marred by a touch of the Slav, a certain heaviness in his features, which he had probably inherited from his Russian forbears. He was always elegantly, if not rather eccentrically dressed – preferring bow ties to ties – an outward expression in his mind at least, that he wasn't entirely serious about life – and never left home without first putting a silk handkerchief in his top pocket. He bought his shirts from the best shirtmakers and his shoes were of the finest quality, although because of his limited means he had only a few shirts and two pairs of shoes. (He was then living on a small inheritance from his favourite aunt, the widow of a minor Belgium aristocrat who, shortly after the first world war, had made a fortune manufacturing racing bicycles). In the summer months he was inclined to wear a Panama hat and a linen suit, and often had a rose in his buttonhole. Because of his appearance Bernard looked more like a nineteenth-century Russian poet, or an old sepia photograph of a man sitting at a café in Venice at the turn of the century, than someone of our own time. This had the curious consequence that women over seventy, especially if they came from Central, or Eastern Europe, seemed to find him almost irresistible.

There was also something of the shabby genteel in the way Bernard looked, which rose on occasion (at least in some people's minds) to the aristocratic. And indeed there was something rather aristocratic about him. He was often capable of being rather aloof and disdainful, and when he wasn't consumed by self-doubt, he could even be arrogant. But the real source of Bernard's aristocratic manner lay neither in the way he dressed, nor in his attitude towards other people, but in a profound maladjustment. The truth was that Bernard Steinway was a displaced person, not displaced in the sense that he was a refugee or an emigré but in the sense of being estranged from his time. In an age when people were addicted to action and were driven by the desire to achieve, or at least to have successful careers, Bernard had what used to be known as a retiring disposition. One of the few things he knew for certain about himself was that he definitely wasn't a man of action. He preferred, above all, the reflective life and even a minute experience could keep him busy for weeks. He sometimes thought of himself as a sort of hippopotamus, standing up to his haunches all day in a muddy pool endlessly chewing things over. He did so little that even the smallest action: changing a light bulb, posting a letter, or going to the car wash, was capable of giving him enormous satisfaction. He didn't envy his contemporaries their endlessly busy lives. Often when he saw men hurrying along the street, briefcase in hand, no doubt on the way to some office or business meeting, he experienced an enormous sense of relief that he didn't have to live like that; didn't have to commute; wasn't cooped up all day in an office; wasn't answerable to anyone. Yet, despite his curiously inert and languid ways and odd outlook, Bernard had always thought of himself as a perfectly ordinary human being. It was only recently that he'd started to become dimly aware that most people found him deeply eccentric, as if he were a latter day Oblomov, or one of those house guests in a Chekhov play who never leave.

But he wasn't happy. Being sceptical about how other people lived didn't in itself provide him with anything to believe in, or a way of passing the time. He felt isolated and without any real sense of purpose. And he worried constantly about money almost as if it had become a part of the very texture of his psyche. The trouble was he'd been born too late, eighty or a hundred years too late, to be precise, because what he was par excellence, was a natural member of the leisure class, a class that unfortunately, from his point of view, no longer existed. If it had, at least he would never have felt lonely, because then the world would have been full of people like him each nurturing their eccentricities in their own way. But it didn't and he was stranded in the present, and feeling intermittently nostalgic for the age of the walking stick wasn't a solution to anything. He needed money. He needed to find a more meaningful and substantial way of life. Nostalgia was no longer enough.

No, it was definitely nothing to do with either his looks or appearance that he almost totally lacked feminine companionship. The real problem was that in the course of his nearly non-existent life he had no job, or career, few friends and hardly ever went anywhere – he simply almost never met anyone he didn't know already. If only he'd been interested in Serbo-Croat, Greek, or even Yoga; interested enough that is to have gone to an evening class, things might have been very different. Yoga, of course, would have been particularly satisfactory, because who knows what beautiful and supple creature might have been lying on the mat in front of him as he struggled to do the postures with that stiff corpus of his, parts of which were practically extinct having hardly been used for years. But there was little point in dwelling on this, because Bernard simply didn't have any interests of that kind. Instead of passing his spare time with other people (and what part of it wasn't spare!) he spent most of his evenings alone at home, making futile attempts to read, an activity he found particularly difficult, since recently his attention span seemed to have shrunk to barely ten minutes. Otherwise he would just sit and stare at his reflection in the dark windows of his study. Although why he persisted in calling it his study was a mystery, as it had been years since he'd seriously studied anything. The only thing Bernard had to console himself with was the thought that, since he hardly ever went out, he must have an inner life.

Bernard's flat which, with its spacious and elegantly furnished rooms, oriental rugs, heavy dark furniture and chandeliers, might easily have been the Moscow home of one of Chekhov's characters (with the most hopeless of whom Bernard had always identified, as if they were his own relatives), became more than ever at this time a place of refuge, an overcoat to wrap himself in, a shelter from reality.

It was on one of those endless solitary evenings, when he had been feeling listless and depressed, having failed to do anything more constructive yet again than to stare for ages at the reflection of his confused looking face in the window opposite his desk, that he began the first significant relationship he had with anyone since Olivia left him. It was about nine o'clock, just after he had finally given up trying to read and turned on the television, more or less at random, something he often did at the time to deaden what was going on in his mind, although he usually regretted it afterwards. Only this time he had no regrets, because it was then that he saw Odette Fitou, the heroine of a series about the French Resistance, for the very first time.

Like other men, Bernard had occasionally been obsessed by one of those delicious looking newscasters, who seem to have been chosen because they make even the most mundane news item absolutely compelling. But this was an entirely different experience, and after watching the programme for barely half an hour, he found himself becoming totally enchanted by her. From then on he never missed a single episode, and during the next few weeks some of his happiest hours were spent lying on the chaise longue with Odette, hours in which, because of his growing infatuation, he was completely oblivious that on any particular evening, he might well have been sharing her with a million or so other men. It wasn't long before he realised that the reason he found her so attractive was because she was so much like Olivia. She had Olivia's eyes, olive skin and long graceful neck. She even had similar small delicate ears. Bernard had always marvelled at Olivia's ears, because they seemed to him the final proof of how well made she was and, much to her annoyance, he occasionally pointed them out to people as if they were a famous tourist attraction. It was her ears also which sometimes made Bernard think that Olivia had been destined to be a gazelle, but owing to some error had entered existence through the wrong door. It wasn't only the way Odette looked that reminded him of Olivia, but also her gracefulness and her aura of tranquillity. This was so evident in a scene where she was nursing a sick airman. He had almost died of envy. Bernard became so obsessed by Odette that it wasn't long before, absurd as it may seem, he began to think that, since both their names began with O, she must somehow have been meant for him.

Their relationship was doomed right from the beginning, because during all those weeks in which Bernard's feelings for Odette were flowering the series was inevitably drawing towards its close. When the end finally came – which fortunately did not entail Odette being either captured, or tortured by the Gestapo, something he could hardly have endured – he still found it almost impossible to hold back his tears as she disappeared beneath the credits for the last time. Even then Bernard did not give up all hope of ever seeing her again. Ever since he first realised how he felt he had begun to try to think if there might not be some way of extracting her from the television set and having her entirely to himself. Once he could no longer depend on seeing her twice a week, what had been little more than a daydream became a far more urgent matter. Ah, if only he'd fallen in love with her seventy or eighty years earlier and Odette had been just an ordinary actress, then there would have been no problem in getting to meet her. All he would have needed to have done would have been to have waited outside the theatre after the show, or sent flowers to her dressing room with a card attached inviting her for dinner. It wouldn't have been impossible that, after a few weeks of pursuing her in this way, she would have ended up as his mistress. But as things were there wasn't much he could do. After all, he couldn't very well hang around outside a TV studio, especially when he knew perfectly well that she was no longer inside. He didn't even know where the programme had been made. So, the only possibility would have been to have written to her. But it seemed to him that a letter from an unknown man would only be construed, at best as a fan letter, or at worst, the letter of an emotionally unstable and lonely admirer. In either case, he doubted very much that he would have received a reply. After thinking about it for several days he decided that there really was nothing to be done, and gradually Odette's face began to fade from his mind until finally she became just another memory.

2

Women were not the only thing that Bernard had to worry about. Everything worried him. Not that there was anything particularly new about that – the truth was he had been in a bad way for years. All through his late twenties and early thirties life had become gradually more and more difficult. Often when he woke in the morning he hadn't the vaguest idea of how he was going to get through the day, or all the other days in his life for that matter, until death, the great full stop, put an end to everything. And there seemed to be so much of it still to get through, not that he knew how much, nobody knew that. Just thinking about the future made him want to stay in bed for an extra couple of hours. Life, his life in particular, seemed to stretch out in front of him like some ominous weather forecast, full of dog days and bleak grey skies. Somewhere in his late twenties, without quite realising it had happened, he had slipped into the dark wood and got completely lost. Only later did he begin to understand that what he must have been doing through all those unbelievably difficult days was rehearsing for his mid-life crisis. But, although he didn't know it at the time, things could have been worse; and when Bernard's marriage finally collapsed he more or less collapsed along with it.

It was a few months later that Bernard first started going to see an analyst. Not that he decided to do this entirely of his own accord. He never said to himself – 'What I need is an analyst'. But then, having found life so difficult for so long, it would never have occurred to him that there was any reason why seeing an analyst, then in particular, could possibly make any difference. He couldn't see how consulting any number of analysts would bring Olivia back to him. Anyway, he was by then so used to feeling awful that he wasn't entirely aware quite how much worse his life had become without her. No, in Bernard's case, it was someone else who persuaded him to go, having sensed that, when Bernard said he was perfectly alright despite everything that had happened – what he really meant was that he was all wrong. After all, how could a man with high blood pressure, a nervous skin complaint (as if even his skin was crying out for help), acute insomnia and no sense of purpose, be alright?

Unfortunately, the analyst his friend recommended (who of course turned out to be their own analyst) was too busy to take him on, which Bernard immediately found very disappointing. He had been drawn to Dr Du Maurier almost from the first, after, that is, he had recovered from an intense feeling of claustrophobia, when he was shown into Dr Du Maurier's tiny consulting room, through two heavy, thick steel doors that were attached to each other by chains. But then even his name evoked pleasant memories of a now defunct brand of cigarettes, that used to come in flat orange-red packets, and which Bernard had surreptitiously smoked whilst still a teenager. But most of all it was Dr Du Maurier's elegant appearance (he was wearing a dark blue suit and silver grey tie that day), his sympathetic and suave manner, and the way he looked at Bernard as if he already knew everything that was troubling him, which impressed him so much. An impression that was only enhanced by the fact that Dr Du Maurier's white hair and beard made him look rather like God, or at least how he imagined God must look. He was also very perspicacious, which became apparent when he suggested that the real reason Bernard was so reluctant to have group therapy (for which he had a vacancy) was not as Bernard thought, because he had always hated the idea of joining any kind of group, but because what he was really looking for was a father figure. An observation which, although it had been made quite casually, struck Bernard as a profound revelation. Straight away he began to think about all those older men he had been drawn to over the years. There had been Leo, a novelist, with whom he had had tea from time to time, and from whom he used to attempt to glean small bits of guidance about life, while trying not to appear to be doing so. Then there was Darevsky, a Russian emigré of independent means, with an incredibly self-deprecating sense of humour who was always saying: 'When I come into a room I want everyone to think someone just left.' Much later there was the poet Hugo Mosco, with whom Bernard had only spent one afternoon, but whose bleak scepticism had nevertheless made a profound impression on him. And of course there was Professor Rubervitch, who always seemed to appear in Bernard's life at crucial moments, such as when Bernard had turned round to find him having lunch at the next table in that hotel in Venice where he and

Olivia were on honeymoon. And then a few years later, there he was again standing in the doorway of Florian's as if he was bearing a message from someone.

He must have been collecting father figures for years. It was also possible that during the time he'd been reading a biography of Freud he'd even thought of him as a father figure as well. He'd certainly been very impressed by Freud's genius and enormous capacity for work, especially since Bernard at the time was finding it tremendously difficult to get up before ten in the morning. Perhaps Herman Praeger, a tailor who'd once made Bernard some trousers and whose flowing white hair and monumental features gave him the look of an Old Testament Prophet, was another one of them as well. Was that why he'd been so reluctant to leave his shop that day? Even Sam, Bernard's father-in-law, had soon become a sort of father figure to him. But that was a rather different case, because he had more or less volunteered for the position, almost as soon as he realised that Bernard hadn't got a clue about life and that if he didn't take this elderly adolescent in hand it was more than likely that he would continue floundering for the rest of his life. Perhaps it was precisely because Bernard was in need of yet another father figure that he had been so disappointed when Dr Du Maurier said he was unable to take him on as a patient. But then what could be worse than to be rejected by someone who looked so much like God, who, after all, was the father figure of all father figures, so to speak.

The analyst who in due course Dr Du Maurier referred Bernard to turned out to be quite satisfactory in the end, even if he never came anywhere near becoming a father figure. But then how could he have since he wasn't Jewish, didn't look a bit like a sage and wasn't even well dressed, as most of the others had been. If he wasn't Jewish, the fact that Dr Lear was Irish was easily the next best thing. Since the man who had presided over Bernard's coming into the world – a certain Dr Shananegan, with whom Bernard's father had often gone to the dogs at weekends – had been Irish. It seemed particularly appropriate, if not poignant, that it should be yet another Irishman he should end up consulting to try and extract himself from the schtuck he'd got into. Dr Shananegan had been a diagnostician of extraordinary powers. On one occasion, when Bernard was driving him somewhere, he remembered hearing him suddenly exclaim, at the sight of an old man limping across the road in front of them: 'Ah there's another poor divil with lumbago.' A diagnostic feat that Bernard only hoped Dr Lear would be able to equal in his own case.

Not that he had been very impressed by Dr Lear to begin with. After that first session he very nearly didn't go back at all. Dr Lear's technique had, to say the least, been rather disconcerting. Instead of asking him all kinds of questions about himself, which was what Bernard had imagined was going to happen, Dr Lear simply sat perfectly still, with his head between his hands and stared at him for what seemed like ages (although it was probably only a few minutes) while Bernard, feeling more and more uncomfortable, did everything he could to avoid looking into Dr Lear's cold blue eyes. He began by trying to make out the titles of the books on the bookshelf behind Dr Lear's chair, some of which he noticed were upside down. Then he looked out at the garden through the french windows. He even studied the ornate plaster-work on the ceiling. After a while it began to occur to him that maybe he was doing something wrong. Perhaps Dr Lear was waiting for him to go and lie down on the couch, which would at least have the obvious advantage that if he were lying down Dr Lear would no longer be able to stare at him like that. But he was much too embarrassed to ask if that was what he was supposed to do. It wasn't until several sessions later that he asked about it and Dr Lear told him that, although most people did end up on the couch, in his opinion Bernard was definitely someone who needed to keep his feet firmly on the ground. But it wasn't long after the beginning of that first session before Bernard began to talk himself, until all his worries came rushing out in a great torrent, which of course, he realised subsequently, was precisely what Dr Lear had intended should happen.

Bernard's suggestion that perhaps Dr Lear might consider accepting a smaller fee if he were paid in cash, didn't help the beginning of their relationship. No sooner had he mentioned it, although he'd only done so very tentatively, than Dr Lear became so agitated that anyone would have thought Bernard had suggested they rob a bank together, instead of engage in a little mild tax evasion. What's more he even started to tick him off: 'In any case Bernard there are people who deserve to have a reduction in the fees I charge and those who don't,' he said, giving him a stern judgemental look, in order to reinforce the point (as if Bernard hadn't already got it) that he definitely came into the latter category. 'No, Bernard from what you've already told me about yourself, I would say that it would be much better for you to pay the correct fee.' That was the end of that. Not that Bernard was very disappointed, because he'd only suggested it in the first place to placate the voice of his father inside his head, who ever since he'd arrived had been going on at him to try and get a better price by offering to pay cash. And it wasn't easy to resist the voice of a man who in this way had managed to get a reduction in the price of his final operation for cancer.

If the beginning of their relationship wasn't very encouraging, by the end of the third or fourth session Bernard began to feel much more optimistic. Dr Lear really was an excellent diagnostician, not that Bernard agreed with everything he said. He certainly didn't care for those sexual interpretations of his dreams that Dr Lear seemed to feel obliged to make, just in case Freud's ghost happened to be right there in the room with them. According to Dr Lear, Bernard was in a state of severe depression, a condition which moreover he insisted Bernard had been suffering from more or less since he'd first stepped out of the womb. He was also told that he was in an anxiety state, which came as a bit of a surprise to Bernard, because in the past few weeks he'd felt so calm he sometimes wondered if he was still alive. But of course he was quite right about that too – it wasn't calm he'd felt, but dead calm. As he listened to the unfurling of his diagnosis Bernard felt a growing sense of relief. At last there was a name for what he'd been going through for all those years. Now if anyone were to ask him what he was, he could at least say that he was a depressive personality with phobic overtones. Oddly enough Bernard found receiving his diagnosis as satisfying as if he'd suddenly been given a title.

During those first few weeks Bernard was often amazed by how perceptive Dr Lear was. Sometimes it seemed as if he'd known him for years instead of about three hundred minutes, which was actually the case. At the same time Bernard was more than a little alarmed by the ease with which Dr Lear was able to diagnose his condition. How was it possible that someone as unique as Bernard had always imagined himself to be could be diagnosed so easily? But fortunately, there was still the consolation that – if the form of his disease was commonplace, at least the content was all his very own. It was also very encouraging to hear – especially as it came after a long discussion of all his problems – that all that was required in his case was, as Dr Lear put it, 'a few small adjustments', although he had admittedly at first been rather alarmed by that phrase, which conjured up in his mind images of trepanning, the instruments for which he had once noticed nestling in a walnut box lined with blue velvet, in the window of an antique shop, and which for some inexplicable reason, for a moment or two at least, he had been tempted to go in and buy. Yes, he could just imagine Dr Lear inserting one of those small drills just above his ear in order to tighten up one of his loose screws.

It was undoubtedly because of his growing confidence in Dr Lear (heightened that day in particular perhaps by having just been told that his normally pessimistic view of life wasn't necessarily true, or unalterable) that after one of his regular sessions, Bernard had the most extraordinary experience. He was standing on the pavement outside Dr Lear's consulting room feeling rather flushed – as if his inner life during the past fifty minutes had somehow made its way to the outside when he suddenly felt that in Dr Lear he had at last found his Virgil. The man who, in time, would be able to guide him out of the dark wood, if not into Paradise, then at least into a better life.

3

Whether this was really true, and not just a momentary feeling, it was certainly the case that in only a matter of weeks after Bernard had first set foot inside Dr Lear's office, his normally passive and indolent attitude towards life slowly began to be replaced by a much more active and positive one. Even if at first this only manifested itself in Bernard's beginning to consult the lonely hearts columns of various magazines, with a view to finding some suitable, if temporary, female companionship, something he would never have dreamt of doing even a few months previously. The trouble was of course, that although he had been convinced by Dr Lear that the world was absolutely full of women who were just waiting for him to come along (almost as if at that very moment a queue was forming outside his flat), he soon discovered that deciding to look at the lonely hearts columns was one thing, finding an advertisement that either applied, or appealed to him, was something else again. There were plenty of ads for bisexual girls (he even noticed one for a bisexual accountant) but he couldn't very well reply to any of those. There also appeared to be any number of women searching for emotionally mature and financially secure men to form a lasting and meaningful relationship with. But he was hardly well off, and anyway he couldn't imagine being able to cope with anything more than a meaningless relationship right then. Almost every week he read the advertisements of professional women who'd reached the point in their careers when they were looking for someone to start a family with, which wasn't for him either. Apart from the fact that he was already married, he had always believed that the essential condition for having a child was to have ceased to be one oneself, and he was still a long way from having achieved that. Who was he to guide someone else through life when he barely knew where the signpost was himself? Then there was the question of cash. Given his meagre resources, adding to the world's population even by one could only mean having to wear polyester shirts for the next fifteen or twenty years, a sacrifice that he simply wasn't prepared to make. Anyway, hadn't he often thought that since there were far too many people already, refraining from reproducing oneself was a way of contributing to the well-being of the human race. He also didn't feel able to respond to those advertisements in which women described themselves as caring. He hated the way that word had recently become so fashionable and anyway he always took it to really mean indifference to the suffering of others. After all, how could anyone care in general any more than it was really possible to feel universal love? No, any woman who was capable of describing herself in that way definitely wasn't for him.

    Although he had grown to enjoy scrutinising these advertisements every week – which in a way wasn't all that different from the pleasure he'd always derived from studying menus outside restaurants – he soon realised it was getting him nowhere. The most effective thing to do would be to insert an advertisement himself. But what should he say? Did he even know what he was really looking for? He spent hours trying to compose advertisements and came up with such gems as: tall, dark and handsome man, early thirties, of aristocratic appearance, wit and poet (yes, well he had composed a few awful poems once so that wasn't entirely a falsehood), Rolls Royce diary owner (that was also true: Sam gave him one every year, perhaps one day he'd give him the Rolls instead), seeks sensual woman for brief affair. Then there was the more laconic: Girlfriend required for middle-aged bachelor. But he knew that wouldn't do. Apart from being too short and far too bland, it was only Bernard who thought that at the age of thirty-three he was already middle-aged. No, had he been silly enough to put that in he might well have ended up being inundated with letters from women in their fifties. In the end of course – the old Steinway personality as yet still not having been entirely replaced by a new one – he did absolutely nothing.

Then, just as he was about to give up altogether, he began to find much more appealing advertisements to reply to. And it wasn't long before he had his first real date with a woman called Monica, whose voice sounded so warm, deep and seductive over the phone that he'd wanted to climb down the line towards it right away. Since she described herself as very attractive, it all sounded very promising. But when he saw her standing outside the exhibition where they had agreed to meet he just couldn't believe his eyes. Poor Monica turned out to have the most infelicitous combination of features he'd ever seen gathered together on one face. Apart from having a huge fleshy nose and a palid complexion, she also had a moustache which, whilst not nearly as luxuriant as the one the cashier at Schmidt's restaurant had, was still quite bad enough. Unfortunately she was also short, plump and incredibly broad-chested, which probably explained her extraordinary voice. A voice as warm and deep as hers could only have been incubated in a chest as spacious as that. As if all that wasn't bad enough, Monica also had ankles that seemed to be as thick as her calves, which was particularly disturbing for Bernard who'd always had such a thing about ankles, so much so that he wasn't adverse on occasion to pulling up his trouser leg to show his own, rather well-turned ones, to other people.

The really sad thing was that Monica turned out to be just as charming as she'd sounded on the telephone, which only made him feel even more ashamed of himself for harbouring such ungenerous and chauvinistic thoughts about her, just because she didn't happen to be beautiful. Yet despite this momentary surfacing of good character, he nevertheless decided that should he run into anyone he knew while they were going round the exhibition he would definitely introduce her as his long-lost cousin from New Zealand.

If Bernard's afternoon with Monica turned out to be disappointing, his evening with Lavinia, the second woman he contacted through a lonely hearts column, was a fiasco. He should have known it wasn't going to work right from the beginning, especially since the way she had incessantly questioned him on the telephone about himself and his attitudes to women made him so anxious that he could feel the perspiration running down his sides. Of all the women he'd known only Olivia had ever had that effect on him before. In retrospect, he simply couldn't understand why he had ever accepted an invitation to go over to her place with such enthusiasm. Unless of course he was simply fascinated that a completely unknown woman was capable of making him so anxious. Yes, that must have been it: he simply couldn't resist the possibility of going to find out what she was like.

But what a mistake that was, because no sooner had he arrived at her place a few days later than she started to interrogate him all over again, as if they'd just put the phone down ten minutes before. Only now she also constantly looked him straight in the eye, as if to make absolutely certain that he wasn't lying, or trying to conceal anything from her. In person Lavinia made him even more nervous and self-conscious than she had over the phone. So much so that when she left him alone in the sitting room for a while (a room that significantly enough was full of books about psychoanalysis and feminism) to go and make coffee, he became so agitated that he wondered if, when she returned, he would be able to pick up his cup of coffee without his hand shaking. He would probably have got up and gone home right away had it not been that he'd found her so attractive, and perhaps he also half hoped that they might end up in bed together. But then how else could he have been expected to react to a beautiful, tall, dark and sensual woman, who over her jeans wore only a black silk camisole top, the straps of which fell down over her beautifully formed shoulders every now and then. Who could blame him for imagining that she had put it on especially for him, although the way she was dressed did rather puzzle him, since it seemed to contradict her whole outlook on life. There was also the not inconsequential fact that Lavinia reminded him of an old girl friend of his, who, years before, had left him and become a Lesbian (was that also more guilt for the pile?), which was significant because he always had a tendency to look for the same woman over and over again. Yes, it could only have been because he found her so attractive that he didn't leave after those first few minutes in which she had managed to make him feel more uncomfortable than he had felt with a woman ever before. Certainly, it wasn't long before he realised that nothing would come of it, and even the most fleeting liaison was far beyond anything they had in common.

There really was something very peculiar about her. Even the way she reacted to the pass he made later on in the evening after they'd come back from the restaurant was very bizzare (if you could really call it a pass, because all he'd done was to respond to what seemed to have been going on between them for some time). They were sitting on the couch and he'd simply leaned over and kissed her, which was so exciting that without thinking he suddenly said how he would like to make love to her. That seemed to make her fantastically angry, so that she pushed him away and went and sat on the other side of the room. At first Bernard couldn't understand what he'd done wrong. But his incomprehension didn't last long because it soon became apparent that what had driven her so mad was that he'd said he wanted to make love *to* her, instead of *with* her. This hardly seemed to Bernard anything worth getting so upset about, but to Lavinia that choice of preposition finally revealed that deep down he really was a nasty male chauvinist. Well, that about finished off what little rapport there was between them, and after that he just couldn't wait to get out of there, although he was such a bad leaver that it was still at least half an hour before he finally managed to get up and go. Anyway, since Lavinia was a trainee psychotherapist, if he had ended up sleeping with her it might well have been a bit like going to bed with a torch. On the way home it occurred to him that the only positive thing about the evening was that it reminded him that there are some women who manage to make even loneliness seem appealing.

After that awful episode Bernard decided that this just wasn't the way to find a woman. There probably wasn't a way, and the only thing to do was to wait for fate to lead one to him, however long it might take. But then a few days after he'd reached that conclusion he received the following letter from someone else whose advertisement he'd responded to:

Dear Bernard,
Thank you for your letter. I shall certainly be pleased
to see you at 12.15 p.m. on Saturday the 24th.
Sexually yours,
Caroline.

At first he just couldn't take it seriously. What woman would ever sign a letter to an unknown man in that way (or even to someone she knew for that matter). It simply had to be some sort of hoax and the only thing to do was to ignore it. The trouble was he couldn't stop thinking about it. What if it was really genuine? Could someone as sexually deprived as Bernard afford to ignore it? On the other hand, if it was a hoax, wouldn't he make a complete fool of himself by keeping the appointment, even if no one need ever know about it? After worrying about what to do for a few days he finally made up his mind to go, although he told himself that he was only going to satisfy his curiosity, which even he realised was nothing but pure self-deception. When he arrived at the modest suburban house from which the letter had apparently emanated, and rushed up the path, his heart beating with excitement – as if Sexually Yours was in the next few minutes about to become Sexually His – of course he found there was no one at home. At that moment he felt both foolish and frustrated. Yet instead of getting back in the car straight away, he stood there for several minutes banging on the door and ringing the bell. The house was completely deserted, and all he could hear when he bent down and looked through the letterbox, was the ticking of a clock and the fridge humming away to itself in the kitchen. Even then he wasn't quite ready to give up and, after looking round to make sure no one was watching, he stepped on to a bed of purple and yellow foxgloves and peered in through the uncurtained window of the dinning room. But there was nothing interesting to see, except arranged on the top of an oak sideboard, stood a whole crowd of alabaster saints in what for a moment looked like compromising positions. Then, a little while later, when he had finally given up and was about to go, he saw someone coming down the road checking the numbers of the houses against a letter he had in his hand, a letter no doubt identical to the one Bernard had himself received. So, at least he wasn't the only one. That was the end of Bernard's pursuit of unknown women. As far as lonely hearts columns were concerned he was resolved that the most he would ever do in future was to read them. All the same he didn't regret – with Dr Lear's encouragement of course – having given it a try even if it had ended in farce. At least that was a lot better than despair.

An African Princess

1

As things turned out it was just as well Bernard had managed to adopt such a stoical attitude towards his emotional life, because it was a long time after he'd stopped answering those lonely hearts advertisements before he met anyone else. Even then, the only reason for this change of fortune was that he suddenly and quite unexpectedly, found himself with a job. Not that he had been even remotely looking for one at the time. When after all had a sloth like him ever done anything as constructive as that? No, if anyone was responsible for Bernard being once more gainfully employed it was his father-in-law, Sam Lowy, who, at the very least, could be said to have encouraged the hand of fate to squeeze Bernard on the shoulder when it did.

This was by no means the only thing he owed Sam. Ever since Olivia's departure his father-in-law, far from refusing to have anything further to do with him, was if anything even more solicitous and friendly than ever. Almost as soon as he'd heard what had happened, Sam was on the telephone to see how Bernard was, and after that he always seemed to be phoning up to invite him out for lunch at one of his clubs, or just to inquire anxiously down the phone – 'Are you alright Bernard?'– in a voice that was so warm, that hearing it made Bernard feel he'd just had a vitamin B12 injection. Sometimes, he would even interrupt an important business meeting to go and give Bernard a ring, as if it had suddenly occurred to him that at that precise moment Bernard might just be placing the noose around his neck. Once, he telephoned from London Airport just before he was due to board Concord to fly to New York for the weekend to make sure Bernard would be alright till he got back. Many people were astonished when Bernard told them about the way Sam treated him. This was hardly how you would normally expect a father-in-law to act towards the man his daughter had just left. But Sam didn't see it like that at all. As far as he was concerned since Olivia and Bernard were still on such good terms, he couldn't see any reason why his relationship with Bernard should be in any way affected by what had happened. Of course, there was more to it than that. What really lay behind Sam's attitude was that he and Bernard had always been very close and it would have been almost as big a deprivation for him to do without seeing Bernard as the other way round. They were so close that sometimes Bernard thought he should have married Sam instead of his daughter, but then perhaps in a sense he had. At any rate, they had hit it off marvellously almost from that first time Olivia had brought him home, and Sam had proceeded to interrogate him about his prospects, as if he already sensed that, sooner or later, Bernard was going to end up as his son-in-law. He didn't even appear to mind all that much that Bernard didn't seem to have any prospects, or even the vaguest idea of what he was going to do with his life; facts which, admittedly, Bernard had tried desperately hard to conceal at the time, but which Sam, who had a remarkable facility for finding out all about people (as well as an extraordinary gift for divining whether or not they were overdrawn, and even sometimes by how much) had elicited from him in no time. It occurred to Bernard that Sam's affection for him was simply because of his enormous sense of relief, that whatever Bernard wasn't, he was at least Jewish. But undoubtedly that wasn't the whole story either. It soon became apparent that they had reciprocal and almost completely harmonious fantasies about each other. Sam had enormous admiration for anyone he considered to be a scholar or an intellectual, amongst whom for some strange reason he numbered Bernard. Whilst Bernard for his part, always held successful businessmen in the highest possible esteem (perhaps because he had been brought up surrounded by them, he somehow always thought of them as the only real grown-ups). But Bernard's image of Sam was hardly a fantasy, since Sam – who was a descendant of the great Rabbi Loew of Prague, the inventor of the first all Jewish robot, the Golem – had managed to work comparable miracles in the world of business, to those his illustrious ancestor had accomplished in the world of the spirit. In just a few years he had become so rich that he no longer knew how much money he had. An achievement which Bernard, who had only recently begun to acquire even the vaguest idea of what real life was all about, found deeply impressive, and which always made him think of Sam as a master of reality, someone who was capable of calling even life itself to heel. And of course, apart from what they thought about each other, they also had in common the fact – which

Sam never seemed to tire of reminding Bernard – that they both loved the same woman.

Sam wasn't simply very rich he was also very generous. In the elevated philanthropic circles in which he moved socially – that included such luminaries of money as the Rothchilds, the Montefiores and the Marks and Spencers – he had long been regarded as a known giver. Sam's compulsion to give away money was such that Bernard had once had occasion to say, that in his opinion, Sam had more money than sense, which must have seemed pretty funny coming from someone who obviously had neither. But then, who but a person like Sam would have begun to give away money long before he'd made any, or would have rushed out in the middle of the night to take some cash to a complete stranger, just because he'd phoned up and said he needed it. There was that unforgettable time in Switzerland when Sam had practically forced a fifty pound note on him, by insisting that if someone like Bernard wouldn't take his money, he simply didn't know what he was going to do with all the stuff. Sam was probably even more generous than Jesus Christ (who, it seemed to him anyway, mostly gave away things such as bogus tickets to the after-life!) Apart from big donations to institutions, anyone who was in Sam's company for an hour or so, always appeared to receive an excellent meal in a restaurant of their choice, or the equivalent in cash.

Sam took enormous delight in helping people in all kinds of other ways as well. He seemed to be constantly collecting people who couldn't cope with life. Years ago he had been obliged to find a place in his office for his cousin Max, a failed newsagent, not so much so that he could earn a living (Sam would have preferred to have given him money to stay away), but to restore his self-esteem. And it had obviously worked, because Max always looked tremendously contented whenever Bernard ran into him at Sam's office. But out of the whole coterie of inadequates that Sam surrounded himself with, Bernard was the only one towards whom he acted like a father.

Almost from the very beginning of their relationship Bernard began to become dependent on receiving regular doses of advice and moral support from Sam. After Olivia's departure, he became more dependent than ever. He could no longer imagine what it would be like to have to get through a whole week without seeing Sam at least once. Not that he had ever been able to take anything like all the advice Sam offered him. Even so, there was something deeply consoling in being constantly told: to get up very early in the morning; to take regular exercise; to be punctual; and never to desist from the struggle to find a worthwhile direction in life. He also gradually began to change, at least in Bernard's perception of him, from a sympathetic father-in-law into a sort of guru. And what other guru would have been prepared to do Bernard's worrying for him? On one occasion, when Bernard had been very anxious about something, Sam said, after listening to him going on about it for over an hour: 'Now Bernard, I'll tell you when you've got to start worrying.' Was it surprising then that Bernard had such a high opinion of Sam?

It was during one of Bernard's Saturday afternoon visits to swim in Sam's private pool (which Sam always rather comically insisted on referring to as his only indulgence), and to receive his usual dose of advice and moral support, that he met a strange American professor who, a few days later, offered him a job. Although the presence of Waldemar Hatrick III in Sam's library that afternoon was itself something of an accident, since he wasn't a friend of Sam's at all, but someone Siggy Wertheimer, Sam's Viennese cousin, had met outside the Vienna Opera House. The fact that Siggy had ever gone back to Vienna was little short of astonishing having insisted for years that he wouldn't return there under any circumstances. On the one occasion in the past that Bernard had ever raised the subject with him, Siggy, who was usually so placid, had suddenly launched into a passionate tirade.

'Tell me Bernard vy should I ever go back zer. Vot did zey ever do for me, except to murder nearly all my family. The Wertheimers used to be sick on the ground, but you tell me Bernard ver are zey now, ver are zey? Of course it's beautiful but zen zo is Bournemouth, and there you have such beautiful surroundings, and no memories Bernard, no memories, sank God!'

Anyway, a particular production of the Magic Flute had lured him back and in the queue for tickets he had struck up a conversation with Waldemar Hatrick and they had hit if off, though it was hard to see what Siggy, who was always so amusing, could possibly have in common with this rather dour and pompous ex-priest, unless it was simply their mutual love of opera.

The exceptionally warm way Sam greeted him that afternoon indicated to Bernard almost immediately that he was less than enchanted by Siggy's friend. This in itself was very unusual since Sam, who was quite the most gregarious person Bernard had ever known, almost always managed to find something to interest him in even the most boring of people. Sometimes Bernard thought he was the only person he had ever met who actually suffered fools gladly. Although, of course, there had been several occasions in the past when Sam had more or less insisted that Bernard attend one of his formal dinner parties, presumably in the hope that Bernard's presence would help to make the evening more bearable (Sam always having had the highest regard for Bernard's witty conversation). Not that Bernard necessarily found Sam's guests on those occasions nearly as boring as he did. He often found them quite exotic, but then where else but at Sam's would he ever have had the opportunity of meeting so many habitués of the Ritz and the Connaught? One of Sam's guests, a certain Mr Hirschman from Ohio, a huge man in a voluminous blue suit with a shiny domed head, had made a lasting impression on him, when he had suddenly got up at the dinner table and declared – almost apropos of nothing, or so it seemed to Bernard – 'That speaking for myself, I have always been a human being first and a businessman second.' A pronouncement that struck Bernard as one of the funniest things he'd ever heard, especially since everything Hirschman had been saying all evening suggested that nothing could have been further from the truth.

That particular afternoon was definitely one of those occasions on which Sam was more than usually pleased to see him.

'Well, I wondered when you were going to appear,' Sam said, jumping up and simultaneously pumping his hand and patting him on the back, the moment Bernard came in through the french windows, 'I was just going to give you a ring. Anyway, now you're here at last let me get you a cup of tea. I'm sure you'll be pleased to hear that there is still some of Irena's chocolate cake left.' Irena was the Lowy's Hungarian housekeeper, whose patisserie was so extraordinary that probably even God himself was looking forward to tasting it.

'Thanks Sam I'd love some. It's so hot today don't you think?' Bernard said, fanning himself with his Panama hat rather theatrically.

'Yes, I suppose it is. Oh, I'm sorry, this is Professor Hatrick and his wife Marilyn. They've come to look at the house. Siggy and Hannah you know of course.'

'Pleased to meet you,' Bernard said, bending over to shake Dr Hatrick's rather clammy hand and then nodding to his wife and the Wertheimers. 'You're not planning to sell the house are you Sam?' He added, feeling suddenly rather anxious.

'No, don't be so silly Bernard. Dr Hatrick is interested in eighteenth century architecture, so Siggy brought him round to see it, that's all.'

'You could always cool off in my car,' Dr Hatrick interjected. 'The air conditioning is absolutely excellent. The best on the market they say,'

'No, thank you all the same. It's very kind of you, but I'll be having a swim in a little while. The tea will do fine for now,' Bernard replied, thinking how foolish he would have felt sitting outside in the courtyard in Hatrick's Mercedes, with the air conditioning full on, while his perspiration slowly evaporated, and how strange it was for him to have suggested it in the first place. Already Bernard was beginning to understand why Sam had been so pleased to see him.

As soon as Bernard had sat down, Hatrick, who had been in the midst of expounding the reasons for which an institution called Dullworth College had been established, an exposition which Bernard's arrival– much to Hatrick's annoyance – had interrupted, continued: 'Well, as I was saying, my, or rather our intention – of course I'm not the only one involved you know – was to set up an international and multi-cultural college, the aim of which is to increase international understanding through combating the innate provincialism and misogyny of modern man. Of course the college was only set up after we had done a great deal of research into comparative approaches to the assessment of the international dimension of higher education. This is the sort of project that, as I'm sure you realise, requires a great deal of preparation. What we hope now is that the college will make its own small contribution to increasing the possibility of achieving world peace in our time...'

On and on he went in this vein, as if for some reason he had suddenly started to imagine he was addressing a meeting of the United Nations and, despite the moments of pure comedy caused by his not infrequent slips of the tongue, listening to this gobbledegook soon became quite unbearable. After a few minutes Bernard felt so oppressed, he began to believe that Hatrick was consuming all the oxygen in the room entirely by himself, and that if he didn't manage to get out of there pretty soon he would be unable to breathe at all.

All the time Hatrick was talking Sam had been surreptitiously winking and smiling at him, which made it fairly obvious that he felt much the same as he did. Perhaps it was just to create a diversion that he suddenly interrupted Hatrick's seemingly endless monologue, to remark that Bernard had done quite a lot of teaching in the past, and maybe they could use someone like him at Dullworth College. A suggestion which, much to Bernard's amazement, appeared to interest Hatrick a great deal, because he immediately began to ask Bernard all kinds of questions about where and what he had taught in the past.

While Hatrick had been boring them stiff about Dullworth College, on the other side of the room Hannah Wertheimer and Evelyn, Sam's wife, had been equally ensnared. For some strange reason Marilyn Hatrick must have imagined that they would be absolutely fascinated by how she kept fit by cycling miles and miles every morning in front of breakfast television. Still, you had to admit that she didn't look her age, or a bit like the ex-nun she actually was, but resembled a faded blonde Hollywood film star from the nineteen fifties. If anything, Bernard found her even more unbearable than her husband. And after they had finally left, which was not without a little prompting from Sam, he just couldn't resist saying to Evelyn that he had seen no point in even attempting to talk to her, when he could watch someone with a ready made personality like hers on television any time he wished.

Although Bernard hadn't been very impressed by Dr Hatrick, the professor seemed to feel quite differently about him. Several times that afternoon he complimented Bernard on his dress, his accent and what he rather mysteriously referred to as Bernard's presence. He even went so far as to praise Bernard's erudition, although this might simply have been in response to Sam's prompting, since Sam didn't let any opportunity pass without making some reference to how knowledge-\able he thought Bernard was. Or possibly Hatrick had formed this opinion entirely by himself, as a result of that remark Bernard made about Beatrix Potter's father, a man who'd made a profound impression on him because he'd never done a day's work in his whole life (people who never did anything always impressed Bernard a great deal, possibly because he'd never entirely recovered from reading Oblomov at too impressionable an age). Bernard didn't think of himself as being at all erudite, but had only read a great deal for the simple reason that he'd never been able to find anything else to do. When Bernard complained during the early stages of his treatment, about the difficulty he was having in concentrating, Dr Lear had quickly understood what this obsession with reading was all about, which he summed up with the neat little formula 'Reading is feeding'; an observation which Bernard found so disturbing that for months afterwards, he was unable to so much as pick up a book, without the image of a giant baby's bottle appearing in his mind.

Whatever the reason was, Bernard must have made quite an impression on Dr Hatrick, because a few days later he telephoned to offer him a job. Much to his surprise Bernard was absolutely delighted, because even if, as he believed, Hatrick was completely wrong about him, this was the first time for years that anyone had offered him a job of any description. It was also particularly congenial that the position was only part-time, since the idea of having to be fully occupied always filled him with horror. This was especially true then, when Bernard felt more than ever that he needed all the time available to deal with his worries. Apart from all the old ones, he had several new ones as well, like trying to understand what Dr Lear's remark – that he still had to discover the real reason why he had chosen to consult an analyst in the first place – really meant. What perplexed him was that he just couldn't understand why Dr Lear had said it, when it must have been perfectly obvious that he was coming to see him because he was completely incapable of doing anything else.

2

When Bernard started work that Autumn it didn't take him long to realise that Dullworth College wasn't the idealistic institution Hatrick had claimed it to be, but that it was a business. He also discovered that practically the whole of Hatrick's tedious monologue had been taken almost word for word from the college prospectus, though admittedly he had written it himself. Even the building – a huge Gothic pile, complete with stained glass windows, turrets, a moat and those little windows for bowmen to shoot from – appeared to have been chosen largely for the impression it would create. There was no doubt about it, Dullworth looked precisely like every foreigner's idea of how an English college should look. The man who was really behind its foundation, knew precisely what he was up to alright. Back in the sixties, L. Ron Taylor, a graduate of the Harvard business school and author of the international best seller *Bio-educational Feed-back and Personal Growth* (Harvard University Press, 1968) and the earlier, but no less influential *Education and the First, Second and Third World* subtitled *Travel Broadens the Mind* (Idaho University Press 1964) realised that since the dollar was so strong at the time, he could bring American students to Europe with the promise of broadening their minds, while simultaneously fulfilling the no less important goal of filling his own pockets. A little while later he also reached the conclusion that there were thousands of Third World students who would be more than willing to pay the hardly modest fees Dullworth charged to acquire at least what looked like an English education.

Since those halcyon days Dullworth had simply grown and grown and now issued its own degrees in subjects ranging from business studies to domestic science (there was even a Major in knitting, which was quite an innovation in its day). At the time Bernard joined the faculty there was still a lot of talk about maintaining academic standards, but he soon understood that the real task of the staff was to keep the customers, that is the students, happy. It was regarded as of the utmost importance that when they finally finished their courses and returned home they would have nothing but praise for the Dullworth experience. Obviously L. Ron Taylor had realised that without a good and ever increasing reputation, even the most assiduous efforts of Dullworth's salesmen, who were constantly travelling through the Middle East and the Third World in search of customers, would be to no avail. The salesmen must also have had clear instructions that no enthusiastic applicant, once of course they'd demonstrated their ability to pay the fees, should ever be refused admittance, however poor their qualifications might be. None of the students Bernard came across seemed to be overwhelmed by a sense of intellectual curiosity, or were ever to be seen reading a book for its own sake; which was just as well since the most striking thing about the library was not the enormity of its collection of books, but that it often smelled strongly of Havana cigars, a smell incidentally, which reminded Bernard of his father who had always smoked them, especially late at night in bed. Sometimes, as he was wandering around the college, Bernard noticed a strange sweetish aroma, which he took to be Marijuana, although he didn't know for sure, having lived through the sixties with his consciousness totally unimpaired by either drugs or alcohol. Not that keeping a clear head had ever really got him anywhere.

What impressed Bernard most about Dullworth was not the library, or the atmosphere of intellectual endeavour (which anyway was nearly non-existent) – but the car park. This was no ordinary car park, but resembled a luxury car showroom and was always full of Porches, Mercedes, Ferraris, Corniches and every other kind of sports car imaginable, all of which belonged to the students who left them there while they endured what little higher education Dullworth had to offer, an experience which could hardly compete with the thrill they must have got from driving one of those cars. There were also distinct advantages to working at a place like Dullworth. For one thing, the teaching was hardly challenging, even if it was sometimes rather trying, and the place was absolutely full of some of the most beautiful girls he'd ever seen. In this respect, the college prospectus was completely accurate, as they appeared to come from every country imaginable; although it was the girls from the Middle East who appealed to him most, some of whom looked as if they had just stepped out of a Persian miniature. He soon became so enchanted by them that sometimes he thought that the most worthwhile thing he could do while he was at Dullworth was to try and form a relationship with one of them; that way, there might at least be a possibility that he would end up spending his declining years somewhere in the Middle East, being waited on hand and foot. Of course he did absolutely nothing about it; firstly because he had moral qualms about trying to pick up girls who were so much younger than he was, and secondly because he soon noticed that some of the most attractive of them seemed to be escorted to and from their classes by sinister looking men with bulges under their jackets, who he assumed could only be their bodyguards. It would be just his luck to fall for one of their charges and be beaten up for trying to become the first Jewish son-in-law of some oil-rich sheik or other. Then one day, after he had been at Dullworth for at least a month, he suddenly became aware of Tissue Olahu (or Princess Olahu as she liked to be addressed) a student in the English composition class he taught on Tuesday and Thursday mornings.

Tissue had been in that class from the very beginning but he just hadn't paid much attention to her. This was hardly surprising, because during those first few weeks he was obliged to try and teach the principles of sentence structure and punctuation to the most difficult group of students he'd ever come across, not least because no two of them seemed to come from the same country. To explain the mysteries of punctuation was in itself no simple matter, especially when, as in Bernard's case, you'd never really understood it yourself. What was more, they weren't exactly enthusiastic to acquire what little knowledge he had to impart, and every time he glanced down at the textbook to check up whether there were five, or was it six basic uses for the semicolon, the class would move that bit nearer to complete pandemonium. And it hadn't exactly been totally silent before. As he subsequently said to Dr Hatrick: all he felt he could do in the circumstances was to try and work with the chaos, although he wasn't at all sure that Hatrick had really appreciated his point of view; particularly since he had had to visit the class more than once to restore order, after some students had gone to complain about what was really going on in English 101. It hadn't helped much either when one student walked out after Bernard had confused the subject and object of a sentence. A pretty funny mistake for him to have made anyway;

after all, who should know better than him that the subject is the 'doer' and the object – grammar's old home from home for the paranoiac – that which is 'done to'. He must have made such a hash of explaining it that the young lady in question just couldn't stand it any more and felt impelled to leave. When it happened, he was a bit shocked and even felt guilty, but then, he remembered his mother saying that you can only do your best (choosing to forget of course what he used to reply – 'And what if your best isn't good enough?') and that made him feel a little better.

On reflection perhaps he should never have agreed to teach that course in the first place, especially since he found the subject only slightly less perplexing than his students did. It was a situation which wasn't all that different from the one he'd found himself in years ago when he'd agreed to teach a course in economics for accountancy students, and had watched as week by week the class got smaller and smaller until there was only one Indian student left, who, Bernard concluded, only continued to attend because his English was too poor to enable him to judge how little economics Bernard really knew. No, he should definitely never have taken on that class. He'd only barely managed to pass the economics exam himself by learning the text-book off by heart. At least that course had given him a sense of adventure, because as his hand moved up the supply curve (or was it the demand curve?) he hadn't the vaguest idea of where he was going, or what it signified. Trying to teach punctuation was almost as bad, only in this case the result was that his own punctuation became even worse than it had been before. He soon became so obsessed with punctuation that he started talking about it during his sessions with Dr Lear, who couldn't understand what he was going on about, 'But sure Bernard there's nothing wrong with your punctuation, a dot here, a dot there, what can it possibly matter anyway.' It was alright for him to talk, he wasn't suffering the way Bernard was, who by then was seeing transparent question marks floating before his eyes during the day and often had nightmares in which he was being attacked by semicolons.

Perhaps he wouldn't have been so upset about it – after all it was unlikely that most of the students realised how little he knew – had not the class also been so difficult to control. This was partly because even the brightest of his students appeared to have an attention span of little more than five minutes, a condition that was no doubt a consequence of the fact that they seemed to spend most of their free time with their heads stuck in the television, or stoned on pop music. He'd realised this one morning when one of the bodyguards had given him a lift to class and he had almost lost his mind sliding around on the pink fur seats of the Cadillac as he listened to the wailing oriental pop music blaring out of the quadrophonic stereo. The other problem was that they soon realised that, however stern Bernard might try to appear, he was really a marshmallow inside, who would put up with practically anything. One morning things got so bad, that he tried to throw one of the students out of the class. He wasn't even successful in that, because Ahmed just wouldn't leave, but kept coming back in protesting: 'But sir, sir, it wasn't me sir. It was the others sir.' In the end he just had to relent and let him sit down again.

Another reason it took him so long before he became aware of Tissue was that there were so many other desirable girls in the class to look at apart from her; especially those from Iran and the Lebanon, who were always so exquisitely dressed that Bernard sometimes thought they must be looking for a husband amongst one of the students, unless of course they were hoping to marry him. Most of the time they were well enough behaved and just sat there gossiping and jangling their bangles, while giving him languorous looks, from under the umbrellas of heavy sensual perfume that they always seemed to wear.

Occasionally though, they would flirt with him quite openly, not seriously of course, but probably just to keep in practice. One morning, as he was peering into the seemingly bottomless, dark, almond shaped eyes of one of the most beautiful of them, while expounding the various uses of the full stop, he was barely able to stop himself from leaning over and kissing her. And they knew perfectly well the sort of effect they were having on him, because at moments like that, someone would invariably ask to go to the toilet, in a voice that was full of sexual innuendo. When this sort of thing happened, Bernard would once again be tempted to try and invite one of them out, and it was only the thought of the bodyguards, who at that moment were probably waiting outside in the corridor, that prevented him from doing anything so foolhardy. But still, there was nothing to prevent him from having all kinds of fantasies about such delicious looking girls as Lola Patuffi or Carmen Herez, who could easily have been two courtesans out of The Thousand and One Nights.

He had noticed Tissue looking at him once or twice during those first few weeks, but whenever he had returned her glance she'd always immediately looked away, as if their eyes had only met by chance. Then something happened which changed everything. One morning she put up her hand to ask if she might leave early because she had an appointment with her bank manager. It seemed like an innocent enough request at the time, but when at eleven-thirty she got up and started to wiggle her way towards the door behind him, he just couldn't believe the way she looked. Someone must have told her that when you had that sort of interview it was a good idea to be well dressed. Tissue had translated this advice in the strangest possible way, because instead of looking demure, serious and respectable, she was wearing a black silk polka dot dress that, had it been even a centimetre tighter, breathing would have been an impossibility, stiletto heels, and a small pillbox hat with a veil; a final touch that added an air of mystery to her already intensely erotic appearance. She looked, in short, the very apotheosis of sexual temptation. In that outfit it wouldn't have surprised Bernard if, instead of giving her the overdraft she probably wanted, her bank manager hadn't locked the door of his office and attempted to seduce her right there and then. She would have had that effect on him. The sight of her dressed like that made his heart beat so loudly, that he wondered for a moment if it wasn't audible to the whole class. But there was no danger of that, because when Tissue started to make her highly sensual progress between the row of desks towards him the class burst into uproar. The South American students, in particular, began to whistle and bang the tops of their desks until Bernard thought they were going to lose all self control entirely. Fortunately, after what seemed like ages, she did manage to reach the door without anything too awful happening. Although Fernandez hadn't been able to resist pinching her bottom as it slid past him at just below eye level. But who could blame him for giving into temptation when confronted with a woman dressed like that. It was only Bernard's position that had stopped him from doing something similar. It took at least five or ten minutes after she'd finally left before he was able to calm them all down; and even then, it was only by pointing to Christ on the cross above the altar (Business at Dullworth having been so good recently that this class had to be held in a rented room of a nearby Church), and shouting out above the row: 'How can you behave like this in a church, and in the presence of your Lord Jesus Christ,' that he managed to regain control of the class at all. Although he wondered later if Christ himself would have behaved much better had he ever been confronted with a woman as provocatively dressed as Tissue was that day.

After what happened that morning Bernard could hardly wait for the next class to see Tissue again. From then on English 101, which he had dreaded so much, became something to really look forward to. He began to arrive early, which was little short of astonishing, since in Bernard's case unpunctuality was practically an illness. A condition which – with Dr Lear's help of course – he had recently begun to understand stemmed from a reluctance bordering on anxiety ever to leave where he was already. It was a malaise which had already resulted in his being reprimanded by Weinberg, the head of Humanities: 'If you don't start getting to class on time Steinway, we'll simply have to get rid of you,' was what he'd said, or rather shouted into Bernard's ear one morning in that incredibly loud voice of his. The effect of which was to make Bernard feel so humiliated that he wanted to hit him, instead of which he simply protested at being spoken to like that. Anyway, at least that problem was solved, since he now found himself frequently arriving for class ten or fifteen minutes early.

Tissue must have been aware that Bernard's attitude towards her had changed in some way, but more importantly, hers too must have changed, because she no longer averted her eyes whenever he looked at her, which he now did at every available opportunity. Soon she began to come to class in a series of costumes in each one of which, if that were possible, she looked even more desirable than the last. Sometimes, the colours of her dresses made her look like a delicious exotic fruit, others were so tight that by wearing them she could only have intended to appeal to him in the most erotic way possible. But whatever her real intention was, Bernard felt as if he were being exposed to a whole symphony of temptations. But it was not only through her clothes that Tissue chose to express her interest in him. She also started to wait for Bernard after class, on the pretext of asking him to go over something she'd found difficult to understand, but in reality just to be alone with him for a few minutes. Once everyone else had left, she would commiserate with him about the difficulties he was having with the class, while carefully packing his books and papers back into his briefcase for him. Before long he started to give her lifts back to college, although it was only a few minutes walk away. These journeys could be extremely disconcerting, especially since, as sometimes happened, she more or less rolled on to his lap as they went round the roundabout.

After a few weeks of this it became obvious, even to Bernard, who had become strangely obtuse as to what women felt about him since Olivia and he had parted, that Tissue must really find him attractive. One day, as they were queuing up for lunch together in the canteen, she took the tray out of his hands and carefully laid it for him, as if he were her child or her lover – a gesture which Bernard took to mean that in due course she would be prepared to do even more significant and intimate things for him. After that he found himself beginning to have all kinds of sexual fantasies about her (sometimes even during class), including one in which they were making love on an enormous aubergine coloured bed into which was fitted a stereo, cocktail cabinet and television, a bed not unlike the one he and Olivia had laughed about so much when they had seen it in the window of a store some years earlier.

Sometimes these fantasies took such a hold on him that he practically had to shake himself to come out of them. But although by then he was completely convinced that Tissue would respond favourably to any overture he might make he would not of his own accord ever have taken it any further. She was so much younger than he was, and he was also suddenly visited by an attack of moral scruples which made the idea of inviting her out seem completely wrong. Much more wrong at any rate than had she been just any student, instead of one of the girls in his class. He realised that he was being slightly absurd. What could it possibly matter that he was older than her and maybe the older man experience was precisely what she was looking for. Anyway, he wasn't that much older than she was. He was also perfectly well aware that lots of the teachers slept with students, and even regarded it as a sort of perk of the job, a compensation perhaps for the relatively small salaries they received. He'd often laughed at stories he'd heard about this kind of thing going on, especially one about a student who'd gone to her teacher to say how much she was enjoying his course, and whose only response was to lock the door of his office and attempt to seduce her.

But perhaps the real problem wasn't his moral scruples at all, but that he was much too timid and self-conscious ever to be able to take the initiative in this kind of situation. He remembered once in the past when he'd taught at a Catholic Teachers' Training College and one of his students – an absolutely ravishing girl called Clare – sat through almost every class in a black leotard, with a belt that seemed to be largely made out of spent cartridges, combing her long auburn hair, while giving him endless, sultry, inviting looks; and how he hadn't reacted at all, as if she had left him completely cold, which couldn't have been less true.

He was also slightly inhibited because he was still prone to attacks of guilt about Olivia, whose face would surface in his mind like a figure in a child's pop-up book, as soon as he found anyone else at all attractive. But of course, what happened next wasn't any longer entirely within his control. Tissue as it turned out was a woman who, perhaps because she was a princess, was used to getting what she wanted. And then, isn't it almost always the case that once a man shows his interest in a woman the initiative subtlety passes from his hands to hers – that much even Bernard understood. Even so, he wasn't expecting things to develop quite as quickly as they did, and certainly not the very next time he saw her after that episode with the tray. It was precisely then, just after he had driven her back to college, that things reached a climax. He had parked the car and they were walking up the gravel driveway towards the main building, from whose narrow windows Bernard had so often in the past felt that he could almost sense bowmen in chain mail aiming at him, when she suddenly stopped for a moment, as if to admire the frieze of embracing couples spread out on the grass a few feet away from them, turned to him and said: 'What do you do on the weekends Professor Steinway?' – the meaning of which was hardly ambiguous. Well, perhaps it wasn't all that sudden, after all she had been complaining recently of being bored, and he'd sensed that something was going to happen all the way back to college. There had definitely been a certain tension, a peculiar atmosphere between them, which had begun almost as soon as the class had ended. 'Yes, this must be it,' Bernard said to himself thinking, immediately and indeed completely characteristically, of that scene in *War and Peace* (for years now he'd looked in literature for clues to the meaning of important moments in his life), when Helen's father, unable to wait any longer for Pierre's proposal of marriage, simply precipitates it by coming in and congratulating the happy couple. Obviously Tissue couldn't wait any longer for him to invite her out either, and had decided finally to take the initiative herself. Even then, he had nearly missed the point of her question and almost began to answer it in detail. Fortunately, he managed to stop himself and instead asked what she did, to which she of course again said how bored she was during the weekends, so that he was left with little alternative (not that he really wanted one) but to suggest they did something together. He still couldn't stop himself from asking her if she didn't perhaps think he was too old for her. She only replied that she couldn't see why age should be at all relevant; although later on he discovered that despite what she'd said, she had nevertheless added on a couple of years to her age, just to be on the safe side, but by then it no longer made any difference. What he mainly felt at that moment though, was enormously fortunate that for some inscrutable reason Tissue had been attracted to him, instead of to one of her other teachers at Dullworth. And of course he could hardly wait for the next Saturday to arrive.

3

After all that, the first evening they spent together was nearly a fiasco. Tissue was late, so late that as Bernard anxiously paced up and down outside the tube station he began to think that perhaps either he or she had made some mistake about where they were supposed to be meeting. Or that perhaps, despite the fact he had arrived on time, she had been and gone while he had been standing there. Could it be possible that outside the familiar context of the classroom he simply hadn't recognised her? But that was very hard to believe, especially since, while trying to appear to be nonchalantly looking in a shop window, Bernard had carefully scrutinised every girl going in or out of the station, who looked even remotely like Tissue; and by so doing, had risked more than one embarrassing scene, because the way he stared at those girls far exceeded the usual rules for the casual appraisal of an attractive woman. Gradually he began to think that she had changed her mind, and simply wasn't coming at all.

It was all beginning to be very disappointing, especially since Bernard had looked forward so eagerly to that evening, and had spent ages getting ready, as if he were an adolescent all over again going out with a girl for the very first time. He had always been very slow getting ready but on that particular evening he really excelled himself. He must have spent at least an hour tying and retying his bow-tie, combing his hair and moustache, and peering at himself in the mirror in a mood that vacillated between vain self-satisfaction and utter dismay. He had even taken the trouble to shave for a second time that day, which was hardly really necessary, but which he did, because he believed that was what a gentleman should do, if he considered there was even the vaguest possibility of kissing the woman he was going to spend the evening with. Then, he applied three, or possibly four, different kinds of aftershave one on top of the other, as if he really believed they had aphrodisiac properties. Finally, just before he was about to leave he was unable to resist going and looking at himself in the mirror one last time, to make absolutely certain that he looked as attractive as he possibly could.

Yes, it was all rather disappointing but then, after he had been waiting for at least an hour, and just as he was about to go, Tissue suddenly appeared, or rather to be precise, almost fell at his feet as she descended from her taxi, mumbling something about having been terribly delayed at her hairdressers, because the beading of her hair had taken much longer than usual. He immediately forgot how irritated and disappointed he had been feeling only a few moments before. He'd never seen her looking so desirable as she did that evening, tottering along on very high heels, her tight silk suit rustling slightly, with her pillbox hat at a jaunty angle. He also noticed, when he looked down to admire her legs, that underneath her silver grey silk stockings she was wearing a fine gold chain around her left ankle, an item of jewellery that he believed had all kinds of erotic implications. She looked so ravishing he felt an almost overwhelming desire to ravish her right there and then. He also felt, for the first time in years, a sudden surge of masculine pride in being with such a beautiful woman. He could hardly believe he deserved such good fortune. Could it be that God had finally forgiven him for breaking his word all those years ago, when he'd promised to go to the Synagogue every Saturday from then on if his parents brought back the two-gun holster set from America, as they said they would? It was a vow which of course he'd never kept, but which he'd felt oddly guilty about from time to time ever since. Was this the sign that he'd been forgiven at last?

But nowhere Bernard took her that evening seemed to be right. In the wine bar, where they had a drink before dinner, she complained that there were too many people, and that she hated crowds. Things weren't made any easier by her sudden revelation that she had a fiancé, even if she had added hastily that he didn't mind at all if she went out with other men. It was still enough to make Bernard feel very uncomfortable, and be unable to stop himself from trying to imagine what it would feel like if her fiancé suddenly appeared in the doorway in a leopard skin and threw an assagai at him, and whether or not the blade would be visible coming out between his shoulder blades if it happened.

When they finally got to the Greek restaurant she refused to eat anything because she said the food was much too dry for her, which made Bernard wonder what food in her country was like – surely it couldn't all be wet. But at least the waiters must have enjoyed their presence that evening because they kept coming over to change the ashtray every five minutes, or to enquire if everything was to their liking, which usually only happens in the very best restaurants – and the Old Cyprus Kebab House wasn't one of those. In all the years Bernard had been going there he'd never had such service, but of course he realised that all they were doing was simply showing how attractive they thought she was. Between Tissue and him things could hardly be said to be flowing. Outside class he hardly knew what to say to her (he couldn't very well talk about punctuation could he?). In the end all that came to mind was to tell her about was a College do that he'd recently had to attend in which Hatrick had made yet another of his superb slips of the tongue, which did at least make her laugh. It was only while they were having their coffee, when he asked what she would like to do next that things really started to look up, because she answered, without a moment's hesitation, that what she would really like was to go back to his flat. A reply which both amazed and startled Bernard, since nothing that had happened between them so far that evening had in any way prepared him for such a delightful denouement. He had been fully expecting her to ask him to take her home straightaway and was so taken aback that he became slightly embarrassed, babbling some rubbish about how he thought she would enjoy seeing his flat because it was very beautiful and there was such a wonderful view from his window across the park, as if that had anything to do with her desire to go home with him. Once all this nonsense had subsided in his head, he simply felt relieved that Tissue's certainty about what she wanted had saved him yet again from having to take the initiative.

In fact, he had nothing further to worry about because Tissue continued to take the initiative for the rest of the evening. Even before they'd got out of the lift, and while he was still feeling acutely anxious in case Harris, Sam's chauffeur, who lived in the basement should see them, she was all over him. Once they had got safely inside, he hardly had time to open the bottle of champagne he was saving for such an occasion, before he found himself being undressed on the chaise longue and having to submit to Tissue's close inspection of his body. In a matter of moments she had pulled down his trousers and was staring at his penis with a mixture of admiration and wonder. Just the sight of it seemed to overwhelm her: 'Oh, you're so strong Professor Steinway, I knew you'd be strong,' she kept on saying over and over. A compliment that took Bernard by complete surprise, but which nevertheless gave him a strange and wholly new feeling of pride. He knew he wasn't under-endowed but he'd never thought of himself as being particular over-endowed either. Just an average sort of penis that's what he'd always assumed he possessed. Not that he'd ever paid all that much attention to other people's; on the contrary, he'd always averted his eyes on those rare occasions when he had the opportunity to make a comparison (he certainly could never imagine showing it to anyone as, in a moment of doubt, Fitzgerald had to Hemingway).

After a while he began to feel rather silly, not to say vulnerable, lying there half-naked with his trousers down around his ankles, but when he suggested that Tissue might like to take her clothes off as well, she simply refused point blank. 'No, I can't do that Professor Steinway. My nurse always said you must never do that, certainly not the first night anyway.' It was a response which although it was initially disappointing, did at least imply that there were going to be other nights like this. And anyway, a little while later, she did take her skirt off, if only as she said to prevent it from getting terribly creased, and that at least afforded him the opportunity of admiring her white suspender belt. An item of underwear that Bernard had always found tremendously erotic, and which in his opinion was one of the two high points in the whole history of lingerie (the other of course being the introduction of French knickers in the nineteen twenties). She also didn't appear to mind if he caressed her under her clothes, which was a real pleasure since Tissue had the smoothest skin he'd even touched. It was like silk velvet and strangely enough reminded him of Panna, a particularly smooth tasting brand of Italian mineral water. And then Tissue was by no means inexpert at caressing that part of his anatomy that she admired so much (not to mention her expertise at oral sex, which it is impossible to describe), so that it wasn't very long before nature had taken its course.

That first evening, although it had begun so badly, was certainly a great success by the time he took her back to college. Especially considering what she told him as they were sitting in the car outside her dormitory (after he had taken the precaution of dowsing the lights, which at the time made him feel like Philip Marlow out on a case). It was then that he asked her why it was she found him so attractive rather than any of her other teachers, a question that had been going round in his mind ever since they had first agreed to go out together. At first she reacted angrily and pulled away from him as if that was the worst possible thing he could have said. She thought he was implying that she was some kind of loose woman who always had affairs with her teachers. She was also absolutely incensed by the suggestion that she could have found someone like Dr Weinberg even remotely attractive, apart from anything else he seemed incredibly old to her, probably because he was almost completely bald, although in fact he was only six months older than Bernard. She soon became so worked up that he really wished he'd never said anything, after all he'd only asked her that question because, narcissist that he was, he wasn't content with just the experience but wanted all the details spelled out as well – a not entirely incomprehensible desire, since there's nothing to compare with giving one's vanity a real feast is there?

Fortunately, he did finally manage to calm her down, but only after he insisted that he'd only said what he had because he was so touched that she seemed to find him attractive at all. Well, that must have done the trick because it was then that she revealed what it was that had attracted her to him, a revelation that made having to pacify her more than worthwhile. As far as she was able to put it into words, this turned out to be based on the fact that she thought he was a real gentleman. A conclusion she'd come to because of his exquisite manners, the way he dressed and his gentleness (it was obvious to her that had he not been a gentleman he wouldn't have had any trouble keeping control in class). She had also been rather impressed by a pair of Bernard's shoes that, apart from being vegetable dyed, had the unusual feature of lacing up at the sides. But then they really were the sort of shoes a gentleman might have worn. Why else would a high court judge have once rebuked a famous M.P. with the words: 'Those are far too expensive shoes for a Socialist like you to even contemplate wearing' – although of course Bernard had bought his in a sale.

Nothing could have pleased Bernard more than that Tissue should have seen him in a way that almost perfectly corresponded to the idealised picture he had of himself, that of an aristocrat or, at the very least, a gentleman of leisure. It was enough to make him slip for a few minutes into his favourite reverie about life on the old family estates in Lithuania before the First World War. As always he could visualise it all so clearly. The white stucco house with the crumbling statues of the Greek gods along the facade (some with broken noses, others with limbs missing). The long summer afternoons sitting by the pond full of pink and yellow water lilies, listening to the water trickling from the lips of a rather overweight and crumbling stone angel. And there was the familiar figure of Boris Denisovitch, rushing to and fro through the avenue of lime trees with the samovar and all kinds of delicacies, including of course caviar, on a heavily laden silver tray. Over by the lake, he could almost make out his grandfather taking his afternoon constitutional, and in the distance the endless dark forests which had been in his family for generations. It was all complete nonsense of course. But even Bernard's sister used to get tears in her eyes whenever he started to reminisce about the old country; or reminded her of the blue and gold ormalu clock that used to stand on a cherrywood table by the french windows in the dinning room, and which played a Chopin waltz on the hour; or when he recalled the wonderful balls they used to have every summer, that went on until those same french windows were completely filled with the rose coloured dawn sky. Sometimes, Bernard got so carried away that he almost started to believe it himself. Once he even came close to having visiting cards printed, embossed with a small crown, and the title Count Steinway, which didn't sound bad at all, at least not to his ears.

What a pity there wasn't a word of truth in any of it. The only thing he knew about his ancestors in the old country, was that story his father used to tell about mad uncle Israel, who had apparently once been a famous lamplighter in Odessa, but even that was probably apocryphal. Of course there was all that talk in the family about his great grandfather, who was reputed to have been Alexander the Third's first Jewish dentist; and who, or so the story went, had received the Russian equivalent of Letters Patent and the title Boyard von Steingluck for his services (the von being added because it was considered more appropriate in view of his grandfather's German origins). The title in particular was a reward for the incomparable artistry of his bridgework, which even the immortal Fabergé had admired a great deal, when invited to peer into the Czar's mouth to examine it. Probably there wasn't a word of truth in that story either, although Bernard had inherited from his grandfather a gold Fabergé cigarette case, which was engraved inside with *From A.R. to B von S*. It was an extraordinary thing, which must have been intended for a chain-smoker, since it opened like a concertina and held at least fifty cigarettes. But the cigarette case didn't really prove anything, since his grandfather could easily have bought it before leaving Russia. That same grandfather – the Norman Hartnell of his day – was said to have hailed a taxi to take him to the Savoy the moment he stepped off the boat from Russia, which was hardly the behaviour of an impoverished immigrant. Bernard himself remembered how old Marks (his grandfather's friend, who had come with him from Russia) used to wander around the house in an old fashioned tail coat, on which were pinned the strangest looking medals. So who knows, perhaps there was some truth in that story after all. There was also that collection of Czarist roubles and railway bonds, which Bernard had inherited from his grandfather and had hung on to in the hope that one day he'd be able to go back there and spend them.

Bernard often thought he'd been born into the wrong age, and that if there was any real justice in the world he would have been an aristocrat in late nineteenth-century Russia (not the time to be a carrier of wood, or a hauler of water); and to have devoted his life to nothing more arduous than changing for dinner, gossip, romantic liaisons, seducing chamber maids, and mild attacks of ennui. Yes, a life in which the most intellectually challenging task was comparing the quality of different brands of caviar was definitely the sort of life for him. He might even have ended up having one of those romantic seeming deaths from T.B. whilst doing his morning exercises in front of an open window in some elegant sanatorium high up in the Swiss Alps. Still, it was at least some consolation to hear himself being described as a gentleman, even if he doubted that Tissue would recognise a real gentleman if she ever saw one.

The second time Tissue came to his flat turned out to be one of the greatest sexual experiences Bernard had ever had; even better probably, than had he been seduced by Shirley Eaton, as he had so longed to be when he was twelve or thirteen, or, if he had spent a weekend with that girl from the Turkish Delight advertisement, who had had such a disturbing effect on his youthful imagination. As on that first night, there was no question of Bernard having to take the initiative. Almost as soon as she arrived, Tissue was demanding to know – in a voice that could only be described as imperious – where the bedroom was. But Bernard really shouldn't have been surprised by her tone since it was completely characteristic of her whole attitude towards sex. In this respect she was as different from Lavinia Smith as could be imagined. As far as Tissue was concerned it definitely wasn't a case of making love *with* but of making love *to*. It was her firm conviction that it was the role of the woman to please the man in every way she knew how. An attitude towards sex which reminded Bernard of Rosalind, an old girlfriend of his, who always insisted that her only desire was to serve him. It was obviously a sign of immaturity that he had left her after only three weeks of this impeccable service. Although he could hardly believe it now, Rosalind was one of the only women he'd ever left in his whole life!

Upstairs on the bed, while Tissue did everything she knew to please him, Bernard could hardly believe his good fortune. Apart from everything else – apart, that is, from the almost infinite pleasure Tissue's demonstration of her amorous technique gave him – her approach to love-making suited him perfectly. Not having to be active mitigated the feelings of guilt he would inevitably have felt being in bed with someone else other than Olivia. It also gratified the narcissist in him, who always assumed he was entitled to the lion's share of whatever pleasure was going. Not to mention his long held belief, that since it was the man who had to contribute his vital fluids, it hardly seemed fair that he should have to do the major part of the work as well. Even with such a chauvinistic attitude, he was astonished by Tissue's skill as a lover. Where could she have possibly acquired so much knowledge about the art of giving pleasure, after all she was only twenty-three. He would never have believed before that there were such a variety of caresses which could be played on the human body, let alone his body, or that so many erotic zones even actually existed. And he would definitely never have thought it possible that toes could be caressed in such a way as to bring one to the very edge of orgasm. So stimulating did Bernard find Tissue's love-making, that he discovered in himself, for the first time in his life, the stamina to make love for hour after hour, and he hadn't even taken one Ginseng tablet either. Not that he'd ever taken such a thing, he'd simply always assumed that was why people bought them. Of course his amazing performance that night must also have had something to with the extraordinary chemistry that existed between them, but whatever the reason, and there really is no explaining these things, Bernard just felt immensely grateful for what he was receiving (thank God it was him and not Weinberg she had chosen to bestow her favours on!). It was as if he had just stumbled into an oasis and was consuming his first mouthful of dates after weeks of near starvation.

It seemed strange to Bernard that whilst they were making love, Tissue had appeared to be almost completely indifferent to his numerous attempts to caress her. She had even seemed to be immune to the most passionate and subtle caresses in his whole repertoire – caresses which had taken him at least ten years of fumbling to acquire – as if by attempting to make them he was in some way interfering in the proceedings. Yet, no sooner had they finished making love than suddenly, slipping into a patois that he'd never heard her use before, she started to complain, for the first time, that the trouble with love-making was that women always had to do the work.

'But we didn't have to make love that way. I thought that was how you wanted to make love,' Bernard said, rather taken aback, and wondering if he shouldn't perhaps have tried harder to join in. His efforts had admittedly tailed off a bit in the last couple of hours, there was no doubt about it.

Bernard leant over and kissed her, feeling as if he had to console her for something while at the same time hoping that she didn't really mean what she said, but was just being playful and that in due course he would receive several more helpings of exactly the same treatment.

Fortunately, as far as Tissue's complaining was concerned, Bernard needn't have worried because she never did it again and, after that first time, they always made love in exactly the same way (which was a kind of missionary position in reverse). All they ever seemed to do was make love; and he soon began to worry if he would be able to sustain the pace – after all he was ten years older than her. Sometimes, he thought she must be completely obsessed with sex, certainly he would never forget that time when she had suddenly exclaimed – albeit in the heat of the moment, or was it the height of pleasure, he was no longer certain – that she wanted to 'fuck him to death', which made Bernard wonder if she might not be expressing – by pure chance of course – what the Elizabethans had meant about the interrelatedness of love and death.

Whatever she really meant and however pleasurable it was being made love to by Tissue, he certainly had no intention of laying down his life for it. But then, he never had been all that heroic. The funny thing was though, the fact that they hardly did anything else but go to bed together soon began to make him feel oddly guilty. Since Tissue was doing so much to enlarge his sexual experience shouldn't he be doing something in return, such as trying to broaden her mind? Maybe he should be taking her to art galleries, the theatre, or something of the kind? Was it really right to go on behaving like this? But it soon occurred to him that this was a very strange way to react; after all, wasn't it only Christians who somehow felt they should feel guilty as soon as they started to experience real pleasure. If he was beginning to feel like that, did it mean that he, Bernard Steinway of all people, had been tainted by Christianity as well?

But Bernard's good intentions came to absolutely nothing, because when he finally got round to asking her if she would like to do something of a cultural nature, she wasn't overwhelmed with enthusiasm. It soon became apparent that her idea of having a good time had absolutely nothing to do with culture, but consisted of doing such things as dancing the night away in a disco – hardly the sort of thing Bernard did for amusement. He realised that he was simply too old and too self-conscious to do anything like that anymore. Indeed, the only thing he really achieved by offering to take her to the theatre or an art gallery, was to make him even more aware than he had been before of how great the gulf was between them.

Unlike Bernard who had never been really good at enjoying himself, Tissue was easily the most hedonistic person he'd ever met. Not that she really knew what the word meant, because when he said that was what he thought she was, she insisted that even if it were true, it still didn't prevent her from being a Christian. An idea Bernard found very hard to accept, since he couldn't see how self-denial which was an inherent part of the Christian faith could ever be reconciled with the unqualified pursuit of pleasure. Tissue couldn't see any contradiction at all. As far as she was concerned God meant her to have as good a time as possible: 'After all I could be dead tomorrow!' Perhaps, Bernard thought when she said this, the God who turned up in her country was entirely different from the one Europeans did business with? But then perhaps it wasn't all that strange that Tissue should think of herself as a devout Christian because she was always full of strange ideas. She even thought – when Bernard revealed that he wasn't Christian himself but Jewish – that it meant he must be some kind of heathen, although maybe she wasn't all that wrong there. After all, he had always felt excluded from something or other, and after thirty-three years on earth, unlike Tissue, he still didn't know how to enjoy life, which seemed to come as naturally to her as going to bed when you were tired.

Where had all that questioning and searching ever got him. 'Happiness is the remission from pain,' Freud once said – which was definitely what it had almost always been for Bernard. The most he'd ever been able to achieve was an hour or two off his anxieties every week. Yes, what was an anxiety-ridden Jew, who was incapable of enjoying life – unless endless worrying was a form of enjoyment – but a kind of modern heathen. He had often felt an outcast, but from what exactly, he had never been entirely sure. Even if her use of the word had been a little strange, maybe there was something in what she said. But of one thing he was now certain – there was no point in feeling guilty for what he was receiving, because it was becoming pretty obvious that he wouldn't be receiving it for all that much longer.

This intuition must have been right, because after the night of that conversation he rarely managed to be alone with her very much ever again. He still saw her in college but then she always seemed to be surrounded by friends, so they did little more than exchange glances; although it was about then that she began to phone him up at all hours of the day and night. According to her this was just to find out what he was doing, but really what she wanted was to reassure herself that he was missing her. Having established that, she would almost invariably proceed to make all kinds of erotic suggestions, as if the sole purpose of her phone call had really been to disturb his peace of mind, not that it had been all that peaceful before she'd rung. If that had really been her intention she certainly succeeded, because after each one of her calls he would wander around the flat for hours, quite unable to think about anything except being in bed with her. Occasionally, he even took the risk of phoning her at college himself (in the hope of arranging a meeting, or at least being excited by her erotic innuendoes) although he always took the precaution of covering the mouthpiece with his handkerchief before enquiring in his best Central European accent: 'If he could please speak vis Princess Olahu,' but she was almost never in. Somehow she was always just about to come over, and then at the last moment she would invariably telephone to say she couldn't make it. Behind all this vacillating Bernard felt he could detect the malign influence of her fiancé, who wasn't perhaps quite as permissive as Tissue had always made him out to be.

The rare evenings he did manage to spend with her often ended in arguments or, worse still, rows. This always happened if for some reason they were unable to go to bed together. On one occasion, after they had been out to dinner to an Italian restaurant and had gone back to the flat afterwards, she had really got angry and accused him of only being interested in her body, after he had become silent and uncommunicative when she wouldn't go to bed with him. And he only finally managed to calm her down by suggesting that the truth was the other way round – and it was she who was only interested in his body! But secretly he knew she was right. Apart from sex they had almost nothing to say to each other. A state of affairs which Bernard, who was used to talking endlessly to women, found more than a little disconcerting. With Olivia there had been no end of talk. In the old days when he left home he would often stop at a call box to phone her to finish a conversation, or to try to rectify some misunderstanding or other. There never seemed to be an end to what they had to say to one another. Even now, just as they were about to part he would almost always hear himself saying: 'Now what was it that I meant to say to you,' as if this was to be the last time they would ever meet.

The last time he saw Tissue alone more or less ended in disaster. But then, he should never have allowed himself to be inveigled into driving her to yet another one of her mysterious appointments with her bank manager (after all how many overdrafts can one person have? Maybe in reality it wasn't because of her fiancé that he had seen her so rarely, but because of some liaison she had been having with him all along?). For one thing, there really wasn't enough time to take her there since he had promised to go and see Olivia in hospital early that evening. Not only that, Tissue's bank happened to be in a part of town where Bernard had his formative experiences of futility and failure. Revisiting those particular places of his infancy, given Bernard's feeling about his childhood, hardly seemed the right thing to be doing at that moment in his life. As he sat in the car waiting for Tissue outside the bank he couldn't avoid seeing the entrance to what used to be his father's garage where, years ago, he had been obliged to spend hours and hours sweeping an enormous cobble-stoned yard, although the dust would start to resettle even before he'd finished the job; and where he had also passed so many mornings polishing cars under the surveillance of his father, who could never resist pointing out the parts he'd missed. And if those memories weren't bad enough, not far away was the ice cream factory where he'd once worked in the holidays as a student; and spent night after night in that vast gloomy and misty fridge, which seemed to him at the time like a frozen version of hell. In the end he'd been given the sack, although the personnel manager had been oddly sympathetic; and seemed to want to make all kinds of excuses for him, including making the suggestion that the trouble might have been that he had been unable to get used to sleeping during the day. But he was all wrong. Bernard had slept perfectly well. The real trouble was that he had never discovered what he was supposed to be doing in that fridge in the first place. An experience that had always seemed strangely symbolic, especially since he still hadn't found out what he was supposed to be doing. Perhaps he never would.

Not only was it disturbing to find himself literally back in the past, but on the return journey Tissue kept on and on nagging him to take her back to the flat so they could make love. 'Come on Steiny (by then she had long since given up calling him professor), it'll only take an hour,' she pleaded, sliding her hand between his thighs. It wasn't as if he didn't want to either, but that he felt agonisingly caught between desire and love. Desire to do what Tissue wanted, and what in a sense he also wanted, and the much deeper need not to disappoint Olivia, who, at that very moment, was probably expecting him to walk through the door of her room in the hospital.

Taking Tissue to the Polish tea room to try and placate her the way one might a child hadn't worked either, since no sooner had he left her for a moment to go downstairs and telephone Olivia to say he'd been delayed, than almost the whole of the Polish Government in exile had gathered round her table and started to proposition her in Polish. Almost every one of them was over eighty and they'd failed to notice that she couldn't understand a word they said. But who could blame them for trying; the way she had wiggled along between the tables when they'd arrived was enough to stir up memories of sexual potency in even the most feeble octogenarian. She looked so provocative that it was almost enough to make one of the life guards in the painting on the wall above the table on which the cakes were displayed, suddenly come to life and carry her off. However, worse was still to come, because when Bernard finally managed to extract Tissue from her newly found admirers (who seemed to be getting more excited by the minute and might be on the verge of doing God knows what), and they left the café to look for a taxi to take her back to college – there simply wasn't one to be found. This wouldn't have been so terrible, had not Tissue refused point blank to take the tube, which, as far as she was concerned was a completely unseemly mode of transport for a princess and the daughter of a king, even if he had been recently forced to abdicate for trying to get the country's gold reserves out of the country on his private plane. And choosing that particular moment to reveal the real reason he couldn't drive her himself was hardly diplomatic either.

As soon as he said it he realised he'd made a dreadful mistake, because immediately she started to shout at him that he was deceitful and not a real gentleman at all. He became so embarrassed at being shouted at in the street in that way, that he caved in and agreed to drive her back to college himself. All the way there he felt more and more anxious and guilty, caught as he undoubtedly was, between the demands of one woman and the expectations of another.

Worse was still to come. When Bernard finally arrived at the hospital, instead of finding Olivia alone, or with her parents as he'd expected, there was someone in the room who he'd never seen before. Sitting as close to the bed as possible (without actually being in it) was a strange looking man with a huge ginger beard, who was staring into Olivia's eyes as if she was some sort of wonder-working icon that was about to perform a miracle. For a few moments there ensued a strained and embarrassed silence during which all three exchanged glances, no one quite knowing what to say. Then Olivia, trying perhaps to make the best of the situation, introduced them to each other. Bernard could hardly bear to look the man in the face, because in those few minutes, he had already begun to sense that there was between them more than mere friendship and that his arrival had interrupted something. What he couldn't understand was what she could possibly see in him. Unless of course it was simply that Christopher (hardly an appropriate name for the admirer of a nice Jewish girl like Olivia anyway) looked remarkably like Donatello's sculpture of John the Baptist, which had made such a deep impression on her when they had seen it in Venice during their honeymoon. He had the saint's look of suffering and intense spirituality, which was the sort of thing that Olivia was always very attracted by, and which generally left Bernard completely cold. In fact, her Christ bearer might even have been mistaken for J. C. himself, if, that is, Christ really looked the way most people assumed he did; and wasn't in fact a short, baldheaded man, who only took up prophecy after being an ignominious failure in the olive oil business. For himself, no doubt partly out of jealousy, Bernard didn't like the look of Christopher at all, and found it hard to believe that she could be seriously involved with him.

Olivia's admirer's feeble attempt to endear himself to Bernard didn't help much either. Having the audacity to offer him a cup of tea, in that almost inaudible voice of his, which sounded remarkably like air being expelled from a soda syphon, practically made Bernard lose complete control of himself. What business had this interloper got to play host anyway! Probably at any moment he would ask him if he would care to kiss his own wife (okay, they were separated, but even so). And just then, looking at her propped up on the pillows, surrounded by spring flowers, in a pure white lawn night dress, her hair up the way he liked it so much, with her beautiful long arms spread out on the covers in front of her, as if they were just waiting to enfold him (she always did look particularly beautiful lying down) he really did feel like bending down and kissing her not once but over and over. Yes, at that moment he hated Christopher, but he didn't reveal how he felt, because he loathed confrontations, and the last thing he wanted was to make a scene, which could hardly do Olivia any good, especially in her condition (not that she was really ill, having only come into hospital for a minor operation on her knee). So, instead of expressing what he was feeling, he simply mumbled something about needing to get some cigarettes and rushed out of the room.

So that's it, Bernard thought, racing along the pavement as fast as his legs would carry him, as if speed would somehow enable him to banish from his mind what had just happened. Yes, it was quite clear now that it wasn't any longer just Olivia's obsession with Gotsky and Potsky's movement for the achievement of higher human consciousness which kept them apart – as if that wasn't bad enough – but the existence of an admirer as well. No doubt, she'd met him during one of those countless weekends she spent at their Institute doing all kinds of crazy physical and mental exercises (including digging in the grounds and avoiding using the word *and* for hours and hours on end) which she rather cryptically referred to as 'The Work', and which was presumably intended to prepare acolytes for the dawning of the new age – whatever that was. Oh, if only he hadn't been so scathing when she'd first told him about the movement. But that time when he was driving her to the airport and she suddenly began to talk about Gotsky's ability to materialise cameos of himself out of thin air, and be – if he so wished – in at least two places at once, he could hardly stop himself laughing. 'After all,' he remembered saying at the time, 'even if he was capable of doing such things, how could it possibly help you?' Not that saying that had done any good whatsoever, because she simply thought he was being cynical. If only he'd kept his mouth shut, by now they might be climbing the staircase of higher consciousness together. Instead of which, he was still traipsing along in the mud unable to see the wood for the trees as always. But it was no use regretting that now; he never had been good at concealing what he felt, least of all from Olivia. Worse still, she had recently told him that she could no longer imagine having a relationship with anyone who didn't share her belief in the movement. God, what an awful night he'd had after she said that! Probably that fellow Christopher wouldn't have any problem in fulfilling that requirement at least, especially if he was right and they really had met during one of those weekends at that Institute.

What a pity he hadn't felt free to do what he really felt like doing when he saw Christopher drooling over Olivia like that. A real gentleman would at least have had the decency to get up and leave when the husband arrived, instead of carrying on sitting there as if nothing had happened. If only it was still possible to challenge someone to a duel. The insensitive way he had offered him that cup of tea would easily have served as sufficient pretext for slapping him across the face with a glove. He could see it all: a park at dawn, the early morning mist rising between the trees, the pearl handled duelling pistols nestling in their case lined with red velvet. But what was the use of dreaming; duelling had gone out years ago. The only modern alternative would have been to have grabbed him by the lapels and thrown him out of the room and then knocked him out with one blow, but alas, he wasn't capable of that either. He didn't even know how to make a fist, and could never remember whether you put your thumb inside or outside after you folded your fingers? If only he'd paid more attention when his uncles – amateur boxers to a man – had tried to teach him the rudiments of the noble art. Even if he hadn't actually punched him on the nose, knowing how to might at least have enabled him to handle the situation better, instead of having to rush out of the room so ignominiously.

But reacting the way he had did at least have its compensations, because when he returned, an hour or so later, Olivia was obviously very impressed by how he'd behaved. Not that he'd risked going back to her room until he had waited around downstairs in the foyer for ages, in the middle of a group of masked arab women and their overweight husbands, and seen Christopher leave with his own eyes:

'Bernie you were wonderful, that was so tactful,' Olivia said, this time lifting those beautiful long arms of hers to embrace him, as soon as he came into the room.

'I did it for your sake,' Bernard said, puffing himself up. 'If it hadn't been for you, I would have punched him on the nose without fail.'

'Bernie, you know that isn't true. You've never punched anyone on the nose in your whole life,' Olivia said, as always clearly enjoying making fun of him.

'There's always a first time.' Bernard said, thinking that it was almost embarrassing how well she knew him. She seemed to know what he was going to do even before he did himself. She even used to know when he was wearing those buckskin brogue shoes she hated so much without even looking at his feet. One look at the guilty expression on his face was quite enough to give the whole game away.

'Anyway, it was very sweet of you to leave like that. It was so confusing. It never occurred to me that you'd bump into each other. I thought you'd have been and gone by the time he arrived. How was I to know you'd be so late.'

'Never mind. It was just a bit of a shock that's all. Anyway, who is he?' Bernard said, not that he really wanted to know the answer.

'Just a friend'

'Someone you met at one of those weekends of yours I suppose. He certainly looks the type alright.'

'Don't be so sarcastic Bernie, he's just a friend of mine that's all. Just because he isn't you!'

'Thank God, I'm not him. All I can say is he doesn't look like a lifetime's companion to me.' But managing to make that witty remark, even if it did make Olivia laugh, was hardly a compensation for not having let Christopher know what he really felt.

The thing was though that, once Bernard had recovered from the shock of finding a strange man in Olivia's room like that, he wasn't nearly as upset about it as he might have been. Perhaps this was because, in some way, his relationship with Tissue cancelled out whatever might be going on between Olivia and Christopher, leaving the feelings that Olivia and he had for each other completely intact. Or maybe, that West Indian mechanic had put his finger on the truth, as they were looking up at the underneath of Bernard's car a few weeks before, when he had said – after searching for a moment for a simile – that a mechanical ignoramus like Bernard would be able to understand that shock absorbers were really just like women. Certainly, Bernard felt much less upset than he would have done had not Tissue been there in the background, waiting, or so he assumed, to console him whenever he wished.

4

A few days later Bernard realised he had been quite wrong to assume that he still had Tissue to fall back on. He didn't. That row outside the Polish Tea Room had not been, as he had thought at the time, a simple misunderstanding that could be easily resolved, but was in effect the end of their relationship. Somehow, concealing and then revealing the real reason why he couldn't take her back to the flat, had resulted in her becoming completely disillusioned with him and there seemed to be nothing he could do to patch things up. Not that he tried very hard, because for some time now he had realised that their relationship was drawing to an end. Even so, he soon missed her, and from time to time wondered if he shouldn't perhaps have tried harder to keep things going a little while longer – at least to the end of term anyway – after which he would not have had to endure the ordeal of seeing Tissue in class and being frequently overwhelmed by a desire to sleep with her. Perhaps his friend Maurice Hasselblad had been right to chastise him for not making enough of a fuss of her right from the beginning. Maybe he really should have sent her enormous bouquets of flowers and bottles of perfume, the way he still did to Olivia. But even if he had, he doubted that their relationship would have lasted more than another week or so, at which point he would have started to want more of her – as he always did after a woman had left him.

And then on top of losing Tissue, towards the end of term Bernard received a memo from President Hatrick saying he wanted to see him in his office in a few days time. At first he couldn't understand what it could be about. Perhaps despite all his attempts at discretion they had finally found out about his affair with Tissue and were about to sack him for gross moral turpitude. But surely no one could possibly have recognised his voice when he used to phone up the college to speak to her late at night, and Tissue would have never told anyone about their relationship herself. No, that couldn't be it, and even if it was, at least now he would be able to say with complete honesty that their relationship was finished. It was much more likely that Hatrick wanted to see him because he'd found out that Bernard couldn't handle English 101, and that far from being the master of his subject, he was mastered by it. Oh, why had he been so foolish as to make all those jokes about his poor grasp of grammar and being haunted by semicolons with other members of the faculty over lunch that day in the canteen. Those jokes really had been far too transparent. After all, they weren't so naive as not to realise that there must be some truth behind them. And then of course, there'd been all those complaints about the rumpus that went on in his class, not to mention the occasion when that girl had walked out. Perhaps Hatrick had also been told by Weinberg how he had to reprimand him more than once for being late for class. Bernard remembered how humiliated he'd felt having to stand there, with all the students milling around outside the classroom, while Weinberg went on and on about it in that stentorian voice of his. The trouble was, although he'd objected to being told off like that, there wasn't anything he could say in his own defence. Weinberg was absolutely right – he had often been late for class, sometimes even three quarters of an hour late. Yes, he felt sure that what was about to happen would only confirm once again that the old man had been right when he used to advise him never to work for anybody else, a piece of advice that Bernard had carried a stage further by hardly ever working at all.

Well, at least now I'll find out what it's all about, Bernard thought, as he knocked on the President's door on the morning of his appointment.

'Oh, it's you Bernard. Come in, I've been expecting you. Take a seat. How are things? Weinberg tells me your English class hasn't been going too well?'

'Oh, it's not been going so badly. They're a bit of a difficult bunch. I just try to work with the chaos, that's all I can do.' So he knows, Bernard thought, expecting the axe to fall at any moment.

'Now I know that isn't entirely true Bernard,' Hatrick said, giving him the kind of suspicious look Dr Lear always gave him when he didn't believe a word he was saying. 'Students have been coming to me to complain you know; they claim they're not making any progress and that you can't even keep control in class.'

He must mean that girl who walked out, Bernard thought.

'What's more, apparently you don't hand their essays back on time. So everything can't be okay, now can it Bernard? Perhaps something's troubling you, something personal I mean, that's interfering with your work. I hope you don't mind my asking, but are you and Olivia still living apart?'

'Yes, we are. I don't think she'll ever come back now. It's been nearly two years since she left,' Bernard said, unable to prevent his voice trailing off in dismay.

'That must be very hard. Siggy once told me how you felt about her. I know how I'd feel if Marilyn ever left me,' Hatrick said, glancing momentarily at the photograph of his wife and children in a red leather frame on the desk in front of him, 'In fact, you don't look at all well to me. Have you been sleeping alright?'

'I'm okay, I suppose, but I must admit I don't sleep well,' Bernard said, beginning to wonder why Hatrick was being so sympathetic, since he never had been before. 'Of course valium helps. Wonderful stuff valium. Have you ever thought that it would take at least ten or fifteen years of yoga or meditation to achieve anything like the kind of inner calm one capsule gives you in ten minutes. The trouble is it doesn't always work. I suppose I must still be too upset about what happened to my marriage even for valium to work all the time.'

But why was he saying all this. Dr Hatrick wasn't really interested in how he felt. In all probability he was only asking out of politeness. He wasn't his analyst. What he should be doing now was putting up a front, not launching into this great confession. But somehow he just couldn't stop himself. He'd been in such a state lately that if anyone asked him how he was, what little self control he possessed crumbled away and he started telling them everything. Even so, he ought to be able to control himself by now, especially in front of someone like Hatrick. He sometimes thought there ought to be huge electronic ears on every street corner into which people in his sort of state could pour their troubles. God knows he wasn't the only one who needed them. Almost every day he saw someone shouting or talking to themselves in the street. Maybe he ought to develop the idea. With modern electronics, they shouldn't be all that hard to produce. All that was needed was a huge ear shaped cubicle to be known as a Steinway, which the customer could enter and unburden himself, and in exchange for a small fee, receive advice or sympathy. Twelve types of advice, or solace would probably be sufficient, since even worries come in relatively limited varieties. If he patented the idea and it went well, perhaps in a few years he would become a household name, and in due course Steinway might be to the psyche what Hore Belisha was to the pedestrian crossing. But he knew that this was just another of his business fantasies that in the end would come to nothing.

'Well, if you aren't sleeping properly Bernard, that at least partly explains why your teaching hasn't been up to standard. Tell me Bernard, how old are you?'

'Thirty-three.'

'The same age as Christ at the time of the crucifixion,' Hatrick said, almost as if he were thinking aloud.

'But what significance can that possibly have for me?'

'Only that it's often the beginning of a very difficult period in a man's life.' Surely, thought Bernard, he doesn't mean that Christ was having a mid-life crisis? Of course Hatrick had once been a priest but this sounded completely crazy.

'Anyway, I can see that this is definitely a very difficult period in your life for sure, and it's not that I'm unsympathetic. I felt much the same when I was your age, but... (Yes, here it comes, Bernard thought, sensing the axe whistling down above his head, yet at the same time feeling a strange sense of relief). The trouble is Bernard, English 101 is too vital a course in the programme for me to allow it to be inadequately taught. Perhaps it wasn't the right course for you in the first place. Maybe it was my fault for suggesting you take it on.'

'I could always try a new approach,' Bernard said anxiously, trying not to sound too much as if he was pleading, which of course was precisely what he was doing.

'No, unfortunately, it's much too late for that now Bernard. Weinberg and I have already decided to take you off the course. We'll be sorry to lose you of course, but the students' needs simply have to come first.'

'Maybe you'll be able to find me something more suitable to teach by next semester?' Bernard said, feeling suddenly mortified by what was happening.

'Why of course Bernard, if anything appropriate should come along we'll certainly get in touch with you.' At which point Hatrick signalled that the interview was at an end by getting up and escorting him to the door.

Well at least he hadn't dismissed my suggestion out of hand, Bernard thought, as he dragged himself along the corridor, feeling distinctly as if he'd just been mugged. The first time he'd ever got the sack (for failing to be able to add up, even on an adding machine) it had been a different story. Then the boss had reacted to his tentative request that they find him something else to do by shouting at him in exasperation: 'But Bernard, what can you do?' A judgement on his abilities that he'd never been entirely able to forget. In the circumstances he should be grateful that he had been fired in the gentlest and most diplomatic way imaginable. Although it was obvious there was no question in Hatrick's mind of his ever being offered a job there again.

But a few days later, Bernard was surprised to find his original feeling of gratitude at having been treated so gently, turning into indignation. No, he wasn't going to allow himself to be got rid of so easily, not without trying to exact some small revenge anyhow. So, before the end of that week, Bernard selected one of the *Notes from the President's desk* in which Hatrick, in that uniquely bureaucratic and humourless style of his (which characteristically included references to such things as exit meetings, invitational workshops and the colleges efforts to achieve reaffirmation of their accreditation) with which he had been bombarded all semester, marked it D, and posted it back to him. Needless to say, he didn't refrain from pointing out the weakness of the sentence structure, the impoverishment of the vocabulary and the overall lack of clarity in the thought that pervaded not only that particular note, but all the other ones he'd received as well. The day he posted it, Bernard felt not only extraordinarily pleased with himself, but absolutely amazed that he could have done such a thing. He would certainly never have thought that he had made such rapid progress with his therapy that he was already capable of acting in such a self assertive way. Yet despite the pleasure making that gesture had undoubtedly given him, by the end of that semester he once again found himself in exactly the same position he had been in at the beginning – without any idea of what to do, or where he would ever again find another woman like Tissue.

A Businessman Second

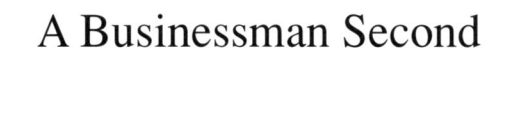

1

Despite the pleasure sending that letter had undoubtedly given Bernard, he was much more upset about getting the sack than he at first realised. It was only that following Friday afternoon, sitting in Dr Lear's pale green consulting room (a room in which by then he'd already spent so many deeply satisfying hours talking entirely about himself), that he began to realise quite how upset he really was. Without Dr Lear's help it's doubtful that he would ever have entirely understood what that experience really meant to him. But then, it was only his analyst who would never allow him to fudge important issues and constantly forced him to confront the truth about himself. Even on those days when he felt he had absolutely nothing to add to the ongoing story of his life, and made some lame joke about Dr Lear taking the wheel for a while, because he didn't feel like talking, Dr Lear wouldn't have any of it. Somehow, he always knew exactly how to get Bernard to reveal what was really going on inside him. All that was ever needed to shake Bernard out of one of his long silences was for Dr Lear to inquire: 'And what about Olivia, have you heard anything from her lately?' And Bernard would immediately begin talking away, primed as it were by his own anguish. Yes, he understood perfectly how reluctant Bernard always was to face up to things like this. After all, wasn't it Dr Lear who'd once called him a master of avoidance.

As usual, Dr Lear didn't say anything for the first few minutes, but sat quite still, holding his face between his hands, in that familiar pose of his and stared at Bernard with his cold blue eyes, waiting for him to begin.

'Well Bernard,' Dr Lear said, after the silence had continued for some time.

'I've been sacked,' Bernard said, looking anxious. 'They finally discovered I didn't know how to teach that subject. I've never been all that good at grammar. Students had been complaining. I don't know what I'm going to do now. I liked going there.'

'Oh come now Bernard, that's nothing to be upset about. That job was just a red herring.'

'A red herring? I don't understand.'

'I mean it wasn't a real job. What did it pay you anyway?'

'A thousand pounds a term, I suppose.'

'There you are, that's what I mean. A few thousand pounds is hardly a respectable salary for a man of your age. It's about time you were earning a real living Bernard.'

Recently Dr Lear had begun to sound more and more like Sam, Bernard thought, only he didn't have to pay Sam for his advice. He also reminded him of an old bank manager of his who, years ago, he'd somehow managed to manoeuvre into the role of analyst. Or was it just that everyone always seemed to be giving him the same advice?

'That money your aunt left you won't last forever, yet you persist in carrying on as if you had a substantial private income,' Lear continued, 'but sooner or later Bernard, you're going to have to face up to reality.'

'But I'll miss going there,' Bernard said, plaintively. 'I hate change of any kind. Whenever I move a chair at home, I invariably move it back to exactly the same position a few minutes later.'

'There's nothing to be proud of in that,' Dr Lear said, rather sharply as if he were a schoolmaster ticking off a dim pupil.

'But what shall I do instead?'

'I don't know, that's for you to decide, but it ought to be something that gives you a decent income at least. That little job of yours was only a way of enabling you to avoid the issue. You're a great procrastinator Bernard. Perhaps being fired will turn out to be a good thing in the end. At least it might force you to do something at last. Weren't you talking about some business venture or other a week or two ago. Something to do with rugs wasn't it?'

'Yes, you remember that friend of mine, Maurice Hasselblad, who made a fortune in the rug business, well he suggested I give it a try. But I'm not sure it's a good idea. I know hardly anything about rugs. I just like them that's all.'

There he goes again trying to get me to go into business. Only last week he went on and on about how the analyst next door was giving up his practice to start an electronics business, Bernard thought, beginning to feel irritated. If he was so keen on business why didn't he try it himself? All this talk about business was probably simple projection anyhow.

'You don't need to know all that much Bernard.'

'But I don't want to be a businessman,' Bernard said, feeling increasingly exasperated. 'I come from generations of businessmen, and the last thing I ever wanted to do was to become one myself. I always believed there was more to life than just making a living. It's only in the twentieth-century that the mad idea that everyone should work has become so popular. A hundred years ago the world was full of people who hardly ever did anything more energetic than changing for dinner.'

'Of course there's more to life than making a living Bernard, I'm not saying that. But think for a moment about the words you've just used. Making a living is awfully close to making a life isn't it? All I'm saying is that if you made a living you'd have more self-esteem; and if you succeeded at something, even if it wasn't absolutely the right thing for you, I'm sure you'd feel much better.'

'You remember Dr Lear how you once said that everyone lays down on the couch in the end, well, I think that moment has arrived for me too now.' Bernard said, putting his hands on the arms of the chair and beginning to get to his feet.

'No, no, Bernard, that's not for you. How many times have I got to tell you, that you need to keep your feet firmly on the ground.' Dr Lear said, with such a look of consternation on his face, that Bernard seriously thought that had he tried to lay down on the couch at that moment, Dr Lear would have physically attempted to prevent him from doing so.

'You see what I mean Bernard, Just the mere mention of reality and straight away you want to lay down.'

'I still can't see how succeeding at something I've spent my whole life avoiding is going to make me feel any better? If you're so keen on business why don't you have a go at it yourself.'

'I'll ignore that Bernard. But you'd be surprised, if you succeeded at anything right now it would be a positive step.'

'I'd rather devote my life to art. I used to think I'd like to be a writer or something like that,' Bernard said dreamily, beginning to feel that he'd had about as much reality as he could stand for one day.

'Now that's a very difficult field Bernard. Do you really think that a life spent raking over the past would be such a good thing for you?

You're too bogged down in the past as it is. You don't even much like looking in my mirror, never mind staring day after day into one of your own making, which is what being an artist often means.'

'Perhaps you're right, maybe I should at least give the idea of going into business some serious thought. It's not as if I've got anything else to do right now,' Bernard said, beginning to slip into a fantasy about becoming fabulously wealthy: having a villa in the South of France, a mixed assortment of mistresses, garages full of Bentleys and Ferraris, monogrammed shirts like his Uncle David used to wear, wild crocodile shoes and only dining in restaurants where the tables were at least five feet apart from each other.

'Don't just think about it Bernard, at this stage in your life you must do something, even if it isn't perfect,' Dr Lear said, getting up to indicate that his fifty minutes were at an end, which, as had often happened before, was precisely the moment when Bernard felt he was just beginning to get somewhere.

Yes, perhaps Dr Lear was right, Bernard thought as he was driving home. At least if I succeeded in business for once in my life I'd be able to gauge exactly how I was doing. Hadn't old Popoff once told him, that all a businessman needed to do to find out how successful he was, was to go to the bank and ask to see his statement. That at least had to be an improvement on Bernard's present, more or less immeasurable, sense of failure. But what if Dr Lear was playing some sort of game with him to see how he would react? Why should he believe him anyway. Weren't analysts supposed to refrain from giving advice? It wasn't that long ago, when Bernard had been considering whether or not to accept the job at Dullworth College, that Dr Lear went on and on about how a teaching career might be just the right thing for him. On the other hand, since he wasn't having proper psychoanalysis, but only went to see Dr Lear once a week, perhaps he felt free to give Bernard as much guidance as he considered necessary. Anyway, whatever Dr Lear thought, maybe going into business wasn't such a bad idea after all.

For the next few days Bernard could hardly think about anything else apart from his new dilemma of whether or not to become a businessman. At thirty-three perhaps it still wasn't too late to become a tycoon. And if he did decide to go into business he had the right background for it. Hadn't his uncle David made a fortune in the furniture business. Even now Bernard could remember the sound of the frogs croaking by the tennis court in his garden. And all through his childhood he had listened to the murmurings of businessmen, not that he had ever understood what they were saying, or even been very interested. But perhaps, despite himself, some of it had gone in. Even Sam once said he had a good business mind. But understanding was one thing. The real question was did he possess all the other necessary qualities to be a successful businessman such as resolution, drive, application, decisiveness, the courage to take decisions and so on. On the other hand, did the fact that for as long as he could remember he'd had business fantasies mean that he had always had an unconscious desire to become a businessman? Was it possible that he'd been avoiding his true destiny for years? Perhaps he'd been making a mistake all along, especially since he'd recently made the discovery (one that was of course perfectly obvious to everybody else) that the whole of life was in a sense business. Was it possible that the reason he was so obsessed now about what to do, was because Dr Lear's advice had stirred up inside him a long repressed wish to become a businessman?

He had once been offered the opportunity of going into business, even if it was only his father's, but he'd been young and idealistic and turned him down without even thinking it over. If only he'd accepted, who knows, by now he might have been rich. Not that if he'd become a businessman then he would have been the same person he was today. He wouldn't have been so perfectly equipped for a life of leisure, even if he had the money for it. On the other hand, being someone else might not have been such a bad thing. As it was, he sometimes dreamed about finding someone to exchange personalities with. Ideally, it would be a person who was insensitive, stable, absolutely never suffered from self-doubt, and of course, was well off. Occasionally, Bernard thought he saw the kind of man he had in mind sitting alone in a restaurant. Usually he was very well dressed, bald, wore a moustache, and had a profoundly vacant expression on his face. Oh, if only he'd known then what he knew now, he would never have turned the old man down. He'd finally realised not long ago that one of the most important things in life was foresight, the trouble was that by the time he usually got it it had turned into hindsight. Well, it was no good thinking about that any more, the past was over and done with as Dr Lear never seemed to tire of telling him. Yet, if that was really true, how did you explain the existence of remorse – or even its weak-kneed cousin regret? But what should he do? He had to do something, if only because his capital just wasn't going to last forever. At any moment the bank would probably begin to charge for the letters they now sent him almost every day about his overdraft. Soon he was going to have to transfer more money. Yes, he had to do something – but what?

Even if he did decide to take the enormous step of going into business, was the rug business the right one to go into? It was obviously perfect for his friend Maurice, who clearly revelled in speeding from capital to capital with a priceless Persian rug on the back seat of his Porsche. But whenever in the past Bernard imagined himself as a businessman, it was always as some kind of financial wizard, or at the very least a captain of industry; one of those modern heroes, whose resolute and determined faces – faces that clearly meant business – stared out at you from the financial pages of the newspapers. In these fantasies he always pictured himself in a Saville Row suit, with a gold chain leading from his lapel to his breast pocket (probably with nothing on the end of it), being driven to his elegant suite of offices in the city. Or he envisioned himself sitting at a huge desk behind a phalanx of telephones from which he conducted his worldwide business empire. He'd always longed for an office to go to, especially if it wasn't too far away and, most important, he didn't have to go there every day. Sometimes in these daydreams he imagined himself as a consultant (a fantasy he'd stolen from his brother-in-law) but what he might be a consultant in he hadn't the vaguest idea. One thing was certain, he'd never imagined that he would ever end up in anything as unglamorous as the the rug business.

Despite his doubts, Bernard was almost completely carried away about the great future that lay ahead of him in business, to the extent that monogrammed shirts had begun to appear on the horizon of his psyche practically every day. Nevertheless, he decided that before finally making up his mind he must first consult Sam. And anyway, there was hardly anything he enjoyed more than finding some pretext for asking Sam's advice.

2

It so happened that Bernard had a long standing arrangement to have dinner with Sam at the Hungaria that following Saturday, which, since it was somewhere Sam had always been very receptive to anything Bernard had to say to him, was obviously the ideal place to ask his advice. It wasn't just that the food was good – although the Hungaria served the best Hungarian food anywhere outside of Budapest. Bernard could think of nowhere else where you could find such delicacies as cold cherry soup, wild duck, smoked goose (served with what the waiters comically referred to as 'Jewish beans'); such paprikashes and goulashes; and the gormand's delight – the Transylvanian mixed grill – not to mention the cheese dumplings in plum sauce, the poppyseed pancakes and the cold summer puddings. Even the ambience, as far as Bernard was concerned, was almost perfect, not least because in the past few years he had begun to have – you couldn't really say he suffered from it – what Dr Lear insisted on referring to as a 'red plush complex'. By this he meant that Bernard had a definite need to spend at least part of each week in sumptuous, if not slightly old fashioned surroundings, in rooms furnished in red plush with gilt mirrors, and with those gilt lights that looked as if they grew out of the wall, or where he would be able to sit and gaze up into the branches of an enormous crystal chandelier. Needless to say, this was almost exactly what the interior of the Hungaria was like. It also happened to be the restaurant that Bernard had been going to all his life, since he was first taken there as a small boy of seven or eight, and had watched the flames curling around the bottom of a copper frying pan, whilst a Debreziner steak was cooked at their table, to the accompaniment of a melancholy tune played on the violin by an ageing Hungarian wearing a toupée. That music always seemed to bring tears into the old man's eyes and started him reminiscing about the wonderful life he'd led in Budapest before the war, although, as far as

Bernard could tell, that largely appeared to consist of going to restaurants almost exactly like the Hungaria and eating the day away. But there must have been more to it than that.

In the years since his father's death Bernard had grown to love that restaurant almost as much as he had. He often thought that he would be perfectly happy to die there one evening, in the midst of transporting a spoonful of poppyseed pancake to his lips. Whether or not such a beautiful end would ever be his, he always thought about his father whenever he went there. It was certainly a better way of remembering him than lighting a memorial candle on the anniversary of his death (indeed, the few times he'd remembered to do that, the candle had always gone out after a couple of hours, which seemed to him to be peculiarly symbolic). But then it wasn't all that surprising that he should have found it so easy to think about his father in the Hungaria with such affection; after all he had been a great restaurant man and was always at his most genial with a napkin tucked into the third button of his shirt, leaning over a white tablecloth on which were arrayed some of the greatest dishes of Central Europe. It was also entirely characteristic of Bernard that he should have chosen to bring up the question of his future in a place that was so redolent of his past.

'Well, are you feeling any better?' Sam said, while they waited for the first course to arrive.

'Not much. It's very difficult living without Olivia.'

'But you've been separated for nearly two years. You ought to be getting used to it by now Bernard.'

'What's a couple of years by comparison with my feelings for her. Let me tell you a story Sam, then perhaps you'll understand. A year ago an old friend of my mother died of cancer. She was a remarkably beautiful woman – very tall, Titian hair, green eyes, cream coloured skin dotted delicately with freckles. A natural nobility of soul. She was just exquisite. Whenever I saw her I thought of a princess in a Tolstoy novel. Well, her husband absolutely doted on her. After she died he just couldn't stay still and was constantly rushing from one city or country to another. I suppose he felt completely rootless without her. He died a couple of months ago supposedly of a heart attack, but I know it was because he couldn't bear to live without her. Well, that's roughly how I feel about Olivia. I don't think I'll ever really get over our marriage breaking up.'

'But in time surely...' Sam said, looking both amazed and rather moved.

'Time has nothing to do with it Sam – the human heart doesn't wear a wristwatch. There are some things in life one never entirely recovers from. A part of me still hopes she'll come back, and if she ever gets over her obsession with spiritual enlightenment she might.'

'Even so, you can't carry on living entirely by yourself. Can't you find a girlfriend, if only for the companionship. If you don't mind my saying so, a middle-aged man like you needs sex,' Sam said, pointing his fork at him.

'Of course I've tried to find one, but it isn't all that easy you know,' Bernard said, astonished by how candid Sam was capable of being at times.

'Obviously you haven't tried hard enough. In your position I'd have had several by now. You give up too easily. It's the same with everything you do. You must learn to be more persistent Bernard. What about work, have you found something else to do now you've no longer got that absurd job at – what was that place called – oh yes, Dullworth College? Not that I ever thought that would lead anywhere. I must say I always found it hard to understand how you could ever have allowed yourself to work for such a pittance.'

As soon as Sam said that, Bernard realised immediately that the moment had come to bring up the subject of his going into business, although he had intended to wait until after they'd had their dessert and were drinking a glass of Tokai. Not that, as it turned out, it mattered, because much to Bernard's surprise, after questioning him carefully to find out what he knew about rugs, which he concluded, though not an enormous amount was probably sufficient to begin with, Sam gave the idea his qualified approval. Of course he might very well have been influenced by the fact that he knew Bernard always had Maurice Hasselblad's advice to fall back on if necessary.

'Yes, I think on the whole it's a good idea. Of course it's not nearly as good as if you'd somehow managed to become a sleeping partner in someone else's business Bernard, or best of all had a rich father.'

Bernard nodded. He'd heard Sam say this sort of thing many times before, especially whilst they were swimming together in the pool on Saturday afternoons, and he couldn't have agreed more. But then, he'd never found it all that difficult to imagine himself stretched out on a couch snoozing the day away in someone else's office. And as far as having inherited a substantial fortune was concerned, that would have been by far the best thing that could ever have happened to him. But there was another attractive alternative – which of course he didn't mention – and that was for Sam to offer him a position in his own office. After all, he'd given his cousin Max one, so why shouldn't Bernard get one as well? Surely, there was room enough for two smos in an office as large as Sam's. He could post letters every bit as well as Max could. What's more, Sam's office wasn't all that far away, and was absolutely overflowing with the most attractive secretaries, personal assistants and receptionists imaginable. But obviously Sam was far too shrewd to land himself with another dope like Max. Giving Bernard advice was one thing, but having him in his office all day and every day, was quite another.

Sam was much less impressed by the way Bernard, excited by having got Sam's approval, proceeded to carry on about his passion for antique rugs and how attractive they would be to deal with. He must have sensed – without Bernard saying as much – that because they were so aesthetically pleasing, Bernard had concluded that being involved with them at least wouldn't detract too much from his self-image.

'That's a lot of nonsense Bernard. The important thing in business is not what it is, but how well you buy it. If you buy something well, you'll always find someone who'll buy it from you, even if the worst comes to the worst and you have to sit on it for years. And another thing – coming back to what you said about not knowing a vast amount about rugs – the important thing in business is not to be proud. You must be prepared to ask advice. When I first went into business I hardly knew anything and I've got where I am today partly by watching other people and listening carefully to what they told me. Also, if you are really serious about wanting to be a businessman you must learn to take care of your capital, and perhaps most important, you must watch your business. If you're going to have a business of your own Bernard you've simply got to look after it.'

When Sam said this it suddenly occurred to Bernard that having a business wasn't perhaps all that different from keeping a pet. Then Sam started yet again to tell him the story of Harold Golding, which to him, was nothing less than the parable of the good businessman. What impressed Sam so much was the way Harold had built up a nationwide chain of garages from scratch and spent almost the whole of the week being driven round the country to inspect them in person.

'You see Bernard, Harold would never have accomplished what he has without taking care of his business; it's a virtue that you must do your best to emulate.'

How mad can you get, Bernard thought, remembering how he'd nearly fallen off the chair laughing when he first heard Sam tell this story one evening over dinner. The idea that anyone would spend their life like that, just to become a successful businessman was almost unbelievable. Fortunately, it was difficult to imagine that his little enterprise would ever merit that much surveillance, which was just as well, since he found the idea of having to look after it to that extent unbearable.

That evening at the Hungaria was one of the most enjoyable he'd spent with Sam for months. Bernard enjoyed it so much that for the first time in years he took out his chequebook (which always seemed to grow visibly smaller in Sam's presence) and made a serious attempt to pay the bill. But as usual Sam wouldn't let him, and instead, pushing Bernard's chequebook aside, took the opportunity to admonish him once again to look after his capital. He then produced an enormous wad of notes from his pocket and proceeded to pay the bill in cash, giving the waiter an excessively large tip to ensure they received the same excellent service on their next visit. He also didn't forget to say, with his usual tact and eloquence what he'd often said before: that it was of no consequence who paid, but that the really important thing was the pleasure of dining together. The most gratifying thing for Bernard about the evening though was that he received Sam's approval. And later on he was able to go to sleep repeating like a mantra the latest instalment of his advice (advice which as always Bernard had listened to as if it had come from an old Testament

Prophet): 'Yes, I must watch the capital, watch the business, buy well, ask advice, watch...'

Well, if he did make untold wealth during his brief sojourn in the rug trade, no one ever told him about it. Even with Sam's blessing things started to go wrong almost from the very beginning. Perhaps it would have worked out better if Sam, instead of giving him all that advice, had offered to come along with him when he went to those auctions, at least then he wouldn't have been so lonely. In retrospect he sometimes thought that the real reason things had gone so wrong was that he'd been far too anxious to do everything right, which in effect seemed to prevent him from doing anything at all. There was also the fact that he probably didn't have enough capital to go into the rug business in the first place. Rugs were very expensive and, inveterate procrastinator that he was, he could never make up his mind whether to spend two thousand pounds of his capital on one rug or, to spread the risk over two, or three, or five or some other number... Moreover, he was so obsessed with following Sam's advice to look after his capital to the letter, that it was only with the greatest difficulty that he could bring himself to part with any of it.

The way he'd felt before the first auction hadn't been a good sign either. That day he was almost as nervous as before his first day at school, when he had galloped miles and miles on his rocking horse upstairs in the bedroom, hoping against hope that his initiation into the real world would somehow be called off at the last moment (which it was because his mother had got the day wrong). Worse than this nervousness, which he could more or less cope with, was that – although he was interested in one or two items he'd seen in the catalogue – when it came to it he was so lacking in self-confidence that he wasn't able to make a single bid. This could partly be attributed to the attitude of the other rug dealers who, more or less as soon as he had come into the room, gave him such antagonistic looks as to make it perfectly clear that should he so much as make a bid, let alone buy anything, they would sort him out afterwards. One of them in particular, a strange looking middle-aged man in a Homburg hat, with a goatee beard, wearing pince-nez, appeared to view his presence with particular animosity. He had given him such malevolent looks throughout the auction, that Bernard gradually became convinced that he wasn't any ordinary rug dealer, but was Gotsky, Olivia's guru, himself, although he didn't look like any of the photographs Bernard had ever seen of him. But that wouldn't have been a problem since, according to Olivia, he was easily capable of assuming any appearance he wished, as well as being in two places at the same time. Certainly, the fact that he was supposed to be abroad that week wouldn't have prevented him from attending the auction if he'd wanted to. And perhaps, since he had once been a prominent rug dealer in Paris, he was still interested in acquiring the odd rug for one or other of his country houses. Yes, this had to be him alright. Why else would he have looked at him in such an extraordinary way?

That they had never met wouldn't have prevented someone of Gotsky's psychic powers from knowing precisely who Bernard was. Oh, if only he hadn't made all those scathing remarks about him to Olivia a few weeks previously. They weren't just ordinary antagonistic looks either, but what he seemed to be attempting to do was to make Bernard feel so uneasy that he fled the auction altogether. He'd never known anyone to look at him like that before, even that Scientologist he'd met years ago, who seemed to enjoy trying to outstare him, hadn't come anywhere near it. Somehow Bernard managed to ignore Gotsky and remain precisely where he was. Not that it did him any good, because worse than the subtle and not so subtle pressures of Gotsky (or whoever he really was) and the other dealers, was what happened towards the end of the auction. It was then, just as he was about to make his last attempt to bid for something, that he suddenly started to hear his father's voice addressing him: 'What are you doing here? We both know you're not grown up enough to understand anything about business. Remember that time in Prague when that man came up to you in the street with a business proposition from which you could have made a handsome profit, even if it was a bit illegal. And what did you do? You were so nervous you turned him down, even after he'd actually said it was business in your pocket. You were a fool then and you're just as big a fool now. So how come you're a businessman all of a sudden?' Well, that did it, and for the rest of the afternoon Bernard just sat there overwhelmed by an enormous sense of inadequacy and defeat.

After the debacle of that first auction Bernard was about ready to give up. It seemed to him that the voice he'd heard – whether or not it really was his father's and not just his super-ego in disguise – might well have been absolutely right. Could he honestly say that anything had really changed to make him suddenly conclude that at the age of thirty-three and a half he had what it took to become a businessman? No, nothing had changed, he was just the same old Steinway he'd always been. He remembered feeling just as bored at the preview to that auction, as he had as a boy of ten when the old man had insisted (perhaps to give him a taste of what real life was like) that he accompany him and uncle Lou to used car auctions. While they were busy examining cars, all Bernard could think of was how long was it going to be before it was lunchtime. Had it not been for Dr Lear more or less insisting that he didn't give up so easily, he would never have found the will power to carry on, even for the short time he did. But then, he had been very impressed by Dr Lear telling him that the voice he'd heard was only his super-ego acting the opportunist and making a bit of a comeback. 'You've got to expect that sort of thing to happen Bernard, especially after what you've been feeling lately. I can assure you it won't continue. Once your self-esteem improves, you'll see it'll stop.' Dr Lear also thought that it was absolutely vital – if not for Bernard's success as a businessman, then at least for his progress as a patient – that he persist a little while longer. In his opinion, if Bernard gave up then, his self-esteem would never recover from the sense of defeat that would follow. So he had no choice – he simply had to give it another try.

Not that the next, and what turned out to be the last, auction he ever attended worked out much better. But at least he didn't have to listen to the old man going on and on about his inadequacies again. Dr Lear had been right about that. It might even have had a slightly better outcome, if he'd not been so foolish as to have bought a rug in near total darkness (It was so dark that winter morning that the grey light filtering into the basement auction room was barely adequate to see what colour his shoes were, never mind be able to judge the quality of a rug). He failed to notice how predominant the orange was, which, as Maurice had told him several times, was a sure sign that a rug was modern and therefore less valuable. Of course, he told himself later that if he had noticed he would never have bought it. But was that really true? He had gone into that auction so full of determination, that he would have probably bought more or less anything to avoid coming away empty handed. Even so, for a few minutes at least, he did manage to sustain a modest amount of confidence in it, especially since until he got it home he still hadn't noticed the orange at all. But then no sooner had the auction ended than someone, who must have been standing at the back, because Bernard hadn't noticed him before, came up and volunteered the opinion that the rug had been wrongly catalogued, and that there was no such thing as a 'Wandering Kazak', and what Bernard had purchased was just an ordinary Belouch. It was Nomadic of course, but not nearly so interesting or as valuable as a real Kazak. This opinion, by itself, would not necessarily have caused Bernard's confidence to give way, since it struck him as just the sort of thing people say on these occasions – rather like the way when you arrive tired out from a long journey and someone remarks: 'But surely you didn't come that way. If only you'd taken my route you would have saved yourself a couple of hours at least.' No, although the defences surrounding his self-confidence were little thicker than rice paper at that moment, he would have been able to withstand that kind of gratuitously offered opinion. And anyway, perhaps it wasn't an objective opinion at all, but was motivated by envy, and the man was simply irritated that he hadn't bought it himself. Maybe the rug was really a great buy and he'd just pulled off a coup, and right under the noses of all those professional dealers as well. He'd read in the papers about such things happening, so why shouldn't it happen to him. Unfortunately he soon realised that he was mistaken, because a little later while he was waiting upstairs in the queue to pay for it, two men immediately in front of him, who he'd been listening to for some time discussing their purchases, suddenly turned round and asked what he had bought. 'I bought the Wandering Kazak, Lot 89,' he replied blithely, still clinging to the belief that it had been a real steal at a hundred pounds. 'Oh,' they said in unison. Just 'Oh'. But that 'Oh' really did it. Bernard could literally feel his confidence draining away as he stood there, finally realising that he must have made a terrible mistake and that far from having got a terrific bargain, he'd only managed to buy that rug because nobody else in the room had been even remotely interested in it.

Worse was still to come, because once he got it home he not only became aware of how predominant the orange really was, but decided he didn't even like the rug. He couldn't bear the sight of it and after looking at it on the floor for a few minutes flung it into a cupboard. Not that doing that really put it out of his mind, because he couldn't resist every now and then taking it out again to see if it was really quite as bad as all that. 'How could I have been such a dumbbell,' he said to himself aloud, banging the flat of his hand against his forehead over and over again, 'How am I ever going to be able to get rid of it?'

All that weekend Bernard was so worked up about what he'd done he could hardly think about anything else. It wasn't the money that bothered him so much, but that he could have been such an idiot. He couldn't have done worse had he been trying to win the Smobel prize for foolishness. Unfortunately, once having reached this conclusion all his mental processes seemed to become inflated, especially three of the most influential ones – anxiety, remorse and regret. And, as if that wasn't enough to cope with, since one thing leads to another (especially in the case of this sort of thing), he started going over everything else he'd ever regretted doing in his whole life. He was so upset he could hardly sleep, and in the early hours of Sunday morning woke up in a cold sweat having dreamt that he'd just bought a Persian rug for ten thousand pounds which, when he examined it closely, turned out to be more holes than rug. Fortunately, later that day he remembered Sam's advice, that if you buy something badly the only thing to do was to sit on it until a buyer came along. But Bernard simply couldn't believe that such a person existed. Who could possibly want such an awful looking thing? Anyway, he was far too worked up about it to calmly sit and wait for this someone to turn up. Right then he would have found it much easier to wait for the second coming of you know who. No, the only thing to do was to somehow get rid of the damn thing as soon as possible. But how?

The problem was that although he knew how to buy rugs, even if badly, he hadn't the vaguest idea how to go about selling them. Buying had always been his strong point. It was after all the perfect mode of expression for his natural extravagance. He always seemed to know where the best things were to be found (from Panama hats to olives), but as to selling, that was a different matter entirely. All he could think of was to try hawking it round from one rug shop to another in the hope that sooner or later someone would take it off his hands; a course of action which even Bernard, naive as he was, realised would definitely minimise the possibility of his making any profit on it. He'd never been any good at selling anything to anybody. To begin with, he had to contend with his obsessive honesty, which resulted in his confessing exactly what he thought about the rug to every dealer he talked to, instead of saying something like how beautiful the colours were, or what a useful size it was. Worse still, he couldn't resist saying what a fool he'd been for having bought it in the first place. Some of the dealers he went to clearly found his total honesty and complete lack of guile quite disarming, even moving; after all, it wasn't everyday they met someone like him. Even so, that wasn't enough to make them buy it. They knew, even if Bernard didn't, that business was far too serious a matter to allow oneself to be influenced by considerations of that kind. Yes, that was a stupid way to have behaved alright, but then Bernard was constantly doing absurd things like that. He had never met anyone else who habitually asked salesmen for their honest opinion about the very thing they were trying to sell him, or tried to get waiters to divulge what they thought the best dish on the menu was, as if they knew what he liked, or could be trusted not to simply recommend whatever was moving the slowest that day. He did in the end finally manage to get rid of it, and even made a small profit. But then that could hardly be called a straightforward commercial transaction, since the ancient Hungarian countess (who had perhaps once resembled Zaza Gabor and had only become a rug dealer out of necessity herself), probably bought it out of pity. Or perhaps she just wanted to help him, because Bernard reminded her in some way of an old flame from her youth in pre-war Budapest, which might explain why, as they sat in her office talking, she started calling him darling or Tibor, and every now and again, even Tibor darling.

That was the end of Bernard's business career. In all it had lasted two weeks, cost him hours of anxiety and worry and earned him exactly ten pounds. Now he knew for certain that he wasn't cut out for business. As soon as the slightest problem had appeared, instead of keeping a cool head, he had practically fallen to pieces with anxiety. He might, as Sam said, have a good business brain, but it was obvious now that he lacked almost all the other necessary qualities, especially the ability to keep calm when you make a mistake. He would have to relinquish all those delicious fantasies about villas, mistresses and crocodile shoes. But then they had already begun to subside soon after the disaster of the first auction, so they could hardly have been as important to him as he'd thought.

The thing that Bernard just couldn't understand was what had suddenly possessed him to think he was capable of becoming a businessman in the first place. Having spent all those years trying not to make a living, it had obviously been far to late to change. Had it not been for Dr Lear, it would never have occurred to him that such a thing was even remotely possible. Yes, that was it, it was all Dr Lear's fault. And if he felt more of a failure now than a couple of weeks previously, before he'd embarked on this mad venture he'd be completely justified in blaming him. After this disastrous experience probably the only thing to do now was to think in terms of an early retirement, at least then he would be assured of making a complete success of it. Somehow or other he would get by. He always had in the past. Something would turn up. The main thing was not to worry. If the worst came to the worst he could always sell his collection of Russian silver, Sèvres china, or some of the other things he'd inherited from the old man. He'd miss their company but anything was preferable to having to go through this kind of experience again. Anyway, maybe he was just about to have another windfall, at least that was what his bank manager had called it when he'd been left that money by his aunt (although he persisted in regarding it as a solution, even if it wasn't really sufficient for a lifetime). Perhaps at that very moment someone was picking his name out of the telephone directory and planning to leave him a fortune. But if this was just wishful thinking, one thing was now absolutely clear – unlike Hirschman, who'd stood up at Sam's that evening and loudly declared how he was always a businessman second – Bernard was definitely not one, second, third, fourth, or even fifteenth. The question still remained what was he first?

The Promised Land

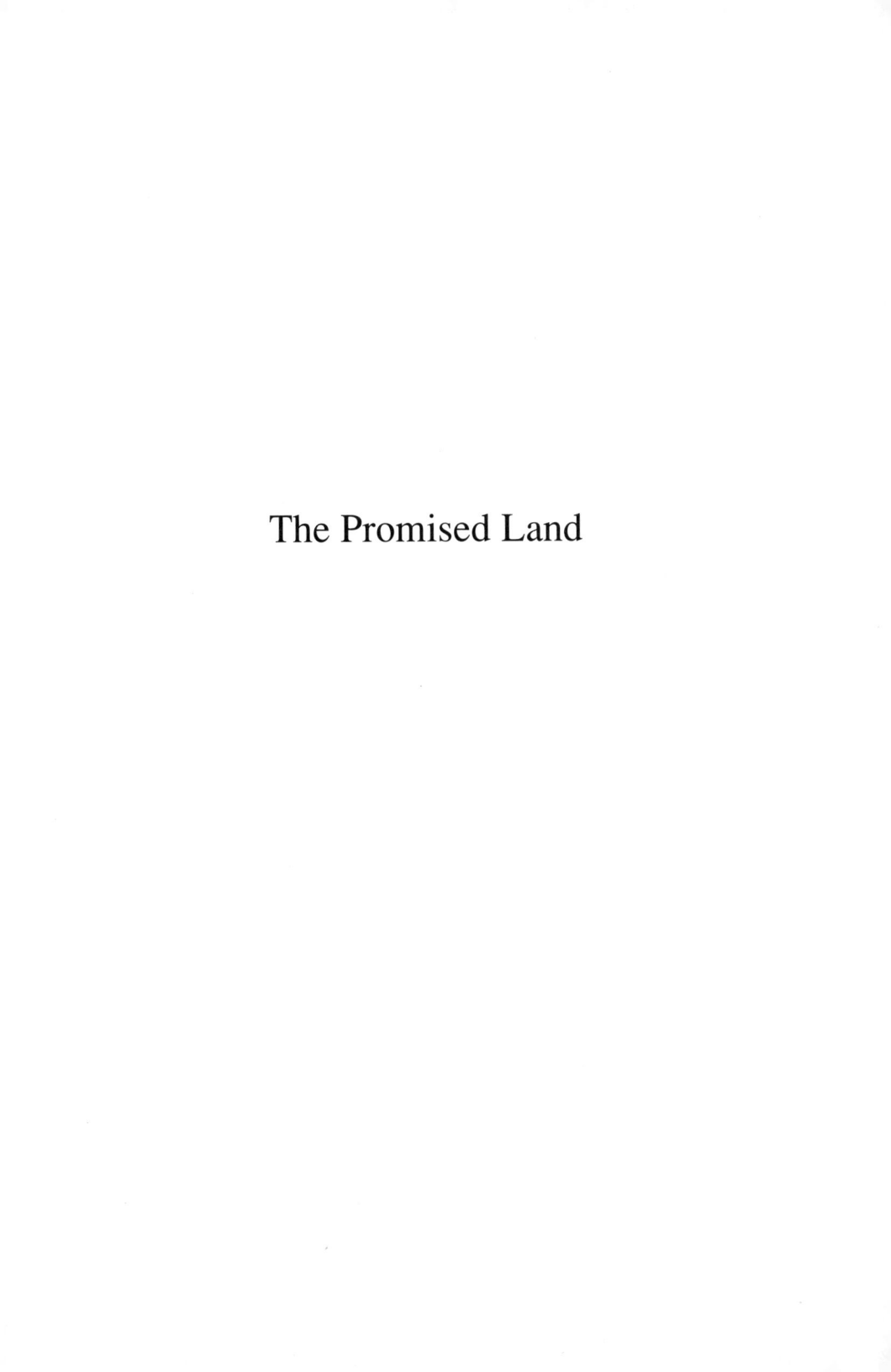

1

What really surprised Bernard, after he had so precipitously abandoned his business career, was that neither Sam nor his analyst appeared to think any the worse of him for it. Of course analysts are a special case; after all isn't it part of their job to support your endeavours however much they may privately doubt the wisdom of any particular decision you have taken, propping up the whim of the moment as if you'd suddenly come upon a profound truth all by yourself. But Sam, that genius of business, who had conjured a fortune out of nothing but imagination and ability, Sam who understood people so well, even he didn't seem to be disillusioned with him.

Bernard just couldn't understand how, by coming out of business almost as soon as he'd gone into it, he hadn't finally managed to expose himself as a truly hopeless case and a complete good-for-nothing. But he was wrong, just as he had always been wrong in expecting – after twenty years of eating at his sister's every week – that his brother-in law would one day stand up and shout across the table: 'I've had enough of him coming here and eating at my expense year in and year out.' Probably he was just being anxious because the only time Joseph ever said anything was that occasion when, just after Bernard had said yes to a second helping of roast lamb, he had been unable to resist observing gleefully that this must be Bernard's meal of the week. The thing he always forgot of course, was that for some reason Joseph liked him. Perhaps it was that, over the years, going to so many family funerals together had forged this bond between them. But it couldn't only have been that, because there was also that time when he'd said, even if it was in a moment of despair, that only Bernard knew what he was really like. How he had reached that conclusion, God knows, since Joseph had never confided anything to him in all the time they'd known each other. But even if he'd been wrong about Joseph, it seemed amazing to Bernard that Sam who had so strangely borne him no grudge for the failure of his marriage (unless that time he drove into the side of Bernard's car was an unconscious expression of resentment) did not on this occasion finally give him up altogether; seeing him for once as he really was, as if Bernard had been suddenly illuminated from above and below by giant fluorescent lights that revealed in minute detail every single one of his defects. Bernard had overlooked one important fact: no-one, least of all Sam, was capable or even inclined to judge him as harshly as he judged himself. Who else had the evidence for the prosecution before them day and night the way he did? At most, all that was visible to the outside world was a mere fragment of his inadequacies. No one else could possibly compete with the way he was able to wipe himself out on a hundred counts, sentence himself to a long fugue of regrets, endless remorse and to hundreds of anxious awakenings.

Sam simply wasn't like that. He might, when he woke up in the middle of the night worrying about one or other of his daughters, stop for a moment as he was looking out of the french windows into the garden, and wonder what Bernard was doing with his life, but if he ever thought Bernard was a fool he would never have said it to his face.

Only occasionally, had he ever looked at Bernard really disapprovingly. A look of doubt, sometimes mixed with bewilderment, even disbelief, spreading across his face until it wore the same severely sceptical expression as in his 'portrait', that hung in the boardroom. It was a painting that Bernard had often coveted, no doubt because he could easily imagine what a beneficial effect looking at it day after day would have had on him. Whenever Bernard happened to see it he could imagine Sam saying: do you really think that's a wise thing to do? or, is that in your opinion a sound money-making proposition? or even, there you are getting up late again and wasting the day before its even begun. Yes, being able to look at that painting every morning would have done him no end of good.

The following Saturday after Bernard had slipped barely noticed from the world of commerce, when he went round to see Sam and have a swim as usual, he fully expected to have to hang his head and listen to Sam telling him off. But instead, all Sam did was laugh. He almost collapsed in the shower laughing when Bernard related in detail what had taken place at those auctions.

'Please stop laughing Sam, it's not that funny,' Bernard said, when he felt he couldn't bear it any longer.

'I'm sorry Bernard, I just can't help it. The thought of you buying a rug you hadn't looked at properly and then falling to pieces with doubt and anxiety is just too funny for words. I was right you see. Business just isn't for you. I didn't like to say so that time when you were overflowing with enthusiasm, but you've never struck me as a businessman, or even really as having the potential to become one. I wish you did. I could really use someone in the office myself. It's a shame really because, as I once told you, I think you've got a good head for business. You certainly appear to understand it very well.'

'You mean I can count my change? I've always prided myself on being able to do that at least.'

'No, you know perfectly well what I mean. You simply have a good understanding of how business works. You'd even quite like to be well off. The trouble is there's something missing but I can't quite put my finger on it.'

'The will to succeed?'

'Something like that, but you also seem to lack ambition, persistence and the ability to do anything that bores you for very long. Perhaps it's just as well, over-abundant ambition without ability often leads to jail, I always think. At least you'll never end up in jail; you haven't got the ambition for it. You like the idea of having an office to go to, the trouble is you don't want to do anything when you get there. I was right all along – the thing for you is a sleeping partnership. I can just see you snoozing through the profits.'

How can he know me so well, Bernard thought, feeling embarrassed at being confronted by such an accurate picture of himself, and wishing that Sam would change the subject. But Sam couldn't stop himself now that the reverie of advice was upon him.

'The trouble is Bernard that you, and to a lesser extent I, were both born into the wrong age. What you really are Bernard is a natural member of the leisure class, anyone can see that because you reveal it in almost everything you say. But that's not much use to you because there isn't a leisure class for you to try and become a member of any more. The thing is what are you going to do now? Let me ask you something: what would you do if you could do anything you liked?'

For a few minutes Bernard just stood there, quite unable to think of anything to say. He certainly didn't want to be a hairdresser, which was what his mother had wanted him to become, and business was now completely ruled out, even as a fantasy. But what did he want to do. A few weeks before someone had asked him at a dinner party what he did for a living and he hadn't known what to reply, but this was worse, much worse.

'Well, I know what you'd do,' Sam continued, probably aware that he shouldn't have asked such a direct question particularly at a time like this. 'You'd get up late, go out to a café, read the papers for a couple of hours and then go home and spend the rest of the day lying down desultorily reading a book. Or you might on occasion go out and visit your tailor. I suppose if you had enough money you might have become a collector of something, of rugs perhaps, since you like them so much. Oh Bernard, Bernard, what are we going to do with you? It's just as well you've still got that bit of capital your aunt left you. You have still got it haven't you, you haven't squandered it?'

'No, I've still got most of it.'

'What a pity it wasn't enough to last you a lifetime. But even if it was a much more substantial sum than it is, what with inflation you could never be absolutely sure it would be sufficient.'

Sam was always worrying about inflation although his capital must have been years ahead of it. Yet even that wasn't security enough for him because he just couldn't bear the idea of his children, or his children's children not having enough money. And he was always making plans so as to be prepared for anything that might happen even long after he'd left the planet.

'You know what I'd do in your position Bernard? – marry an heiress. Someone who could keep you in the style to which you are accustomed.'

'But I already did. Not that I was really aware of it at the time.'

'That's no reason not to do it again. I could introduce you to several, not as beautiful, or as young as Olivia of course, but then you can't have everything, at least not twice you can't.' Sam said, smiling to himself at the thought of how beautiful Olivia was.

'Well, I suppose if I did what you suggest at least it would redound to my credit, because it would mean that I had finally become realistic enough to accept that I was completely incapable of earning a living.

The trouble is I just don't like the idea of it.'

'Then if that doesn't appeal to you, how about writing, I've always thought you'd be good at that. With your natural gift for words, maybe that's what you should do,' Sam said, suddenly gazing at him appreciatively as if he were looking at a potential Tolstoy, 'It's not as if you lack imagination. Only a few weeks ago you were capable of believing you could become a businessman. If that isn't imagination I don't know what is.'

This was an old story. Sam was for ever going on about how Bernard ought to write, although he'd never seen a word he'd written, which was hardly surprising, since Bernard had barely written anything for years, the years he always thought of as those in which he'd been lost in the dark wood.

'The main thing is not to worry Bernard. Something will turn up, it always has before. Just enjoy life, after all it doesn't last for ever.'

Bernard didn't worry for long because shortly after seeing Sam that afternoon he met a woman who, for a while at least, preoccupied him to such an extent that he entirely forgot about what he ought to be doing with his life. Racquella was no ordinary woman, but seemed to Bernard, to begin with anyway, to offer all the consolations of a second mother. Although in the past Bernard had never wanted anything like that, feeling a failure as he did then made the idea of someone who could offer him a refuge and protect him from reality suddenly very appealing. But then, if that wasn't the moment to lose himself in a woman, what was? And hadn't he sometimes thought that he'd been happier with his mother than with any other woman he'd ever known? It might even have been the best romance he ever had. They had spent some very happy times together, especially when the old man had stopped talking to her during those holidays in Belgium, and they had gone off together to the circus, or to a café, or spent hours walking along the seafront early in the morning. What wonderful breakfasts they'd had alone together afterwards, their eyes meeting over the hot rolls, which she had of course buttered for him. Who had ever done that since? True, he had only been six at the time, and he couldn't very well have carried on like that. If he had listened to her he would have spent almost his whole life lying down, wrapped in a blanket, only getting up now and then to eat a bowl of chicken soup. No, he couldn't have continued in that way, not that he had ever been very active since. If there was ever a time when he felt he could do with a second helping of maternal love, this was definitely it. Olivia once said that what he needed was a nurse. Well, another mother would be even better.

Not that Racquella – a diminutive, plump red-head with green eyes, who appeared in the café that afternoon (the same café as it happened where Tissue had almost been assaulted by the Polish government in exile) looked like his mother. The only thing they had in common was that they were both short. Bernard's mother having been a peroxide blonde for as long as he could remember. That didn't seem to matter much, what mattered was that he must have sensed she was Jewish, which set off all kinds of archetypal longings inside him. This may also explain why he had found her so attractive from almost the first moment he saw her, because although she was good looking, she really wasn't the sort of woman he was normally drawn to. They, like Olivia, almost always had olive skin, almond shaped eyes and dark hair; indeed he'd sometimes thought that all the women he'd ever cared deeply about were in reality all the same woman who happened, like those Russian wooden dolls, to come in different sizes. Nevertheless she must have had a profound effect on him because when she appeared in the café for a second time, although she was not alone, he immediately decided that he had to somehow get to talk to her. How he ever got up the courage to follow her downstairs, when she went to make a phone call, was astonishing. Especially since, he not only did that, but also had the presence of mind to go straight past her into the gentlemen's and stand there, his ear pressed to the wall, until she seemed to be nearing the end of her conversation (or so he judged) and then to rush back along the corridor to make an assignation with her for the following day. For months afterwards he persisted in regarding the way he'd picked her up that afternoon as one of his greatest amatory triumphs ever, although of course it was true, that before she'd gone to make that phone call, Racquella had given him one of the most enticing smiles he'd ever received from a woman. So it was just possible that it was really she who had picked him up. It did seem providential that she should ever have appeared in that café a second time at all, since he was sure he'd never seen her there before. Moreover, when he discovered she was also from the Promised Land he began to imagine that perhaps fate had intended that he should meet her. Was it possible, he thought, that she was its promise to him?

He had already begun to think of Racquella as a possible second mother when, soon after she had telephoned to invite him for dinner, he began to have fantasies about what her cooking would be like. This in itself was very peculiar, because he'd never wanted to be cooked for by any woman before, imagining that if he ever allowed that to happen, some terrible price would be exacted in exchange. It had never happened since he'd left home years ago, and as Olivia was quite unable to cook it was now she who missed his cooking, rather than the other way round. But now here he was quite incapable of preventing himself from picturing Racquella standing beside a huge silver tureen, ladling out bowls of steaming chicken soup in which small sailboats of Jewish ravioli were floating backwards and forwards just below the surface; a sight that had first captivated him at his grandmother's when he was still barely tall enough to reach the table. And afterwards, there would be boiled chicken with raspberry-coloured horseradish sauce and sweet and sour carrots, and finally that heaviest of delicacies – Lokshen pudding, with its beguiling aroma of cinnamon and hot sultanas.

But of course nothing like that happened, because Racquella it turned out was – like almost every other woman Bernard knew – a vegetarian. Naturally, he was disappointed when he realised that instead of any of those childhood dishes, he was going to have to eat a vegetable casserole and salad and, since there wasn't a desert spoon on the table, there obviously wasn't going to be any sweet either. But he didn't mind all that much, because he had recently discovered an old fashioned Jewish restaurant where all these things could be had without any emotional complications.

Goody's, where Bernard often went when he felt lonely or overwhelmed with nostalgia, held other attractions as well. He liked almost everything about it, especially the ambience, which if it wasn't red plush, was at least almost entirely pink – there were pink mirrors engraved with Stars of David, pink Venetian chandeliers, pink damask tablecloths, even the walls were a dusky pale pink. When he was there he never felt lonely. Almost any of the other clients could have been one of his relatives; the portly men in camel-hair coats, with their big Havana cigars; their sumptuous blonde wives in minks; the bachelors who were always complaining how the quality of life had got worse and worse, while the waiter nodded and cut up their pickled cucumbers exactly how they liked them; and the elderly couples who looked as if they'd become glued together with the passing of the years, and who always seemed to be reminiscing about their holidays in Marbella. Any one of them could have been a relative of his, but it was part of the particular charm of going to Goody's that they hardly ever were. He was also drawn there by the two delicious Polish blonde waitresses, one of whom was apparently so obsessed by the colour green that she not only always wore it but had green highlights in her hair and painted her nails green as well. But the supreme delight of that restaurant was of course the food, which was the best food imaginable simply because it was the food of childhood. It was also at Goody's one Friday evening that Bernard discovered a way of alleviating depression, well his depression anyway. He had ordered Chicken en casserole – that is boiled chicken immersed in about two pints of chicken soup – and had followed it with three, or possibly four, cups of black coffee, and suddenly found himself suffused with an extraordinary feeling of well-being. For a while at least he might almost have said he felt happy. But then, if that combination didn't induce a feeling of well-being what would.

Unfortunately, Bernard had discovered Goody's far too late. Shortly after he started going there he often found he was the only customer, and Fritz, the proprietor, would be sitting in the corner looking mournful, as if God knows what was about to happen. Then one evening the pink damask table napkins had been replaced by red paper ones, which was a very bad sign. One day soon he would arrive at the door to find Goody's had vanished. Then where was he going to go?

It wasn't just Racquella's cooking that was so disappointing, although that was bad enough, since there was so much ginger in the casserole that Bernard had frequently to rush to the bathroom to pour cold water over his face. Yes, she made him sweat alright, and not only because of the food. Once again Bernard had been completely wrong about a woman. Instead of being soft and maternal, Racquella turned out to be aggressive and judgemental. She wasn't nearly as understanding as Sam had been when he told her about his recent failure as a businessman. She reacted in precisely the way he had imagined Sam was going to and accused him of lacking backbone (a judgement which, it so happened, he was rather inclined to agree with himself) and not being a real man, all of which she said while giving him the kind of look that seemed to suggest there must be something fundamentally wrong with him. Nor was she sympathetic when, once again, he had been unable to stop himself from going on and on about Olivia, but that at least was understandable. The way she treated him that evening really made him wonder if it was such a good idea to get involved with such a difficult woman who, although she was beautiful, wasn't even his type. On the other hand, he had once had a brief affair with a red-head and spent wondrously sensual nights in a postgraduate hostel for girls, where the pleasure of being a lover was made all the more piquant by also being simultaneously a trespasser. Not that that relationship had worked out all that well in the end. He also wondered, since she attacked him so often that evening, if perhaps he wasn't the wrong sort of man for her. Perhaps someone who could manipulate life, whom she in turn could then manipulate, would be far more suitable?

Despite the disappointment of their first evening together, there must have been something that drew him to her, because over the next few weeks he often found himself driving over to see her. Perhaps all it meant was that Bernard had finally come to realise that in life you don't get what you want, and a woman about whom you have reservations is far better than no woman at all. At the very least, it was consoling to be able to warm himself on her womanliness, as she bustled around her flat, arranging flowers, draping shawls over mirrors, or brushed out her heavy copper-coloured hair. It was also true that the pleasure he got from the smell of her perfume, or from watching her earrings swaying to and fro (something he had always found intensely erotic) was quite independent of anything annoying she might say. And then, although they might both be uncertain whether they really liked each other, that didn't prevent them from being physically attracted to one another. Almost always they would end up lying down on that ancient couch of hers which she had covered with a saffron yellow shawl, kissing and cuddling for hours on end like a pair of teenagers. But Racquella soon got fed up with it, and more or less insisted that either they went to bed together or he should stop playing around. And they probably would have done so, because Bernard certainly desired her enough, had he not more or less insisted that they take things slowly for a while at least. It was a decision with which she was never entirely happy, and every now and then she would accuse him of prevaricating by always wanting to stay in the kitchen (since she only had two rooms the choice always had been between the kitchen and her bedroom). Although it annoyed her, Bernard was glad he'd insisted they didn't rush things, because he still found her very threatening, and for some reason felt that once they'd slept together, there would be no going back. Then, quite suddenly, without realising it was going to happen, he did spend the night with her, which proved far more disturbing than he would ever have thought possible.

2

Why it should have happened that night of all nights was almost inexplicable. The only reason he could think of later to explain it was that somehow going to see Don Giovanni that week had awoken in him an aspect of himself – that of the seducer – which he'd barely realised existed before. It hardly seemed likely otherwise that he would have found himself at Racquella's door late that night because he wanted to add her to his list of conquests. Nothing in Bernard's relations with women had ever been as simple as that before.

What made it even more incomprehensible was that he'd spent most of that afternoon with Olivia during which they'd been closer than they had been for months. He had been so excited by the prospect of seeing her that he had got up early that morning and rushed off (in so far as anyone as slow as Bernard could ever be said to rush) with the idea of buying some perfume for her birthday. Not that when he found himself in the department store this proved such an easy thing to do. It wasn't a question of knowing which perfume she liked, which of course he did, but of whether or not it was any longer really appropriate to buy her such an intimate gift, since they had been apart so long. He felt so confused that when a young Chinese sales girl came up and asked if she could help him he took her completely literally (after all, didn't he as always need all the help he could get?), and began to pour out the whole story of his marital difficulties; how he still loved his wife; and how he couldn't decide because of the state of their relationship whether or not it was really the right thing to buy her perfume at all. Why he should have confided all this to her, God knows, especially since it was obviously her job to sell perfume, not to give therapy to the customers. It must have been that her offer of help struck him as so sincere. And of course it was rather soothing to find himself standing there in the nearly deserted perfume department at 9.30 a.m. with a beautiful woman holding his hand and rubbing perfume into it, whilst she looked at him almost lovingly with her dark eyes, as if he were a small boy who'd got lost instead of a grown man. He found the experience so enjoyable that quite often during the next few months he contemplated going back there in the hope that he might receive the same treatment all over again.

It wasn't only the appropriateness of buying her perfume that worried him, it was also that if he did, there was no telling who else might plunge their nose into Olivia's beautiful neck to enjoy it. Just as he was about to write out the cheque, the awful image of Christopher's nose doing precisely that suddenly appeared in his mind, and made him hesitate for more than a minute or two. Oh, if only he'd managed to summon up sufficient aggression and punched him on the nose, when they had come face to face across Olivia's bed a few months ago in the hospital, he might well have permanently impaired his sense of smell and now at least there would have been one less nose to worry about. In the end of course, after deliberating for ages, he went ahead and bought the biggest bottle they had. The desire to please her easily outweighing the paranoia he felt at the idea of any number of strange noses enjoying what after all was his perfume! Although he only managed to accomplish this feat of magnanimity by forcing himself to concentrate on the difference between the gesture he was about to make and what would happen to the perfume afterwards. Yes, generosity of spirit definitely triumphed that morning, even if it was tempered by the awareness that one of the noses dipping into Olivia's neck to enjoy the scent of that perfume would, at least on occasion, be his.

Often during that afternoon with Olivia, Bernard felt as Odysseus must have done when he finally reached home after all his adventures. That they had decided to meet in that café where he'd first taken her made the occasion especially poignant; particularly since it was somewhere they always seemed to feel very happy together. It was almost as if the place cast a spell over them so they had only to pass through the swing doors to begin to experience those times once again. Like so many of the places Bernard was drawn to, it had a fin de siècle atmosphere with dark green walls, worn gilt mirrors, chandeliers and, behind the bar, a wonderful mural of an endless summer on the Côte d'Azure, on which you could warm yourself on a cold winter's day.

That meeting was almost perfect. Olivia arrived with her glistening black hair piled up on her head, which was how he liked it best, looking as if she'd just stepped off an ancient Greek vase, and wearing that amethyst necklace he had bought her years before in Florence. It made him feel that she was trying to express how much his love still meant to her. And then, when shortly after they had sat down and he gave her the perfume, a look of such pleasure appeared on her face that he knew instantly that he had done the right thing after all.

It also seemed significant that Olivia chose that particular day to tell him more about what she'd always in the past elusively referred to as 'The Work'. She became so intense and passionate when she was trying to convince him of the existence of angels, that he almost began to suspect that the old lady sitting at the next table, wearing a black velvet beret and smoking a cigarette in a long amber holder, might be one of them. Olivia had never before allowed herself to be so open about her belief in the presence on earth of beings with divine connections (which perhaps meant, Bernard thought, that God left them messages on their answerphones), beings who were already on their third or fourth reincarnation and who, because of their knowledge of ancient teachings, were constantly working for the good of mankind.

Needless to say, both Gotsky and Potsky were leading figures amongst them. In the past whenever she'd carried on like this Bernard had never managed to restrain himself from making some ironic or cynical remark. On this occasion he did, because he knew that if he said anything at all critical he would have ruined the whole afternoon, and also because he sensed that behind her sudden desire to say all this might be the wish to come back to him. After all, hadn't she more than once said that one of the main reasons they could no longer be together was because he was so totally unsympathetic to the spiritual path she had chosen to follow. And she was absolutely right. All those jokes he used to make about being perfectly content to find out about the afterlife, afterwards; and that as far as he was concerned the journey to the East ended at the nearest Indian restaurant, hadn't exactly contributed to producing greater harmony between them. But he could have been completely mistaken. Probably she wasn't interested in coming back to him at all, and had confided in him for some other reason. Olivia was always so unpredictable anyway and if she felt something today it didn't necessarily mean she would feel the same way tomorrow. He remembered how right he'd felt Dr Lear had been when he'd insisted that Bernard should only ever allow himself to believe Olivia was coming back to him when she'd already arrived.

But whatever Olivia's sudden desire to tell him all this meant, there was no doubt about how close they felt that afternoon. Those three hours passed like minutes, as if they were Harlequin and Columbine locked in a timeless embrace, so that when Olivia went to the loo Bernard suddenly felt as lonely and bereft as if she had gone to Australia, instead of just across the room.

It was hardly surprising then, that when the time came for them to part it was so difficult, not that they had ever been very good at partings. Bernard in particular, was terrible at saying goodbye and was always going back to kiss or embrace her one more time, and would almost invariably think of several things he absolutely had to say to her at the very last moment, although he knew very well that what he felt so desperate to communicate was really nothing but an expression of his reluctance to be parted from her yet again. It was worse than usual that day because, just as Olivia was putting on her coat, he suddenly couldn't remember why they weren't any longer together; almost as if his desire to be with her had obliterated from his memory all the reasons why it was the case. Although he had been very restrained until then, at the last possible moment, he had brought the subject up and they had to go through it all over again, the ways they were and weren't compatible, which made it even worse. When shortly afterwards, they finally managed to separate, he stood on the pavement watching her turn and wave to him several times until she disappeared into the inky blue darkness of that wet evening, before he could bring himself to go home. For hours afterwards he went on feeling her presence as if she were still there, sitting across the table from him.

How strange then to find himself, late that night driving over to see Racquella. What was even stranger, was that she seemed to have been expecting him to come all evening. Not that standing there in that dimly lit doorway in an old flannel nightdress, over which she had thrown a shawl, she looked exactly enticing. No, that was hardly the way a woman who wanted to seduce you would dress. That Racquella was dressed in such an unappealing way probably didn't mean anything. It was a very cold night and she was far too subtle and liberated a woman to ever resort to anything as crude as erotic underwear.

She certainly didn't look anything like any of those women in the glamour wear catalogues that had mysteriously begun to arrive in the post over the past few months. Pouring over those pictures first thing in the morning made his blood rush around so fast he found himself awake even before he'd had his first espresso.

He did momentarily feel rather disappointed, although that soon passed when he realised how pleased she was to see him.

'I knew you'd come tonight,' Racquella said, kissing him and drawing him inside.

'How? I didn't know myself till half an hour ago.'

'I suppose I just wanted you to come that's all. Perhaps I even willed it. I often think I can sense what you're going to do.'

'You and your psychic powers,' Bernard said, remembering how Racquella had once told him that she sometimes made some money by doing horoscopes, and feeling irritated that she might be capable of knowing what he was going to do even before he did himself. He never minded when Olivia seemed to know he was wearing those brogue shoes she hated so much, without even looking at his feet, but he found it annoying when it came from anybody else.

'It doesn't really matter whether I knew or not. The main thing is that you're here now,' Racquella said, leading the way upstairs.

There was no doubt that she was pleased to see him that night, because a little while later when they were once again sitting in the kitchen she suddenly put her arms around him and announced that she wanted him to spend the night.

'Tonight! Why tonight especially?' Bernard said, feeling alarmed and remembering how he'd spent the afternoon.

'Just because I want you to.'

'But I'm really not sure this is the right night. I only intended to come for a little while.'

'Well, if you don't stay, I may not ask you again. You should never spurn a woman Bernard,' and then after kissing him again she added, in a playfully imploring tone of voice, 'Stay Bernie, I really want to be with you tonight.'

Why had she suddenly called him that, she never had before, Bernard thought, wondering if it could be significant, and feeling trapped and tempted all at once.

'Oh, alright,' Bernard said giving into the inevitable but still feeling far from certain that he was doing the right thing. 'But I'm not sure I really feel like making love.' He was aware that, although it might not be the perfect night for him, it would almost certainly be the only time she would ever ask him to stay if he rejected her now. Then again, the fact that he had come to see her so late in the evening, could mean that the moment had finally arrived when he really did want to sleep with her.

Perhaps his first reaction had been the right one. Once they had gone to bed and begun to make love, he soon found that he was only able to make the most tentative of gestures towards her. It could just have been shyness, he had often been like this the first time he slept with someone, but on this occasion it was much more likely to be because of a lack of feeling, as if some message was just not being sent from his heart to his hands. It was a strange experience, almost like being an adolescent again who didn't know how to make love to a woman, or as if his life were a game of snakes and ladders and he had been sent back to the beginning.

Still, however limited Bernard's participation he nevertheless enjoyed making love to her. But then what more pleasurable activity exists in life. Even smoking, which was undoubtedly one of the things Bernard enjoyed most, and was perhaps what he did best, didn't really compare to the pleasure of spending the night with a beautiful woman. Though if he were ever forced to decide between the totally predictable and uncomplicated pleasure of smoking and a relationship with a difficult woman like Racquella, he really wasn't sure which he'd choose.

Fortunately, when it came to it he had been able to make love to her (impotence at least was one thing he never suffered from) and she even appeared to enjoy it. But how could she really have enjoyed making love with a man who'd barely touched her?

Yet when Bernard woke up in the early hours of the morning, far from feeling happy, he just couldn't understand what he was doing there, and why it wasn't Olivia lying in bed next to him. He'd often heard that jocular remark about going to bed with one woman and waking up thinking about another, but this didn't seem at all funny. Racquella was the first woman he'd ever spent the whole night with since he had parted from Olivia. But this anguish wasn't the end of his troubles, because when Racquella woke up around eight, she immediately wanted to make love again as she put it – 'to release her energies' – and became incredibly angry when he didn't want to, so angry that she pushed him out of bed, which hadn't happened since the first time he'd ever slept with a woman (that at least had been completely justifiable, since how you made love to a woman was then still a complete mystery to him). Even that didn't appear to satisfy her, and shortly afterwards she started to harangue him and accuse him of all kinds of things, including being a homosexual. Well, that really made him angry, because if he was sure of anything about himself it was that he wasn't homosexual. What was even more irritating was that she absolutely refused to explain why she'd said it.

All he was able to get out of her, then or subsequently, was that she had felt that way about him for some time, a remark she made with a knowing look on her face, as if she knew him better than he knew himself, which only made him even more annoyed. Nevertheless, by the time Bernard left later that morning everything seemed to be smoothed over between them. Racquella, for her part, appeared to have entirely forgotten what she'd said, and even flirted with him over breakfast to such an extent that he began to want to make love again himself.

All that day Bernard was aware of a distinct feeling of well being. He even felt a hint of masculine pride, as if it was he who'd initiated what had happened the previous night and not her. For a while he forgot how upset he'd felt when he'd woken up in the early hours. But, by the time of his usual appointment with Dr Lear, this light-hearted state of mind had long since turned into anguish. He was convinced, that by having spent the night with Racquella he had finally become a traitor to his feelings, because he had allowed, however slightly, something alien to encroach on that part of himself which was exclusively bound up with Olivia. It wasn't that Racquella threatened this as such – he didn't feel in any danger of falling in love with her – but that by sleeping with her he had opened himself to the movement of life again, which, if he let it, would eventually carry him away from Olivia altogether.

All of this came rushing out of him almost the moment he had sat down in the familiar refuge of Dr Lear's consulting room that afternoon. After, of course, they had concluded their inevitable argument about precisely what the correct time was, because as usual, despite his particularly desperate need to talk to Dr Lear that day, Bernard had somehow contrived to arrive ten minutes late. That he did this so often always astonished Dr Lear, as well as anyone else he ever mentioned it to. How could anyone be late for an analyst when their hour was only fifty minutes long, and you paid for each and every minute.

'Why do you feel this way suddenly? I thought you were feeling so much better now you've found yourself a girlfriend,' Dr Lear said, after Bernard had finished telling him what had happened.

'It must've been sleeping with her that did it. I really didn't want to spend the whole night there. It was her idea, and now I feel as if I've unhinged myself. I suppose I feel worse because I was with Olivia all afternoon.'

'Ah, it's Olivia again is it. That was a big loss for you Bernard, a big loss,' Dr Lear said, mournfully as if he were beginning to recite a dirge.

'But I thought that I had recovered from that now, at least to the extent that I can have some sort of relationship with another woman. I'll never stop loving Olivia of course, but I'm not in love with her any longer. There's a difference, isn't there?'

'But surely what you're feeling contradicts that? You're still much more involved with Olivia than you're prepared to admit, even to yourself Bernard.'

'Isn't it enough that I've just admitted that I still love her.'

'It's much deeper than that Bernard. Somehow your whole sense of identity, your security is tied up with her. Didn't you once tell me that without her you felt you had no one to talk to? You cling to her like Prometheus to his rock. But you won't drown without her Bernard. It really is about time that you began to accept that she isn't coming back. The fact that you can feel this way shows you've still got a long way to go Bernard.'

Yes, perhaps he's right, Bernard thought. He certainly thought about Olivia all the time. Even the female characters in the novels he read had a way of turning into her. It was even worse if he happened to read a book about the concentration camps because inevitably, at some point, her face full of suffering would appear in his mind, until he couldn't stand it any longer, and he had to close the book and go for a walk. Even the geese in the park, craning their necks towards him for bread, made him think of her, perhaps because he always felt so guilty for forgetting to bring them any. 'I suppose you're right. I certainly cannot imagine a life totally without her.'

'But what's the sense in it Bernard. You're not together. You don't sleep together. You must stop mourning her and learn to live in the present. You must carry on with your life.'

It had started to get dark and the room was full of shadows. What light there was came from the standard lamp just behind Dr Lear's chair, just as the only illumination in Bernard's life at that moment seemed to come from him.

'What can I do about it? Go to a clinic and get myself exorcised!' Bernard said, picturing himself in an enormous white room surrounded by psychiatrists and marriage guidance counsellors who were busily engaged in reciting selected passages from Freud over him.

'Ah, if only there was a magic cure like that Bernard, things would be much easier for us. But there isn't; the only thing we can do is to go on talking and hope that gradually you begin to change. A little more freedom, that's all you can hope for Bernard. Anyway, we've got to stop now,' Dr Lear said, glancing at his watch and wearily getting to his feet.

'Already!' Bernard said, once again feeling that his session with Dr Lear had ended far too soon and still quite unready to be sent back into the world to cope with life on his own.

A few minutes later, when once again he found himself outside in the street, he felt like a starving man who had been dragged away from a table in a restaurant, just as the main course was about to arrive. True, his immediate reaction had been one of relief from having emptied himself, but by the time he got back to the car, he had begun to feel so upset (as if what he'd actually done was not just to empty himself but to empty himself all over himself) that he wondered if being forced to face up to the truth was such a good thing after all. Maybe it would have been better to have remained only vaguely aware of what he really felt, and to have left the murky aquarium of his inner life undisturbed. Maybe his brother-in-law was right to get up and walk out of the room whenever Bernard tried to discover what was worrying him. Perhaps getting things off your chest wasn't as beneficial as people thought. Right then he would have been perfectly happy if they'd climbed back on again. On the other hand, if he wasn't prepared to go through all this, if he didn't allow himself to become the archaeologist of his own heart, how could he ever expect things to be any different.

He must have carried on sitting in the car for at least twenty minutes going over all this, before he decided that the only thing to do to regain his composure was to go to Guggenheim's café. He always felt at home there among its clientele of ageing German Jewish refugees, some of whom always seemed to be arguing about whether the apple strüdel was better there, or at the Dorice on the other side of the road. There were always one or two people there who were recovering from visiting their own analysts so what better place to go and wait for his inner life to gradually settle back into its usual somnolent state.

But even before the lemon tea he'd ordered had time to arrive, and long before he began to feel at all composed, he found himself rushing compulsively to telephone Olivia, as if he were intentionally trying to confirm everything Dr Lear had just been saying about their relationship. More than ever he felt the need to reassure himself that the bond between them still existed. Above all perhaps, he wanted to hear her call him beloved, as she still did, despite everything that had happened, and which always had such a soothing effect on him, more soothing even than when his mother used to rub Vick on his chest in the winter when he was a child.

But why after having received all the reassurance he needed did he have to go and confess everything (or nearly everything) that had happened at Racquella's the night before, especially when he had no intention of doing so. Was he so neurotic that his unconscious was capable of taking his actions by complete surprise. Not that he had ever been able to keep anything of any significance from Olivia for very long. Even if he didn't tell her directly she always seemed to be able to intuit what was going on in his life. Why hadn't he had the presence of mind to resist telephoning her, at least until he had calmed down a little? Surely he should have known how she would react. Yet at first he was completely surprised by how upset she was, so upset that she kept repeating over and over: 'but Bernard how could you, how could you'. What was so awful was that there seemed to be nothing he could do to pacify her, and saying that what had happened didn't mean anything to him, appeared to make no difference at all. Soon Olivia's distress turned into long silences until he felt he could almost hear her heart pounding (something she used to complain happened whenever something he'd said, not said, done, or not done, had upset her deeply).

Worse still, she wouldn't allow him to go round to see her, although it was as much to calm himself down that he was by then almost desperate to see her. It was no use, she just wouldn't let him come and a few moments later, after they had said the hollowest of goodbyes that perhaps they'd ever said to each other, he found himself standing with the phone in his hand, full of guilt and remorse, feeling completely desolate. At that moment he really believed he had finally hit the bottom, because it was completely inconceivable that there could be anyone else underneath.

He must have been ages on the telephone shoving in money and getting back agony in exchange, but even so when he finally dragged himself back to his table there was still no sign of his lemon tea. He was just about to try and attract the waitress's attention, when a little old man sitting at the next table, who with his bald head, childlike expression and small pointed ears, looked like an elderly angel, seeing Bernard looking perplexed began to apologise.

'I'm terribly sorry, you were such a long time on the phone, and since your tea was getting cold and I was thirsty, I just drank it.'

'Don't worry. I'll simply order another one,' Bernard replied, more anxious not to be drawn into a conversation, than worried about the disappearance of his tea.

'As long as you're not angry.'

'Of course I'm not angry. It's nothing. Don't give it another thought.' At which point the old man, apparently reassured, turned round and went on with his conversation.

How could he have been angry about something as trivial as that. He was much more disturbed when he noticed opposite him, under that strange painting of a group of baboons marching through a forest, was that middle-aged man with the concentration number on his arm, who as usual, was sitting with his head in his hands. Seeing him, Bernard wondered how he would ever have been able to cope with what he must have been through, when, especially on days like this, he found life in peacetime almost unendurable. But his train of thought was soon interrupted because the little man next to him had stood up, and was putting on his coat, and seemed to be about to say something.

'Please allow me to apologise again for drinking your tea like that,' and then pausing for a moment, he added smiling, 'Well anyway, if that's the worst thing that ever happens to you,' which at least made Bernard laugh, feeling as he did that that was precisely what had just happened to him.

3

Bernard's naivety seemed to have no limit. When Racquella came round to see him a few days later, he seriously expected her to be sympathetic about what had happened with Olivia. He couldn't have been more wrong, because instead of being sympathetic what she did was to attack him. Yes, he really was, as he'd once said to his mother-in-law, the man who was born yesterday, whatever day yesterday happened to be. Of course, it had been stupid of him not to remember to remove Olivia's photograph from its usual place on his desk, since its presence there must have made it completely obvious how he still felt about her. Even so, he was rather shocked when she picked up the photograph, glanced at it for a moment, and said how she couldn't understand why he was so upset over a woman who wasn't even particularly attractive.

It wasn't difficult to understand the way she reacted to seeing Olivia's photograph, but he was surprised that she could be so completely indifferent to how beautiful the flat looked that summer's evening, with the samovar glowing in the sunset and the shadows cast by the wrought iron roses outside the window slowly dancing up and down on the wall, especially since that was the first time she'd been there. All she could think of was to question why he was still living in what she quaintly referred to as the 'marital home', when every room must remind him of Olivia (who as usual she referred to as 'your wife' rather than by name). There was some truth in what she said; the flat was full of memories; there were even some of Olivia's clothes upstairs in the wardrobe; and maybe he would never be entirely free of the past until he moved out, but it wasn't up to her to make those kind of observations. What surprised him most, was not her lack of aesthetic feeling, or her tactlessness, but that she could be so unsympathetic, when sympathy had invariably been the one thing he'd always been able to elicit from almost any woman. How else had he managed never to pay a library fine, or sew on a button for himself?

Racquella's behaviour that evening finally made Bernard realise that far from being like a Jewish mother, her tendencies to be stern, judgemental and undermining, were much more the qualities of a Jewish father. If anything, she was worse than his own father, whose attitude to him had always been so negative that he sometimes appeared to Bernard to be working for the other side. Bernard had never been able to forget him saying, when he had finally got his degree, 'that a degree wasn't everything' – although what was everything was something Bernard had been trying to find out ever since. And one of Bernard's last memories of him was of that afternoon when, in front of his girlfriend, his father had asked him to pierce a hole in a cigar for him and then almost immediately snatched it out of his hands, as if to demonstrate to her that Bernard was incapable of performing even such a simple task. If that wasn't an attempt to castrate him psychologically he couldn't imagine what would be. But even the old man was never as bad as Racquella, who always seemed to be criticising him about one thing or another, in particular, about his attitude to life which, according to her, was so unassertive that she seriously doubted if he would ever amount to anything. She was also constantly telling him that it was about time he got a divorce, and that he hadn't done so already was a clear sign that he was too weak even to be able to let go of the past entirely. On balance, Racquella was probably rather more judgemental than God himself, who at least had the reputation of forgiving the odd human weakness from time to time.

Even after he'd reached this conclusion Bernard still continued going to see her almost as often as before, although by then they had both realised that it could never lead anywhere. Sometimes they ended up kissing and cuddling on that old couch like they used to but they never slept together again. Whatever she might feel, it was obvious to Bernard that he was definitely the wrong man for her, yet he was in some ways still fascinated by her. Of all the women he'd ever known, he'd never met anyone quite so aggressive and volatile as Racquella, but since he no longer felt in the least bit vulnerable to her constant criticism now it just seemed amusing. Possibly he only continued to visit her out of lassitude, or because he'd simply got used to seeing her two or three times a week. But this relatively tranquil state of affairs could hardly last and it wasn't long before Racquella began to talk about some other man she'd recently met, a philosophy professor called Smoshine, who according to her was everything Bernard wasn't – a real man, a success and a rising star in his field. It did seem rather strange though that at that stage of their relationship she should suddenly want to try and make him jealous, especially since it soon became apparent that she had reservations about Smoshine as well. But then Racquella was the sort of woman who always needed to be surrounded by admirers, even if she didn't particularly care for any of them.

It wasn't simply having to listen to her singing Smoshine's praises that was so irritating, but that now almost every time Bernard dropped round to see her unexpectedly, who would he find there already but Smoshine, ensconced in what used to be his place on the couch, with a self-satisfied look on his face (as if he'd just discovered the meaning of life), holding forth about some philosophical problem or other. Racquella would be sitting there giving him admiring looks as if he were Wittgenstein or somebody, so that pretty soon Bernard felt like a complete interloper.

It was the night of Racquella's birthday party that things finally came to a head between them. The evening had begun terribly, because instead of appearing with some sort of lavish gift, he had arrived bearing a bunch of flowers which looked as if they might well have been taken from a cemetery. Racquella realised immediately what sort of a gesture he was making and said, a rebuking edge to her voice, 'That's just the sort of present I would have expected from you'. Yes, to have turned up with such a miserable looking bunch of flowers was a mistake alright, because it must have looked as if he was trying to demonstrate just how little he really cared for her. And perhaps also, it couldn't help but remind her of the tentative way in which he had made love to her. But what else could he have done? All afternoon he'd wandered around trying to think of some suitable gift for her, and absolutely nothing had occurred to him. No feelings of love or even of affection arose to inspire him, and even the desire to possess her, which he certainly still felt on occasion, didn't seem to be enough to suggest anything. Nevertheless, it was a terrible error of judgement; much better to have brought nothing. Nothing says nothing but there's no mistaking the meaning of a tired looking bunch of flowers.

And then, as if making that mistake wasn't bad enough, although Racquella hadn't said anything about Smoshine being invited, almost the first person Bernard saw at the party, standing near a buffet table heavily laden with middle eastern delicacies, was Smoshine who was proclaiming, in a voice that was almost as loud as Weinberg's, that had he known there was going to be so much food he would never have eaten before he came. Bernard was simply astonished. He could very well imagine someone thinking that, but to actually say it!

It wasn't just Smoshine's presence that irritated him so much, but that for the rest of the evening Racquella practically ignored him. When she wasn't fussing over her guests she always seemed to be sitting in a corner with Smoshine having, what looked like, the most intimate of tête à têtes. Although Bernard thought that she was probably only acting like this because she was still furious about the flowers it suddenly made him realise how absurd the whole situation was. There he was feeling what could only be described as jealous, about a woman whom he knew perfectly well he didn't even want. So what was the point in carrying on with it? Even if Racquella had been the tender, loving second mother he'd thought he'd wanted, it couldn't have worked, because as Dr Lear said, he was still far too bound up with Olivia to become seriously involved with anyone else.

By the time Bernard left the party that evening he'd finally made up his mind that before anything like this ever happened again, he would do everything he could to try and get Olivia to come back to him, even if it meant taking an interest in the spiritual life. If necessary, he was prepared to try and follow the same path she had taken, and who knows, with a bit of luck, he might catch up with her after a while. Even making a serious attempt to believe in the absurd, esoteric teachings of Gotsky and Potsky would be worth it, if it meant that they became reconciled at last. And anyway, if in the end he failed to achieve higher consciousness or spiritual enlightenment, no one need ever know, since success or failure in that world at least, unlike in business, was practically invisible.

Under the Spreading Yoghourt Tree

1

Bernard threw himself into fantasising about the new life he was going to lead pursuing higher consciousness with all the passion and enthusiasm he'd felt a few months previously, when he'd been on the verge of beginning his business career. The whole idea of it suddenly began to appeal to him enormously. Of course, Olivia was always saying that if he was really serious about their being reunited he would at least make some effort to understand the kind of path she'd chosen to follow (she'd even mentioned it again that afternoon when they had tea together). But that wasn't the whole story. No, what really made him decide to do it then, was that since he felt such an enormous failure, he'd once again started to wish he was someone else. Of course he realised it was far too much to hope that he would be able to change to such an extent that he would be unable to recognise himself. Still, attempting to become more spiritually enlightened was probably as big a change as he was capable of. And if it worked, it would definitely help to persuade Olivia that he had become the sort of man she could bear to live with: someone who was lighter, more sensitive, spiritually aware and open to all kinds of cosmic and transcendental possibilities.

It also seemed the ideal moment to try to change other fundamental things in his life. For a while he even contemplated becoming a vegetarian. Apart from the fact that Olivia would obviously approve, wasn't it reasonable to assume that if he was going to become more finely tuned spiritually he would require a more appropriate diet thus purifying his body as well as his spirit. Olivia was forever going on purifying diets and she must have had some reason for doing so. He'd always thought there had to be more than just a phonetic connection between yoga and yoghourt. Perhaps it was even true that eating that sort of food automatically helped to put you on a higher spiritual plain. Surely a new self must require a new diet. For years Olivia had claimed that Bernard's ability to eat absolutely anything he felt like without experiencing even a moment's discomfort, showed how unaware and insensitive he really was. Could it be that one of the minor benefits of becoming more aware was that, for perhaps the first time in his life, he was going to be able to experience the pleasures of indigestion? There was no reason to stop at vegetarianism either. Perhaps this was also the moment to give up smoking as well, although as soon as the thought came into his head, he couldn't resist reaching into his pocket for yet another delicious Gitane.

What really excited him was the awareness that if he did manage to become more spiritually enlightened there was no telling what else might follow from it. Perhaps he would even begin to appreciate the pleasures of nature the way Olivia did. At the very least, he might be spared such experiences as the one that occurred while he was having breakfast on the terrace of his hotel in Switzerland a couple of years previously. He had been sitting enjoying what he assumed was the smell of wild flowers when he suddenly realised, much to his embarrassment, that what had been giving him so much pleasure was nothing other than the scent of his own aftershave.

It wasn't long however before he decided that it was vital he didn't let himself get too carried away. Olivia, who was not without a sense of humour even in these matters, might very easily doubt his sincerity when she found out what he was up to. He didn't want to look like that buffoon he'd recently observed at a party loudly proclaiming how he was an ardent feminist, in an obvious attempt to avoid being rejected by his girlfriend, who clearly took her feminism more seriously than she did him. It wasn't inconceivable that an appreciation of the higher meaning of existence might lead to such things as the enjoyment of the simple life. Olivia was forever talking about something being simple as if that automatically meant it was good. Maybe after a while he too would feel the same way. But even if he didn't, he might at least hope to find contentment and inner peace, which presumably was why other people, lost souls like himself no doubt, went in search of eternal truths and spiritual enlightenment in the first place. Olivia always appeared to be much calmer and more content than he was. Perhaps he'd been wrong to have been so critical and ironic about her beliefs all these years. Yes, peace of mind was what he needed alright, instead of all that anguish, which going to see Dr Lear only seemed to stir up even more. He'd been feeling very dissatisfied with him lately. Somehow, they just seemed to go over and over the same ground, without ever really getting anywhere. But however things worked out he decided he definitely wasn't going to tell Dr Lear what he had in mind. After all, you don't tell your barber when you're contemplating having your hair cut by someone else do you? Whichever way he looked at it, trying to follow a similar path to the one Olivia had taken at this particular juncture in his life was obviously the right thing to do. But carried away as he was by the fantasy of becoming an entirely different person, it never once occurred to Bernard that he just might not be capable of it.

Bernard's decision to radically change his life happened to coincide with one of Olivia's regular visits to the East. This time it was to stay at the ashram of some new guru she'd heard about called Fakir Baksheesh, whose love for each of his followers was reputed to be equal in power to that of a thousand mothers – a description that filled Bernard with horror, since he couldn't stop imagining what the love of a thousand Jewish mothers would be like. Nevertheless, her trip made it the perfect moment to begin putting his plan into operation (after all he didn't want Olivia to know what he was up to until he'd actually accomplished something). And he couldn't imagine a better coming home present than to be able to greet her with a completely new self, and moreover one that, for the first time since they'd known each other, would be perfectly in harmony with hers. He could even picture himself – after weeks spent in meditation, reading the lives of Indian saints and devoting his weekends to attending self-enlightenment workshops – on the day of her return dancing up and down outside her flat in long flowing orange robes, his head shaved, banging a tambourine and chanting Hara Hara Krishna at the top of his voice.

Bernard hadn't always been so enthusiastic about Olivia's periodic trips to India. When she'd first told him she was planning to go yet again he'd been overwhelmed with feelings of anxiety and apprehension. It was already bad enough that they were no longer living together without her going thousands of miles away (as it was she had recently bought a flat that was equidistant between her father and him – a choice that seemed to have been made with the specific intention of making Freud's ghost happy). When he'd first heard about her plans, he'd tried to pretend it really wasn't going to happen. But every time they met she was incapable of talking about anything else apart from this Fakir Baksheesh (a name which Olivia in her innocence didn't appear to find in the least bit off-putting) and he realised that she was really serious about it. The way she went on and on about him anyone would have thought that he had the answers to all her troubles (and everybody else's for that matter). Apparently, he was some kind of divinity (albeit a minor one) and capable of all kinds of miracles, such as being in at least two places at once (a talent which she believed her favourite guru Gotsky also possessed); materialising endless cameos of himself to give to his followers; and producing little packets of healing white dust. Such feats he did whilst uttering profound insights about life such as: God is love, love is selflessness and self is lovelessness (though how his followers reconciled this with all those pictures of himself he was constantly handing out, was a mystery). It seemed that Baksheesh not only knew the meaning of life but also didn't hesitate to tell his disciples precisely what to do with theirs. Bernard found listening to her talk about him so disturbing that on one occasion, when Olivia seemed to be even more obsessed with him than usual, he'd attempted to stop her in mid-flow and suggested that perhaps they could talk about something else for a while and go back to the subject of God later on. Not that it had made any difference. That afternoon he had been so alarmed by her state of mind, not to mention the other worldly look on her face, that he'd attempted to talk her out of going altogether, something he hadn't tried to do for years knowing exactly how futile it was. In any case, he really didn't have anything new to say on the subject. It wasn't much use pointing out yet again that he could see no reason why all the wisdom in the world should be crowded into one continent. Or that – even if this Fakir Baksheesh could do everything she said he could – that was all very well for him, especially if it made him happy, but what possible difference could it make to her life? It was all useless. Once Olivia had decided something there was absolutely no talking her out of it.

A few years before Olivia had tried to persuade him to accompany her on one of her trips to India. An invitation which, although he didn't want to be separated from her (they were still living together at the time), he found impossible to accept, especially after she told him how they would be spending their time in the ashram. Bernard simply couldn't imagine himself getting up at four a.m. to go and fetch flowers for the temple and then having to wait around for hours in a great tumult of the guru's followers (it was Rag somebody or other at the time) in the hope that they might get a glimpse of the great sage himself, or that he would send them a telepathic message, or perhaps best of all, that he would pass by near enough so that they could prostrate themselves and, if they were really fortunate, kiss the hem of his robes. A personal interview with him more than once during their visit would be too much to hope for, and even then you had to queue all day for it. The rest of the time would be spent in meditation, chanting and various other rituals, except for short breaks during which they could go to the canteen for their meals, which were of course strictly vegetarian. It would have been more or less exactly the same day after day, without ever having a real espresso, or so much as catching a glimpse of a Gitane (not that if he had it would have made any difference, since smoking wasn't allowed either). It was probably precisely because every day followed this identical pattern that Olivia always stayed so long when she went to India. She never had a particularly good sense of time, and the very sameness of the days, blending into each other as they must have done could easily have led to her losing touch with it altogether. Bernard knew very well that two days of that would have been more than enough for him. He'd never had much time for gurus, who he'd once rather derisively defined for Olivia as people who live alone but insist on telling others how to live together. His attitude wasn't all that surprising since he'd never been religious or believed in God. Praying at the age of six or seven, that his parents would bring him back a cowboy set from America hardly counted. He'd never prayed since, and although over the years there had been occasions when he might have wanted to go to a synagogue (if only to experience a sense of belonging to something), he never had because he wouldn't have known whom to address his prayers to when he got there.

But if he didn't have much of a feeling for God, he certainly knew what it felt like to be Jewish. He'd once given a talk about it at a Catholic girls' boarding school. Although almost as soon as he'd taken it on he began to feel enormously anxious about it, which is of course a very important part of what it feels like to be Jewish. On the way there in the car he'd felt so anxious that the hands on his watch seemed to be racing round the face even faster than usual. And when he arrived he was only able to force himself to go into the room where the lecture was to be held by throwing down two glasses of sherry and taking a tranquilliser. Even then he'd wanted to ask one of the nuns who ran the school to hold his hand while he talked, which would hardly have been considered seemly. When he finally got himself in there though the talk went well enough. But then how could it have been otherwise when the first thing that happened when he stepped inside that oak panelled lecture room was that fifty ripening teenage girls jumped to their feet. What's more, as soon as he'd put his lecture notes on the lectern under the huge crucifix on which Christ was stretching out his arms in agony, and looked around the room he noticed that several of them were very beautiful, and had even begun to look at him in a way that was hardly pure. If only he'd had the courage to have pointed to the most attractive of them and declared in a loud voice: 'I'll have that one, that one, that one and that one,' which was what his old mentor Issidore Popoff would have done. But in those days, perhaps because he was still not sufficiently progressed in his treatment, he couldn't imagine doing anything as bold as that. Still, the way they looked at him that evening at least gave Bernard enough of a frisson to ensure that he was sufficiently relaxed to launch into all kinds of jokes and stories, although what they responded most to was his, hardly entirely serious observation, that the main difference between Judaism and Christianity was that in Judaism you cut out the middleman and got God wholesale. Yes, he'd made an impression there alright, if only because apparently – he had no memory of it himself – on seeing a wooden sculpture of the Pieta near the front door, he'd put his arm around Mary's shoulder and remarked to the posse of girls who were accompanying him back to his car, 'that she was definitely every Jewish boy's dream'.

All that irony and cynicism about God and the world of the spirit would soon be a thing of the past. Bernard now fully expected that should Olivia ever ask him to accompany her to India again, his new self would be only too delighted to accept. The prospect of a such a trip, which once seemed unbelievably tedious, would by then no doubt have become completely enthralling.

2

Fortunately, Bernard had at least some idea of how to go about getting onto the right path to spiritual enlightenment. Olivia had often told him about a course of evening classes at the School for Higher Consciousness and Traditional Wisdom, known as Wiso for short, where he would at least be able to learn the rudiments. Not that he wasn't, for a while at least, tempted by all kinds of other gurus, communes and spiritual teachings that, now he was open to such things, he saw advertised all over the place. Spiritual growth being all the rage at the time there seemed to be a lot of paths to choose from. There was even one movement which purported to offer not only education and personal growth but assistance in the development of business skills as well. Apparently, success as a businessman could be much enhanced by being developed in harmony with the additional dimensions of love, awareness and meditation. As soon as he saw that advertisement, it was all Bernard could do to prevent himself from joining straightaway. His brief business career might have been an abysmal failure, but he had never entirely relinquished the hope that one day he would make one last attempt to become a tycoon. He had also occasionally thought that Sam's enormous success in business might have been partly due to the years he'd spent assiduously practising an obscure form of Japanese yoga. Was that the reason for his enormous energy and drive and why, although he was often manic, he never got in the least bit depressed?

Yes, what could be better than to achieve higher awareness, personal growth and enormous wealth all at the same time. But he soon became disillusioned. Bernard found it difficult to see how love, meditation and awareness could really help you to become rich. Sam's yoga was all very well, and indeed probably did help him to keep a clear head, but Bernard was absolutely certain that it wasn't the real secret of his business success. Even before he took up Yoga Sam already had what it took to become a successful businessman. No, whoever thought up that advertisement was simply playing on everyone's desire to be a success and he wasn't going to allow himself to be taken in by that – no more than he had been by that Pyramid selling conference he'd once attended. He might be a dope but he wasn't that big a dope. He'd only gone to that meeting because he'd been inveigled by a taxi driver, who'd asked him, just as he was fishing in his pocket for his wallet to pay the fare (always an anxious moment) if he was interested in making some money. What else could someone in Bernard's position have said but 'who wasn't'. Thankfully, one evening of that was quite enough for him.

That movement wasn't the only road to spiritual fulfilment Bernard was tempted by. For a while he considered joining the Rosicrucians, but then how could he possibly resist the temptation of having his awareness extended beyond the five senses and his personality entirely transformed? And he hadn't hesitated to write off for their free booklet, *The Mastery of Life*, which after all was precisely what he was looking for. Yes, with the deeper psychic aspects of his self at his finger tips, Bernard thought, who knows what he might not be capable of – telepathy, extra-sensory perception, and of course a whole new world of insights. The problem was now that he was open to such things almost every movement or teaching he read about seemed to have its good points. He contemplated attending Joyous Choy's Happiness Workshops, that he'd seen advertised in *World of the Spirit* magazine. Now, when Bernard peered into the window of the Hara Krishna centre at the group of dummies depicting the cycle from birth to death, instead of laughing to himself as he used to, he began to think he understood what they were getting at. If he were to become one of their followers, he would not only beat death, but open himself to the possibility of being transformed into all kinds of other beings as his soul sailed through the millennia.

In the end Bernard decided on the School of Higher Awareness and Traditional Wisdom, which not only had the advantage of being recommended by Olivia, but was also extremely cheap. For a mere eighteen pounds a term they offered to teach you not only the meaning of human existence and the aim of life but the art of knowing yourself as well. This was certainly a great deal cheaper than Dr Lear who didn't even pretend to know what life meant himself (or indeed if it was even a meaningful question to ask). Whenever Bernard so much as mentioned his anxiety about such matters, Dr Lear invariably responded by asking him what he thought himself, as if he would even have bothered to ask the question in the first place if he already knew what the answer was. Perhaps now at long last he was going to begin to get some answers.

Attending that course of evening classes turned out to be, at least in retrospect, the most satisfying part of Bernard's whole spiritual quest. Not that this was entirely because of how enlightened he became as a result. In the beginning he hadn't felt it was going to be at all satisfactory. That first evening, after he'd enrolled and been shown into the room where the lectures were going to be held, and saw those rows of tiny chairs, which appeared to grow smaller and smaller the more he looked at them, he'd suddenly felt far too old and that he really couldn't go through with it. It was almost as disturbing as if he'd been informed that he had to go back to school and start his life all over again. But as the weeks passed Bernard gradually came to look forward to the evenings he spent in that vast room, packed out with lost souls like himself, under a painted ceiling on which angels were reaching out to embrace one another. That they were angels seemed particularly appropriate, since Bernard soon began to think that he might eventually end up one himself. Somehow just going there once a week made him feel, for the first time in years, that he was making progress at last (although admittedly he probably felt something similar after his first few sessions with Dr Lear). Why he should have felt that wasn't easy to explain. It was deeply consoling to be able to listen to those lecturers (who themselves had been on the spiritual path for years and years) expounding the mysteries of the universe and the nature of human existence. According to them life on earth was guided by beings with the best supernatural connections, people who, Bernard imagined, were linked to the divine, rather in the way some saints in early Renaissance paintings are connected to God by barely visible, gold threads. Not that Bernard could always follow what they were saying – although he often tried to take notes and always carefully copied down the diagrams from the blackboard. This became especially evident if he ever tried to explain it to someone else, when, what he thought he'd understood perfectly, literally seemed to evaporate. Perhaps that was hardly surprising, since what they had been discussing was after all ineffable.

No, the real reason that those evenings seemed to be so beneficial was not so much because of what was said, or whether or not he'd grasped it, but that simply listening to those lectures had a strangely soothing effect on his whole being. It was as if he were a child again listening to his mother reading him a bedtime story. He often felt so peaceful and relaxed that it wouldn't have seemed at all inappropriate had they suddenly handed round blankets and suggested that everyone lay down on the floor and rested for a while just as at primary school. It would have fitted perfectly with the period of meditation with which the evening there always commenced. For Bernard just being able to meditate at all was a great step forward in itself, because whenever he'd attempted to in the past he'd never been anywhere nearly calm enough even to begin. Sitting trying to think of avenues of lime trees, or other idyllic scenes, had been of little use when his anxieties were racing around inside him in a state of near frenzy.

Bernard also soon discovered that he enjoyed the refreshment breaks at the school almost as much as what went on in the classroom. For some reason, being on the receiving end of all that spiritual nourishment, always made him feel enormously hungry. And the food, being absolutely pure and organic, naturally added a feeling of moral uplift to the spiritual sustenance he'd already received. But it wasn't simply hunger that made him look forward to those breaks so enthusiastically. No, the truth was that after only a couple of weeks he had become infatuated with Terresa, the flaxen-haired cashier whose heavy plait reached down right to the bottom of her spine. Not that even momentarily, with a look or a smile, did she once respond to any of Bernard's overtures. Although he should hardly have been surprised by that, since her aura of tranquillity and other worldliness suggested that she must at least have glimpsed some higher truth which would have made her totally immune to the charms of someone like him. But then those humourous and insensitive remarks he made about the books on sale in the refreshment room, which included such titles as – *The Imitation of the Buddha, Christ's Secret Diary* (which Bernard thought probably contained the real truth about his relationship with his mother) and *The collected works of Gotsky and Potsky* – must have seemed extraordinarily crass and irritating, almost as if they were intended to put her off him entirely. Not that this particular amorous failure really bothered him all that much because, although he might well have been in love with her for ten minutes or so – why else would he have lingered by the cash register so often making futile attempts to tune into her wavelength – he knew almost from the first moment he saw her that she really wasn't his type, or he hers. Nor was he so frivolous as to have forgotten so soon why he'd come to the school in the first place, which certainly wasn't to look for a woman.

Gradually Bernard realised that it wasn't only Terresa who looked as if she'd been taken over by a higher power but practically everyone else he encountered there. It was a look which appeared to suggest that once having accepted the teachings, the followers had been able to abandon their self-doubt and uncertainty about life altogether. Some of them looked so bland and contented it was as if their personalities had become extinct. To Bernard – for whom the experience of self-doubt was almost a religious rite (Indeed perhaps it was his sole religious activity) – seeing people in that state was deeply disturbing. Of course, not everyone was as devoted to self-doubt as he was, or indeed had even experienced it very much. Joseph Barnett, the self-made businessman who lived next door, was like that. Either he'd given up questioning things years ago or as Bernard suspected, he'd never experienced a moment's self-doubt in his whole life. Joseph, however, who was in his late seventies but acted as if old age simply didn't exist (recently he'd told Bernard that he was contemplating starting yet another business), was like that for quite different reasons – the most important of which was that he appeared to possess the most perfect ego Bernard had ever encountered. He was always brimming over with self-confidence, so much so that unless Bernard was feeling in a particularly good frame of mind he preferred to wait in the car, rather than have to travel up in the lift with him. He would never forget the day he forgot to follow that procedure, and in the lift had risked saying what a dismal grey day it was, to which Joseph's only reply had been, that he'd been in meetings all day and hadn't noticed. And only someone as self-confident as Joseph could use expressions such as 'I'm not going to worry about that now', which always amazed Bernard, for whom yesterday wouldn't have been soon enough to get started if he had even the slightest thing to worry about. But the acolytes Bernard saw at Wiso were constructed entirely differently. What they had done was to hand over all their worries and doubts for something they'd never even seen. And now they were almost literally munching away on the pie in the sky.

It wasn't long before Bernard realised that staying on at the school beyond the introductory course would mean having to make the supreme sacrifice of giving up his cherished self-doubt and becoming exactly like one of them. Not that the choice was entirely his. In a variety of ways, including the gradual imposition of a more authoritarian atmosphere in the lectures, it was made clear that unless you were prepared to accept the teachings without reservation sooner or later you would have to leave.

Although Bernard was aware how much he would miss listening to those soothing talks, as well as having the opportunity of admiring, if not flirting with the voluptuous Terresa, whose exquisite ankles he'd just begun to appreciate (since women at the school were obliged to wear long skirts, Bernard's fantasies had recently taken on a curiously Victorian hue), these pleasures, such as they were, were not worth paying any price for, particularly since he'd lately discovered (as a result of overhearing two of the lecturers talking in the corridor) that what was taught at Wiso was a diluted form of the teachings of Sergei Gotsky himself anyway. He definitely wasn't prepared to sacrifice all his precious anxieties and doubts for something that wasn't even the real thing.

Sometimes, after leaving the school, Bernard wondered if that might not be the end of his attempt to achieve higher consciousness altogether. It wasn't as if he'd ever understood very much of what he'd heard in those lectures, and even weeks afterwards he still couldn't decide whether they were right or wrong, or for that matter how anyone could judge. He wasn't in any great rush to make up his mind what to do next. The only important thing was to have reached some sort of decision by the time Olivia got back from India. Although by then she'd already been away for more than four months (which in itself was beginning to give Sam sleepless nights), there was still no sign that she was anywhere near ready to return. What was delaying her so long, as she'd said in her last letter, was that almost as soon as she'd arrived Baksheesh had been taken mysteriously ill and had spent practically all his time secluded in his quarters, being cared for by his favourite devotees, so that she'd hardly seen him at all. And naturally she couldn't see any point in coming home until she'd had the opportunity to find out for herself if he really was as miraculous a being as she had been led to believe. Although her decision seemed perfectly reasonable, he had recently begun to miss her so much that not long after Bernard received that letter, he went out and bought Baksheesh an enormous get well card, and knowing how much gurus relish adoration, covered it with literally hundreds of bogus signatures and posted it off to the Ashram. It wasn't that he cared about Baksheesh's health, or believed that it could possibly make any difference but, feeling as powerless as he did, he just couldn't think of anything else to do. And the principle was definitely right: the sooner Baksheesh recovered, the sooner she would see him and the sooner she'd come home.

A week or so after posting it, Bernard was awoken in the middle of the night by a phone call.

'Hallo, hallo. Is that Mr Steinway?'

'Yes it is, but do you realise what the time is.'

'This is an emergency. Fakir Backsheesh speaking. I've been trying to get hold of you for days .'

'Why... What's the trouble... Olivia isn't ill is she?' Bernard said, feeling the anxiety rising in his chest.

'No, no, nothing like that. She's as fit as a fiddle. No, the trouble is your wife, ex-wife, or whatever you call her, is driving everyone in the Ashram completely crazy.'

'Well I know she can be a bit difficult but...'

'It's her questions Mr Steinway, her endless infernal questions. Well, I can't take it anymore Mr Steinway. I haven't been at all well lately myself and...'

'Nothing serious I hope?'

'No, it's nothing much, just a recurrence of my old nervous trouble – I've been meditating too much again I expect. Thank you very much for asking anyway. As I was saying. I haven't been well lately, and on top of that she's driving me crazy about what the meaning of life is. It's too much Bernard, you don't mind my calling you Bernard I hope?'

'No, I don't mind.'

'Well I don't know myself what the meaning of life is! Bernard I simply can't put up with much more of this. I'm already coping with two thousand hysterical women as it is. That's enough for any man don't you think? These days India is full of European girls. They come here in pursuit of eternal truths. Sometimes I think every single one of them is here in my Ashram. I don't see why I should be expected to deal with all of them. It's just not cricket Bernard. It wouldn't be so bad if it was just me your wife plagued with those infernal question of hers, but it isn't. She goes round the Ashram asking absolutely everyone she meets what they think. You must help me Mr Steinway. You're my last hope. Please come and take her away. Nothing less than the tranquillity of the Ashram is at stake.'

'But surely you of all people can cope,' Bernard said, not entirely able to prevent himself from sounding ironic.

'No Bernard, I can't. You must come as soon as possible. I implore you. If you don't come and fetch her I don't know what I'm going to do.'

'It's a bit difficult for me to drop everything and come straight away.'

'Oh I see, so you won't be able to come then. I'm so sorry, so sorry.'

'No... and it wouldn't necessarily help if I did. Olivia may not listen to me, she doesn't always.'

Then there was such a long silence. Bernard wondered if they'd been cut off, or if Backsheesh was so disappointed by his refusal that he'd simply put the phone down on him. But a few seconds later he was back again.

'Hallo Bernard are you still there?'

'Yes, I'm here.' Clearly Baksheesh hadn't put the phone down. He'd been thinking.

'Well, by golly, I've got it. I'll tell her that it's most urgent she return to the West and carry on with my work there. Yes, that's it. Thank you very much Mr Steinway. You've been most helpful, most helpful indeed.'

'But I didn't do anything,' Bernard shouted down the phone, but it was too late; by then Baksheesh really had hung up.

Not long after receiving that call Bernard decided that since Olivia would be coming home soon (if not quite as soon as Baksheesh would have wished) that if he was ever going to make any further progress along the spiritual path, this was definitely the moment to try and do it. Whatever doubts he might have about his ability, it was clearly now or never. But it wasn't just that phone call which put a stop to Bernard's procrastination but also that Sam – who wasn't entirely convinced that he hadn't made up the whole story of talking to Baksheesh on the telephone altogether – if only to allay his anxieties had decided to go to India himself and bring her back. As he said to Bernard not long before he left, 'Even if your account of that call was accurate in every detail, it still doesn't follow, knowing Olivia as well as we both do, that she will be on the next plane home, or anything like it.' Bernard was so impressed by Sam's determination to go there himself – despite his aversion to everything Olivia had told him about Baksheesh, and indeed to gurus in general. He immediately made up his mind, that if Sam was prepared to go that far, he simply had to carry on with his spiritual quest at least until he'd come face to face with Olivia's favourite guru, Sergei Gotsky.

3

Bernard had no difficulty in finding out where Gotsky, or Count Sergei Gotsky, as he called himself, had his headquarters (years earlier Gotsky had assumed this title to which he had only a very dubious claim). All he had to do was to look in the phone book and there it was – Count Sergei Gotsky, President, The Easthouse Institute for Human Harmony, 1 St Petersburg Mansions, St Petersburg Place. It was a part of the city that was full of memories for him. As a child he'd gone there with his father who liked it because its numerous cafe's and restaurants reminded him of pre-war Budapest. It was also not far from his late Aunt Jessie's old fashioned patisserie, where they stopped off every Sunday to collect a box of perfect white meringues for tea after their walk in the park. Gotsky's flat also happened to be in the same street where Dr Shenanagan once had his practice, although by now of course he must have been dead for years. The last time Bernard saw him was that day the old man had consulted him to get a second opinion about the operation for cancer he'd been advised to have. Despite the sadness of that memory Bernard couldn't help feeling that the very location of Gotsky's Institute was somehow a good omen. Later, he found out that Gotsky had simply chosen it because it was very near a Russian Orthodox church where, although he had abandoned the faith long ago, he still sometimes liked to go and stand at the back, candle in hand, and join in the singing. But if finding the address was simple, getting to see him proved to be much more difficult. Gotsky never answered the phone himself and the young American woman who did (who was, as Bernard discovered subsequently, his mistress) seemed to be completely indifferent to Bernard's anxiety to speak to him. It was always the same story: the Master, as she referred to him, was either meditating, or simply far too busy seeing his disciples to come to the phone in person. Bernard must have phoned twenty or thirty times before he was finally informed, by that same impersonal voice, that Gotsky was at last prepared to meet him. But although Bernard conscientiously went to every one of those rendezvous, which were either at various cafés near to his flat, at Lebanese restaurants at four or five in the morning, or even, oddly enough, in the lingerie departments of various big stores (Gotsky, it turned out, had once worked for a New York lingerie manufacturer called Intimate Apparel). But he never showed up, or if he did, Bernard didn't recognise him. Of course, if what Olivia always said about him was true, he could well have been there in any number of guises without Bernard necessarily recognising him. For all Bernard knew he was that dog which for no apparent reason had started to bark at him outside the French patisserie where they were supposed to meet that first time. Bernard would have found being stood up like that extremely annoying (although waiting around in lingerie departments had its compensations, since he was often virtually the only man there in a sea of bras and camisoles at which he looked and pretended not to look at the same time) had he not quickly realised that what Gotsky was doing was testing him to see how serious he was. He was certain this was the case because he had once spent a profoundly tedious evening reading the *Tibetan Book Of The Dead*, in which a great sage was forever putting obstacles in the path of his prospective followers for exactly the same reason. If anything, what Gotsky was doing was far harder to endure, because whereas they were expected to perform various tasks, such as building a house for the guru, before being admitted to the way of knowledge, Bernard hadn't the vaguest idea what was expected of him, except perhaps that he didn't give up phoning for yet another appointment directly after he had been stood up for the last one. Then quite suddenly Gotsky changed his tactics, and the very next time Bernard telephoned he was informed that there were to be no more rendezvous but instead he was to attend a meeting of Gotsky's followers, who would be able to assess whether or not he was the right sort of person to be admitted to the Institute.

God only knows how Bernard managed to get through that awful evening but somehow he did. Somehow he contrived to conceal both his mirth and his irritation from all of them. Yes, he fooled them alright. He even managed to participate in their bizarre spiritual exercises. They avoided using the words *and* or *but* and so did he. They scorned the expression of negative emotions and he did the same. Yes, the way he acted that evening must have made him seem like a model candidate, which was quite an achievement since almost everything about those people irritated him enormously; especially the impression they tried to give of being in possession of a higher truth; the way they exuded inner calm; and the look of profound tranquillity on their faces. Even the flat where the meeting took place, with its carefully positioned bowls and sculptures, which looked as if they too had achieved inner peace, the pervasive sickly sweet smell of incense and the photographs of various Indian holy men in loin cloths hanging on the walls was deeply alien to him. But Bernard was so determined to be allowed to see Gotsky in person, that the whole evening he never once said anything ironic or even vaguely sceptical, that would have led them to doubt the seriousness of his intentions. Although what he had really felt like doing, was to have tipped over that table laden with various wholefood delicacies, and then got up and walked out of there into the infinitely preferable cold, uncertain, darkness of the night. Later on in the evening he even accepted a cup of decaffeinated tea with good grace when it was offered to him, when the very idea of it would normally have provoked him to make any number of humourous remarks. Yes, there he was amongst the citizens of Smodonia and he didn't say a single word that would make them doubt that he wasn't sincerely interested in becoming one of them. That was quite an achievement for someone who normally felt a compulsion to say exactly what he felt at all times to an extent that was virtually pathological. Anyway, his act must have convinced them that he really was the earnest seeker after truth that he purported to be, because a few days later he was finally invited to an audience with the master himself.

It was certainly worth enduring the almost intolerable tedium of that evening, because when the following week he was invited to meet Gotsky in person he soon felt he was in the presence of one of the most extraordinary people he'd ever met. Not that his initial reaction to either the Institute, or to Gotsky himself, was all that favourable. In fact, more than once while he sat in that incredibly crowded waiting room, which with its flickering brass oil lamps, nomadic rugs and bright red canopy suspended from the ceiling resembled a Bedouin tent (or perhaps even a Turkish bordello), he'd felt so oppressed that he was tempted to give up the whole thing and go home. And then when after nearly two hours, he was finally ushered into the room where Gotsky was waiting to receive him, reclining on a great mound of cushions inside a strange black tent, Bernard found his whole appearance so exotic and contrived that it was almost impossible to believe he could really be the great sage and teacher Olivia talked about. What Gotsky – a heavily built man in his sixties, who wore an iridescent Egyptian cotton suit that seemed to change colour from moment to moment, a fez, the tassle of which dangled half way down his face, and a thick luxuriant moustache, the tips of which pointed upwards towards heaven – most resembled was a sort of old fashioned music hall magician. For a few minutes Bernard felt deeply suspicious. Surely Gotsky's appearance could only be that of a man who had quite consciously set out to give a very particular impression? He looked the way he did because he imagined, rightly or wrongly, that was how people would expect a spiritual leader to look.

Once he sat down and Gotsky began looking at him with those strange hypnotic eyes of his – eyes that made Bernard feel that he had experienced everything and understood everything – and he commenced speaking in that peculiar, vaguely middle eastern accent of his, Bernard found his initial doubts begin to evaporate.

'I have been expecting you for many months Bernard.'

'But I only decided I wanted to try and find you a few weeks ago myself.'

'I know all things. There's nothing I don't know. I knew long ago you would come and why you would come. I know you're Olivia's husband. You don't think you've come for yourself but to find a way back to her. You think this is the way. But you have not only come for that reason. You come here to me because you are lost yourself also,' Gotsky said, in a voice which increasingly sounded to Bernard as he imagined an oracle would sound (albeit in an accent that you would be more likely to hear in a Lebanese restaurant), or like a sort of verbal equivalent of the writing on the wall (a biblical story which for some reason had long ago made itself totally at home in his mind, perhaps because he had often hoped to receive written instructions about what to do next himself).

Gotsky's initial remarks absolutely astonished Bernard. How could he possibly know that he and Olivia were connected in any way. She had never used his name after they were married but had carried on with her own as if nothing at all had changed. Could this mean that Gotsky really was, as they said, the man who knows? The longer Gotsky stared at him with those extraordinary eyes of his, the more Bernard felt that he was able to see right through him into the tangled mess of his innermost being. It was as if, not only did Gotsky know who he was and why he'd come, but had always known him. This must have been why – although he really had believed that his main reason for seeking out Gotsky was as a means of drawing closer to Olivia – he now suddenly began to pour out all his worries and anxieties (including the whole story of his failure as a rug dealer), as if he really was someone who had the power to guide him towards the light at last.

There was no exaggeration in anything he told him, because despite having been a patient of Dr Lear for more than a year he was hardly any better than before his treatment had begun. It was a situation which sometimes led his sister to ask him why Dr Lear couldn't give him something to make him feel better, as if there was some equivalent to an aspirin which could instantly banish despair. As far as his state of mind was concerned he wasn't much less confused than old Mrs Gestetner, who he sometimes saw lingering downstairs in the entrance hall unable to decide whether she was coming in or going out. Nor had he been entirely joking when she rang his bell late one night to say she couldn't go on and he suggested that maybe they should jump together.

During the whole time Bernard had been obsessively pouring out his troubles Gotsky didn't say a word, but sat almost impassively puffing slowly on a Romeo and Juliet cigar (which he made the mistake of smoking with the band on) and occasionally stroking his moustache from the centre outwards to its upturned waxed tips. It wasn't until Bernard had finally reached the end of his agonised soliloquy, or had at least become too exhausted to continue, that Gotsky made any comment at all.

'You in sorry state. Not make a living very bad thing. The practical in life very important Bernard.'

Bernard could hardly believe his ears. Had he really been so persistent in his efforts to meet this man only to have to listen to the almost identical thing that Dr Lear was always saying. For a few moments he felt as frustrated and angry as the man in that joke must have felt, who sells up everything he has to be able to travel to Tibet to find a guru who is supposed to know the meaning of life, only to be told as soon as he's ushered into the guru's presence, that the meaning of life is chicken soup. But it was what Gotsky said immediately after that which made a really profound impression on him.

'You are a broken automobile Bernard, you need repairing. You must work on yourself. Work on yourself is the most important work. First work on yourself then everything become easy for you, even earning a living.'

It was being called a 'broken automobile' that really stirred Bernard up. It would have been hard to think of a more appropriate metaphor for describing someone in his state, especially since his father had spent several years as a secondhand car dealer and had put as his occupation on Bernard's birth certificate that of garage proprietor. It turned out later that he had been quite wrong to imagine that Gotsky had used that expression because he had real knowledge of Bernard's past. He almost invariably said the same thing to prospective pupils, and its use owed less to divine insight than to a passion for old cars. But it wasn't simply that which moved Bernard so deeply. How could anyone as indolent as Bernard possibly resist the idea that the most important work was not real work, but work on yourself (whatever Gotsky precisely meant by that) and which seemed to Bernard infinitely preferable to working. And even supposing the opposite was true, and Gotsky really did believe making a living was so vital, having to work on himself first, would at least enable Bernard to put off for some considerable time to come trying to make a success of that all over again.

'But you can't do this alone Bernard,' Gotsky continued, 'you come to my Institute and we show you how to work on yourself. Here we prepare you for life. With my help you achieve self-mastery and then life become easy for you. As they say in your country – a piece of cake.'

This seemed to Bernard absolutely amazing. Was it really possible, after years of being a victim of himself, that he was going to achieve self-mastery at last. This was simply too attractive not to give it a try. There was nothing else for it, he just had to join Gotsky's Institute, even if it did mean parting with ten per cent of his income to do so. It wasn't only what Gotsky said that made the idea so attractive. There was something about him – his charisma, or the sense he conveyed of being all knowing perhaps – that made him an almost perfect candidate to become yet another of Bernard's father figures. It was also not insignificant that Gotsky rather resembled Bernard's father. They had a similar build, the same sallow complexion and hazel eyes that were slightly tinged with melancholy. They had both gone bald in that same, rather classical way that leaves a tarmac of flesh running between two patches of hair on either side of the head. Only Gotsky's moustache was different, but even that was merely a matter of the way his pointed up at the ends. Or perhaps it would be truer to say that what Gotsky really looked like was a strange combination of Bernard's father, and Bernie, an ex-professional wrestler, who at one time had been his business partner, and who had always given Bernard one of those enormous white five pound notes on his birthday, notes which it turned out later, were really his father's whom he'd been cheating for years. But whoever he looked like, Gotsky's face was definitely one which made Bernard feel completely at home.

Ah, if only Bernard had known what that work on himself was really going to entail, he would never have allowed himself to become involved with Gotsky's crazy establishment. And there wasn't only work on yourself to do either, but real work as well. Somewhere along the way Gotsky had become a great believer in the therapeutic virtues of work as a way of promoting spiritual growth and all his followers, whatever their degree of enlightenment (whether they were number ones, or number fives in Gotsky's estimation), were expected to contribute to the running of the Institute. Suddenly poor old Bernard, incorrigibly lazy as he was, found himself devoting a large part of the weekends, like many of Gotsky's other followers, at the Institute doing domestic chores. If Bernard achieved nothing else during his time with Gotsky he certainly became expert at that and pretty soon he found himself becoming a virtuoso performer with the hoover, the broom and the dustpan and brush. For Gotsky, being a good householder, as he called it, was at least as important as any of the other activities of the Institute. So there was no slacking, no leaning on brooms, or missing out corners, or else you very soon found yourself being instructed to do your allotted task all over again. And if that ever happened it was regarded as a very serious misdemeanour indeed, because the attitude the pupil took to his work was regarded as at least of equal importance as the results of his labours. But if the domestic chores Bernard was obliged to perform were arduous, the real work, the work on himself was almost unendurable.

To begin with, there were those interminable meetings and study groups which took place on both Saturday and Sunday afternoons when the master's works were carefully studied and discussed in detail. This was necessary, as far as Bernard was concerned anyway, because by himself he could hardly understand a single word of *Life And How*

To Live It – An Esoteric Guide; and as for *The Meaning Behind Things, a Letter to Beelzebub's Grand-daughter*, attempting to make sense of that drove Bernard so crazy that one evening when he'd been trying to study it at home, he tore it up and threw it across the room. Unfortunately, there was no skipping those meetings either, since they were considered to be essential for progressing towards a more wide awake state; that is, becoming a more conscious being. In those meetings pupils were supposed to help each other to be more awake, by acting like human alarm clocks. This was partly the meaning behind the crazy language exercises which had so astonished Bernard when he'd first encountered them that evening he'd spent being vetted by Gotsky's disciples. The idea was that by avoiding using *and* or *but* you would become more conscious of what you were doing and therefore more awake and in the present, although for Bernard the result was only to make communication more or less impossible. Most often he found the easiest course of action to take was to say almost nothing, whilst trying very hard not to fall asleep, which would have been regarded as a tremendous insult to the ethos of the Institute, even if becoming more awake obviously wasn't meant absolutely literally. Fortunately, he didn't find it all that difficult to keep quiet because he very quickly realised that he had almost nothing in common with anybody else who attended those meetings, least of all with Gotsky's followers from the Californian branch, who with their clean-cut good looks, white shirts and blue suits looked remarkably like the born-again Christians he sometimes noticed in the Polish tea room. It didn't help that those meetings were often led by Karen, an incredibly cheerful woman from San Diego, who had the infuriating habit of saying right at the beginning of every meeting: 'Now then let's begin this afternoon's session with a good *do*,' – as in do, re, me, fa and so on. The musical terminology having its origin in their belief that Mozart had been a follower of Gotsky during one of his previous incarnations, and had composed the greater part of his music whilst under his influence.

Those attempts to study the master's works were light hearted diversions by comparison with the practice of those strange physical exercises (they seemed to Bernard like a sort of metaphysical P.T.)

which Gotsky had apparently learned from the monks in a remote Tibetan monastery. These were carried out under the direction of two diminutive, very old, Russian aristocratic sisters, Princess Potava and Princess Dominicina, both of whom with their spindly legs and jerky movements could well have been relatives of Pinnochio. They had both been with Gotsky for years and had followed him from one country to another, in the course of which they had given him almost the whole of their inheritance, which included the exquisite Sèvres china (amongst which was a coffee pot, with a spout in the form of an elephant's trunk), the bohemian glass and old Russian silver that were frequently used for the banquets held regularly at the Institute. The hours and hours the pupils spent marching on the spot and attempting to perform exercises like rubbing your stomach in a clockwise direction, whilst simultaneously patting the top of your head, were supposed to help overcome laziness and at the same time build up the stamina needed for a completely wide-awake existence. To Bernard what they really seemed to be were exercises in the art of awkwardness, and as such nearly as crazy as some photographs he'd once seen of great yogis, who after years of practice, are able to contort their bodies into the most bizarre postures; thereby apparently gaining complete mastery over them, although God knows to what purpose.

What everyone looked forward to most during those weekends at Gotsky's were the opportunities to hear the Master read and discuss his collected works, and to listen to him chanting and answering questions about life. This generally took place on Saturday evenings after dinner, when everyone would gather in the big assembly room and sit cross-legged in a semi-circle outside Gotsky's study house (the small marquee where Bernard had first been received by him and where Gotsky spent most of his time). Often these occasions lasted far into the night (once he got going, Gotsky would have made even Fidel Castro look laconic). Despite the difficulty Bernard always experienced in sitting in that position for more than a half an hour at a time, he found listening to Gotsky's voice rising and falling affected him like a very soothing kind of music which, far from awakening his true self, tended to send him to sleep. This might also have been partly a consequence of the abundant splendours of the master's culinary genius: the great silver salvers of chicken cooked in yoghourt, the vast dishes of couscous, the pigeons baked in the lightest flaky pastry, the mounds of Persian rice with raisins and sultanas, the figs from Smyrna; all of which were accompanied by great quantities of white Burgundy. Not that those dinners could by any means be described as tranquil affairs. On the contrary, quite often Gotsky would behave in the most provocative way imaginable towards his followers; accusing the women of being more interested in his body than in anything he had to teach them, and the men of being unbelievably lazy and totally impractical. At some point in the evening he would almost always threaten them by saying things like – 'Well, If I died tomorrow you all be in right old mess.' Everyone would become extremely anxious because although Gotsky only looked about sixty, sometimes he would claim to be a hundred and twenty-seven, or give as his date of birth eighteen hundred and two – or even amazingly at some point in the distant future. Nearly everyone realised he behaved like this largely to wake them up, but even so the atmosphere by the end of those meals was hardly harmonious. Not that Bernard found Gotsky's post-prandial ruminations terribly illuminating when they'd all finally settled down to listen to him speak. Gotsky's personal elucidation of his own writings made them hardly more comprehensible than Bernard's attempts at understanding them by himself. As for his spontaneous observations on life, most frequently they just seemed banal, rather than, as Bernard had hoped, the profound and wise reflections of a great savant. But then perhaps he missed the true esoteric significance behind such remarks as 'In the rain an umbrella is sometimes a useful thing'. Although almost everyone else appeared to hang on Gotsky's every word, as if his slightest utterance had the power to transform their lives totally.

After barely a few weeks of this, Bernard gradually found himself becoming disillusioned with the whole enterprise. After all, it wasn't as if his consciousness was even a millimetre more developed than it had been at the outset. He had applied himself as assiduously as he was able to the activity of becoming a good householder; not even once when he had the hoover in his hand had he allowed his mind to wander, or permitted himself to feel a moment's discontent. Even during those endless meetings he'd always tried his best to follow what was going on. Then there were those hours and hours he'd spent at home listening to tapes of Gotsky chanting and philosophising about life. But none of it seemed to do much good. He couldn't say he felt all that much at home with any of the other disciples either, but then he might have anticipated that would happen. The instinctive revulsion he'd felt at the age of six when he'd been sent to the cubs for the afternoon had obviously been formative. He was, as his mother often said, a lone wolf, and so perhaps it was his fate to howl the rest of his life away by himself. Despite his growing doubts though, he would probably have carried on spending almost every weekend at the Institute for a great deal longer than he did (his character having often in the past revealed an oddly tenacious streak). Yes, he might very well have still been there now, had it not been that after a few weeks, Bernard had begun to receive private tuition from Sergei Gotsky in the hope that this would speed up his progress towards becoming a more fully conscious human being, but which had the opposite result of making the progress of his disenchantment even faster.

After only a few sessions Gotsky started to behave much more like a real father than the father figure Bernard had previously seen him as. Instead of being supportive and understanding, he constantly criticised and cajoled him about his inadequacies, especially his laziness and impracticality. It wasn't long before, unlike Dr Lear who always believed in Bernard discovering such things for himself, that Gotsky started to tell Bernard exactly what he ought to be doing with his life. In particular, he was always going on and on about how it was vital Bernard make at least one further attempt to make a success of the rug business. He never seemed to tire of saying the same old thing over and over.

'Carpet business beautiful business Bernard, much better than restaurant business. I should know I bin in both. In Constantinople, Rome, Bucharest, I always had the best clientele, everyone know me. You listen to me and you become rich in no time Bernard.'

This idea of Gotsky's absolutely astounded Bernard. It also made him wonder yet again if Gotsky really hadn't been the man in the Homburg hat at the auction that afternoon, whose behaviour had had such a strange effect on him. But what was even more astonishing was that he seemed to be completely set on the idea of becoming Bernard's silent partner in the undertaking, although Bernard could hardly imagine him ever being able to remain silent for very long about anything. He even had the name of their new business clear in his mind. It was to be called Gotsky & Steinway Oriental Carpet Merchants. The problem was, however hard he tried, Bernard just couldn't see it working. He wasn't at all convinced that he really trusted him. He was certain that if the business was a success Gotsky would make off with most of the money and spend it on yet another Bentley or Lagonda, or a holiday in the South of France, and if it was a failure he'd end up being blamed for it. Although they had parted years ago Gotsky still blamed Potsky for failing him in their war against sleeping mankind; and he wasn't even above occasionally accusing him of having had his hand in the till.

No, he just couldn't see himself going into business with Gotsky whatever happened. He also found it extremely irksome to suddenly find himself landed with another father, particularly since he still hadn't fully come to terms with the one he'd had. Even now, although it was years since he'd died, he would occasionally wake up in the night hearing his father telling him off for some failing or other. A supportive, indulgent, understanding father figure was one thing, but another father like his own was just too much. He also had absolutely no desire to go back into the rug business ever again. After that last fiasco he had at least discovered one of his limitations, which was that he was utterly incapable of starting a business. He might, just might, if the conditions were right be able to adequately carry out his duties in some well established family firm (would that one existed that would open its arms to him), especially if it was really a sinecure. Perhaps, if he had to have a worthwhile occupation, the ideal one would be that of evaluating the expressions on the faces of teddy bears in a toy factory as they came off the production line: this one a little too depressed, the next too stoical, that one too optimistic and the legions of those that were too childishly insouciant. But he was sure no such post existed. Beyond that he simply couldn't go. Even Bunuel's father's daily walk bearing a pot of caviar home for lunch might be too much for

Bernard's well established indolence. Better the absolute lethargy of Oblomov's couch and the pleasures of the table, or the near pointless existence as one of that dying breed of great restaurant men, whose aimless lives were once celebrated in obituaries in the Times. For Bernard, Lao Tsu's dictum – that any act was an interference with the divine harmony of the universe – had become more or less a catechism. The last thing he wanted was to make a living, or be a success in the real world, no matter whether it was Dr Lear, or Gotsky, or anyone else, who said that his only hope of salvation lay in that direction.

With Gotsky suddenly beginning to act like a father, and his general feeling of disenchantment with his progress at the Institute, Bernard soon concluded he had little choice but to abandon going there altogether. He was sorry about it, because whatever his reservations, spending nearly every weekend with Gotsky definitely added a little something to his sense of purpose, and whilst he carried on he could always hope that tomorrow he would wake up more himself than he was today. Still, he had learned something from the experience. Now at least he was certain he was incapable of becoming someone else. It might, as Dr Lear had often said, be possible to make a few slight adjustments to his personality, but that was about it. He would simply have to struggle on to the end as he was now. He also found out yet again that he lacked the necessary qualities to become a follower. But that suited him fine, better to be completely lost on your own than an acolyte. Ironically enough, the way things turned out, it didn't matter at all that Bernard had failed to take the same spiritual path as Olivia had followed, because when she finally returned from India, a few weeks later, he very quickly found out that she had switched her allegiance to Fakir Baksheesh by comparison to whom, Gotsky apparently hadn't even reached the first rung on the ladder of spiritual enlightenment.

Bernard hadn't only failed to attain higher consciousness, he'd also failed in his resolve to give up his beloved Gitanes, develop a passion for the countryside, or become a vegetarian (not that Gotsky had ever pretended to be one himself). The one visit Bernard had forced himself to make to a wholefood restaurant hadn't been a great success. Though he'd been stoical about having to sit at a long wooden refectory table surrounded by all those excessively healthy looking dinners, and had even managed to eat that great mound of vegetables and roast tofu they'd put in front of him, he had ended up spending the night in the bathroom feeling as if his centre of gravity had gone for ever. Apparently even being able to digest tofu properly requires a period of adjustment. And he'd hardly touched all those totally pure provisions he'd spent a small fortune on at the very same wholefood shop that Olivia patronised (an establishment, it so happened, which was run by a group of people who themselves were on some sort of spiritual path, which perhaps explained why they always looked so completely at peace with themselves). Now the tubes of tartex spread, the Japanese zipcon soups, the bottles of decaffeinated Cola, the organically fed free-range eggs, the Swiss, incomparably pure, carrot and beetroot juices, were nearly all still there keeping themselves company in the larder. Yes, it hadn't taken him long to conclude that vegetarian food wasn't a cuisine at all but a branch of philosophy in which the key words were whole, pure and natural and though it might be worth thinking about, it definitely wasn't worth eating. And as for all those different sorts of yoghourts he'd bought (including both the living and the dead), he'd never been able to bring himself to touch any of them. But then, if you think about it, isn't life sometimes quite sour enough without having to eat that sort of thing every day?

Bernard's Luck

1

Bernard's complete failure to achieve higher consciousness turned out to be, if not the last straw, then definitely the one next to it. It wasn't long before he found himself slipping back into the dark wood, if anything to a far deeper level than he'd ever reached before. Having failed to achieve something that was after all invisible it seemed to him that there really was nothing left to fail at. This wasn't simply another failure but signified to Bernard the end of his hopes of ever being reconciled with Olivia. No wonder he felt so lost and depressed.

Not that anyone noticed how terrible he felt. Nobody else knew anything about his latest failure, since fortunately he had had the good sense to keep the story of his brief excursion into the world of spiritual enlightenment entirely to himself. Fuelled by his despair, Bernard was outwardly even funnier and wittier than usual. At the dinner parties he occasionally went to – at least after he'd had a couple of glasses of wine – he was like a social star rising over the hors d'oeuvres, although anyone who was at all observant would have soon realised that those self-deprecating monologues of his were really only signs of profound desperation. But of course no one recognised this, and instead people just egged him on until he became even funnier and more manic. Perhaps it was no coincidence that it was about this time that Olivia's mother began to suggest that he was so funny he really ought to be on the radio, although she never said how exactly you went about achieving such a thing. After all, he couldn't very well just phone them up and say that his nearly ex-mother-in-law had said they could really use someone like him on one of their chat shows.

Bernard wasn't fooled by his apparent good humour. He knew perfectly well that this tendency to be at his funniest when he was really at his lowest, was normal for him and was yet again something he'd inherited from his father, whose melancholy self was almost always instantly transformed into that of the gayest of bon vivants the moment he set foot inside a good restaurant. Yes, the old man was always at his best when tucking a damask serviette into his shirt and summoning the head waiter over to take his order. Bernard had to admit that he too had experienced some of his happiest moments in old fashioned, expensive restaurants (during the early years of their relationship Olivia would always rush him off to one of his favourite restaurants if ever he complained of feeling depressed), which was perhaps why Dr Lear had once suggested that he suffered from a red plush complex.

But when he was alone in his room overlooking the park, a room he had made into a nearly perfect replica of a nineteenth-century Russian gentleman's study (the only things missing perhaps were a boar's head on the wall and a snarling bearskin rug on the floor) he lay down on the green chaise-longue and looked out of the window at the monotonous, almost motionless, grey sky (which, it sometimes seemed to Bernard, had been pasted on to the window specifically to seal in his despair). He often felt as downhearted and listless as Oblomov must have felt caught up in his waning life of torpor and inaction. It was on one of those many, seemingly endless afternoons, that Bernard spent almost entirely lying down, looking out of the window and in at his past life (during which he sometimes felt he could literally feel the passing of time), that he remembered another one of his mother-in-law's observations about his character. It was something she had said one morning during the time they had been staying with Olivia's parents after they returned from living in Italy. As usual Bernard had been wandering aimlessly from room to room, his hair uncombed, a newspaper in his hand, his shirt hanging out at the back, when, for want of anything better to do, he had accompanied Olivia and her mother to the front door to wave goodbye to them. This would have been a perfectly unexceptionable thing to have done had it not been that they were only going down the road for half an hour to do some shopping. Evelyn was so astonished, that she couldn't resist saying to Olivia that she thought Bernard must be the laziest man she'd ever known. But it wasn't true at all. He was slow – yes, painfully slow – but there was nothing he could do about that, since it too was a characteristic he'd inherited from his father, who was easily capable of spending three quarters of an hour trimming his moustache in the morning. No, what obviously seemed to her laziness was in fact nothing other than the almost perfect expression of Bernard not having even the vaguest idea what to do with himself, a condition he'd suffered from on and off for as long as he could remember.

Only occasionally was Bernard able to interrupt his endless obsessive going over of the past (a phenomenon he later referred to as his misery-go-round) and do anything as simple as read a book. But even then all he ever seemed to be capable of concentrating on, and then for barely half an hour, was Beatrix Potter, or a few pages of *Wind in The Willows*. It might have been true that at that time he was even beginning to think of Badger as a kind of father figure. But he never managed to escape from his overwhelming sense of failure for very long. Often it seemed to him that he had achieved nothing in his life, except perhaps to have been in the avant garde of those who were pushing forward the frontier of depression. While other people had been fully occupied developing their careers, or getting rich, all Bernard had managed to do was to explore his despair to yet deeper and deeper levels.

If he felt bad when he was at home things weren't much better when he went out. But then how could they be, when almost the first thing he discovered was that his old friends – anxiety, claustrophobia and guilt – whom he thought had finally begun to disappear from his life for ever, were once again rushing towards him with open arms. On one occasion, when he had gone by tube to visit a friend, his feelings of claustrophobia and anxiety were so acute that by the time the train arrived at his station, he felt such a hero for having forced himself to stay on it, that he fully expected someone to step out of the crowd and pin a medal on his chest. It was almost as bad if he took the car, because he only had to see a police car in the rear-view mirror, to be instantly consumed by the fear that he was about to be stopped and arrested, which showed just how guilty he was feeling – certainly there was nothing wrong with either his documents or his driving. He wasn't even immune to experiencing banal feelings of failure at the traffic lights, when he compared the new cars other people were driving to his own ancient heap. But easily the worst experience he had was during a visit to an exhibition of African bronzes. He'd only been inside a few minutes and had stopped to admire the sculpture of a tiger, which made a deep impression on him, partly because it appeared to be so full of pent-up energy (something he never had) and also because it reminded him of the one at home, that had been carved out of a piece of walnut as a wedding present for his parents in Italy before the war, when suddenly, although he'd felt perfectly alright a few moment before, (well, nearly alright anyway) he became aware of a voice in his head. Soon the voice was practically shouting that he was a total failure and a completely hopeless human being, who was not only incapable of making a living, or of sustaining a relationship with a woman but who didn't even know how to punctuate properly. What's more he couldn't even speak French! Why the voice picked on that particular failing wasn't quite clear, unless it was that recently he had brought up the subject of his feelings of inadequacy about being unable to speak any foreign languages in a session with Dr Lear who had pointed out that the real truth was he didn't want to speak French, Italian, Russian, or any of the other languages he'd ever attempted to learn, but wanted to be the kind of person who knew several languages. Well, perhaps his saying that hadn't made as big a difference as Bernard had thought at the time. On and on the voice went, if anything increasing the scope of its denunciation of his character until Bernard felt he couldn't stand it any longer. But what could he do? He couldn't very well shout back at it to stop without attracting attention to himself. And if he had, it wouldn't have been long before the attendants had come over and escorted him from the gallery. He doubted if even that would have made it stop, because he soon realised that that voice was not just inside him, but was him, or at least a part of him; his super-ego perhaps, that had finally become determined to deliver its last judgement on his whole personality. The only thing to do was to leave the gallery immediately and keep walking until it subsided, which, no doubt, if what he'd once read in a biography of Kierkegaard was correct, was what the Great Dane himself would have done in the circumstances.

That awful and terrifying experience had one positive result. It made him suddenly aware that all those weeks of despair and cascading self-esteem had had a very destructive effect on him, and if he didn't do something to pull himself together soon, he might well be in danger of losing his mind altogether. Admittedly, it wasn't all that long ago that he would have found that prospect really rather appealing, especially if it meant being able to find a better one to replace it with. But the reality, or at least the intimation, that it could happen was a different matter entirely and certainly quite enough to make him resolve to do something to improve his state of mind as soon as he possibly could.

He began by telling Dr Lear the whole story of his failed attempt to achieve spiritual enlightenment. Naturally Dr Lear was aware that Bernard had been in a bad way for some time, although he had no idea what he'd been up to during the past few months. What was surprising was that Dr Lear didn't appear to be at all angry that Bernard had been deceiving him, only puzzled at what conclusions he had drawn about his experience. As far as he was concerned, the way Bernard was feeling was simply the result of one of his usual attacks of Autumn Melancholia.

'Sure Bernard, aren't you always depressed at this time of year. In any case, I simply can't see why you should find this latest failure so significant, even if you'd got on like a house on fire with this Gotsky fella. How could it have made any difference to your chances of getting Olivia back, especially if what you say is true, and she has now switched her allegiance to another guru altogether. If that's really what's happened, how could any amount of success with her fallen idol possibly have made any difference? There's no logic in it at all Bernard.'

And it was no good Bernard trying to insist that success at any spiritual pursuit would have made Olivia much more likely to come back to him, because Dr Lear simply couldn't see how that could have been remotely possible.

'No, the real point Bernard is that I don't understand how you could ever have persuaded yourself in the first place that you had the faintest chance of succeeding. As far as I know, you have absolutely no inclination towards the spiritual life and always profess to be a complete sceptic as far as religion is concerned. Weren't you telling me only the other week that if you saw God himself coming along the road you'd cross over to avoid meeting him?'

But although confessing to Dr Lear definitely gave Bernard an instant feeling of relief (deceiving him all that time had always made him feel uneasy; one's therapist after all is without doubt, the one person one should be absolutely honest with), he still didn't find anything Dr Lear had to say either helpful or very insightful. He wasn't convinced that this was just another one of his seasonal attacks of depression. And it really didn't help to be told – especially when he was feeling so low – that one obvious way to combat it was to be even more determined to face reality and carry on trying to find a way of making a living. Listening to him go on about how it was vital for Bernard to succeed at something at this stage in his life, he found himself beginning to hate the reality principle more than ever. He had long ago accepted that Dr Lear had no pills or magic remedies to make him feel better, but having to listen yet again that the only course of action open to him was to carry on trying to discover the truth about himself wasn't exactly encouraging either. The way his therapy had been progressing lately, he could just see himself having to carry on waging a personal war against depression for the rest of his life. No, he simply couldn't see how he was going to be able to face carrying on like this endlessly. So when, a little while later, he heard of a psychologist who claimed to have a new technique, which in a matter of weeks could alleviate the worst symptoms of depression, if not eliminate it altogether, Bernard could hardly wait to make an appointment.

Dr Steele, the discoverer of this technique, whose cold grey eyes looked at Bernard through the kind of rimless glasses once favoured by scientists (or at least scientists in the movies), in a way that seemed to suggest Bernard ought to just pull himself together, was a very different kind of therapist from Dr Lear. In his expensive double breasted suit, monogrammed shirt and bespoke shoes (which a shoe aficionado like Bernard couldn't help admiring enormously), Dr Steele looked like a very successful businessman, which was precisely what he was. Having made a fortune as an industrial psychologist advising multi-national companies on how to improve their productivity levels, by doing things that ranged from reorganising the group structure to changing the light bulbs, he had recently founded a luxurious clinic which specialised in putting top executives back together after their crack-ups. Almost every one of the signed photographs of satisfied customers that lined the walls of his office, was of one of those tough, determined looking men; those modern heroes who really did get up at six in the morning and come out fighting, and whose faces Bernard always found so intimidating when they stared out at him from the newspapers. He'd always found it impossible to believe that men like that could ever get anywhere near having a nervous breakdown, although he knew from experience that they did. He had never been able to forget the haunting recitative of Mr Gold, his first landlady's husband, calling out from the top of the stairs every time he went round to pay the rent: 'Why did I do it, why did I do it,' because he'd completely gone to pieces only a few weeks after taking early retirement from his firm.

What Dr Steele's technique amounted to in practice was that the therapist appointed to deal with his case (Dr Steele himself only ever handled executives of the highest rank) would, in a maximum of twelve sessions, tap into Bernard's thought processes and endeavour to restructure them in a much more positive way. Unlike Dr Lear, they were not remotely interested in burrowing into the aetiology of his condition, but in getting him back into the ring as soon as possible. Apparently the results could be dramatic and, if all went according to plan, pessimism might soon be a thing of the past and he could well end up an outgoing optimistic doer, as vigorous and dynamic with his newly released energy as the men in the photographs. As Dr Steele said as he was showing him to the door: 'I can assure you Mr Steinway, we'll make a new man of you. Once you've had the treatment your depression will be a thing of the past.'

All of this sounded to Bernard far too much like a bizarre mixture of brainwashing and that old adage: 'It's better to look on the bright side'. He was also not at all sure that he wanted to be changed so utterly, certainly not if that meant ending up with a personality like one of Dr Steele's reconstructed executives. Perhaps, when it really came to it, he was far too attached to his old depressive self to want to give it up. He also doubted whether Dr Steele's method would work in his case. If what Dr Lear was always saying was true, depression was far too deeply embedded in his psyche for a technique like that to have even a remote chance of working.

Even if he had been able to overcome his instinctive reservations, at one hundred pounds a session, it would cost at least twelve hundred pounds to make any impact on his condition whatsoever. And unfortunately, Dr Steele's wasn't amused when Bernard suggested that maybe he would like to give him the treatment for nothing, in exchange for having the opportunity of working on such an interesting and unusual case as his undoubtedly was. Oddly enough, Bernard was really surprised that his offer was turned down with such alacrity, but he soon concluded that perhaps Dr Steele just wasn't interested in making such a gift to someone like him, in whom the achievement orientation was so obviously completely lacking. Or perhaps, he thought that Bernard was simply trying to get something for nothing, which, as it happens, was quite true.

Still that visit to Dr Steele's extraordinarily luxurious establishment with its exquisitely beautiful Chinese nurses, cordon bleu food, and swimming pool on the roof wasn't a waste of time. It was heartening to be told (even if he had heard it before) that whatever treatment he finally opted for he definitely wasn't hospitalisable; although oddly enough, he initially reacted by entertaining the bizarre thought that if this really was the case all his years in the depression business really had been futile, since this meant, if it came to it, he would never even be able to make a living by being institutionalised. That he could have reacted, to what was after all a favourable prognosis, in such an idiosyncratic and strange way, subsequently made him wonder if he shouldn't perhaps have paid his money and had the treatment. But even if Bernard's determination to find a new way of dealing with his depression hadn't amounted to much, thankfully he never had to listen to that voice again. Perhaps it, at least, had been impressed by his efforts, impressed enough anyway to retreat back into the depths of his psyche from where presumably it had come from in the first place.

Despite that minuscule triumph, Bernard didn't on the whole feel any better. And finding himself a week or so later being obliged to accompany his mother to visit an old uncle of his in hospital was hardly destined to improve his state of mind either. This was rather surprising, because normally he found doing that kind of thing deeply satisfying. Only recently, when his sister had been taken into hospital suffering from vertigo, he had gone and sat by her bedside for hours every day. And that was by no means the first time he'd shown himself so assiduously attentive to the sick. He'd been like that for years. No doubt if Dr Lear had known about it he would have said that it must have satisfied some deep inner need. Probably he would have been right too. Feeling sympathetic with people who couldn't cope with life, for whatever reason, had always come easily to Bernard, perhaps too easily. Normally he would have looked forward to visiting Uncle Jo in hospital if only for the sense of purpose and feeling of satisfaction it would give him. The problem was his mother. He never wanted to see her when he was in a bad way like this, which was precisely the reason he'd avoided telephoning her for weeks. He didn't want her to know the state he was in. Once, years ago in an unguarded moment, he'd told her he felt suicidal and she hadn't slept for a week. No, he didn't want to do anything like that again. What would be the point? If confessing every week to Dr Lear didn't help, how could telling her do any good. And even if he pretended to be absolutely okay he knew that somehow she would sense the truth. Then she would bring the conversation round to the subject of his relationship with Olivia, whom she never ceased to blame if he was feeling depressed. Or what was nearly as bad, she would bring up yet again, the – at least to her – deeply mysterious phenomenon of his inability to make a living. 'What I don't understand Bernard is how with all those letters after your name you can't make a good living,' was how she always put it. As if having the whole blasted alphabet after his name could possibly have made any difference!

But there was no letting her down this time as he had on the day of his grandfather's funeral. Then he seemed to have no choice and with only an hour to go before they were due to leave for the cemetery, he had suddenly rushed out of the house on the pretext that he had just remembered something urgent he had to do up in town. Once he was alone he had just walked and walked till it was too late to go back. But that time at least he knew his behaviour hadn't been entirely incomprehensible. His father's funeral had taken place only a few weeks previously and if he couldn't face throwing earth on someone else's coffin so soon afterwards he knew they'd understand. In fact, his sister told him later that the moment he'd gone she knew he wouldn't come back, which was remarkably perceptive of her, because he hadn't realised it himself at the time. But on this occasion there was no getting out of it and he would just have to get through the afternoon somehow or other.

Even if Bernard had gone by himself to visit his uncle that afternoon it is doubtful that the experience would have left him with the usual profound sense of satisfaction. In his present state of mind, it was far too easy to identify with that lonely old man lying propped up in bed under one of those mass produced crucifixes of Christ writhing on his cross (in itself hardly an inspiration to get well for anyone's uncle, let alone his Jewish one). It was really far too easy to see himself ending up the same way. Wasn't that precisely what happened to men who couldn't sustain a relationship with a woman. Not that you could say that Jo had ever seriously tried. As far as Bernard knew, he'd never slept with a woman in his whole life, and at more than seventy years of age was in all probability still a virgin. Instead of trying to make a go of a life on the pillow next to a woman, he'd simply stayed at home, rationalising his behaviour by saying that somebody had to look after the Guvnor, as he always referred to his father. Then after the Guvnor died he simply found himself a housekeeper, who cooked him vast, life-threatening six course meals every evening, or at least so family rumour had it. And when, a few years later, she in turn died, he went to live in a guest house by the sea. Bernard never did know precisely where, and he spent his days doing God knows what, nothing probably. By then he must have been really used to it, having sold his sweet shop and retired in his mid-forties. No, you couldn't really say Jo had ever done much. Probably retirement suited him better than anything. By far the strongest childhood memory Bernard had of Jo was of the way he frequently appeared just as lunch was about to be served (although he lived several miles away, he used to walk all the way over to Bernard's home, he claimed for the sake of his varicose veins, though everyone suspected that he really did it to save the bus fare), eat an enormous amount, including several pieces of Bernard's mother's incomparable fried fish and then proclaim in his incredibly loud voice 'That was a very nice snack Stella.' Yes, Uncle Jo's life hadn't amounted to a great deal: probably enjoying his food and taking it easy was about it. His enormous bland face, which conveyed nothing except perhaps a kind of benign silliness, didn't look as if a thought had ever passed across it. Bernard only hoped that Jo never got around to examining his life the way he did. But even if they were differently made, it wasn't all that hard to imagine himself in later life ending up as someone else's neglected bachelor uncle. Already he found himself eating round at his sister's far more than he used to, which was hardly a good sign.

Perhaps it was only natural that Jo should have tried to give the impression of perfect equanimity and well-being while they were there. Over and over he kept on insisting how nice everyone in the hospital had been to him, and how he had received fruit or flowers, or at the very least a card, from practically everybody he knew. 'Do you know Stella, even the boys at the guest house sent me a card. Can you beat that.' But he was obviously deceiving himself. Why else should tears of relief have appeared in his eyes almost the moment they arrived, and there certainly wasn't any sign that anyone else had ever visited, or sent him anything. In fact there was nothing in that bleak hospital room apart from a bottle of lemon and barley water and Jo's false teeth grimacing in a glass on the bedside table.

It didn't take long for Bernard to find being there very depressing, especially when Uncle Jo began to hum to himself and twiddle his thumbs; a sign, ironically enough, that he was feeling particularly relaxed and content. Even staring out of the window didn't help, since Jo's room overlooked nothing more uplifting than the car park of the local supermarket. But fortunately, just as he was beginning to feel that he really was going to have to make some excuse to leave, if only for a little while, Jo interrupted his humming to ask if he wouldn't mind going out to get him some more of a particular brand of boiled sweets, that he had become very fond of since his years in the confectionery business.

As Bernard made his way along the dark corridor, listening to the hollow sound his feet made on the worn linoleum, instead of the feeling of relief he had expected, he suddenly began to imagine that at any moment someone was going to put a restraining hand on his shoulder and insist he admit himself to the hospital immediately. 'No, there's no question of your leaving,' the man would say, 'when it's obvious you're terminally ill.' Bernard soon realised that this was only anxiety, tinged perhaps with a hint of paranoia, since he was never ill and hadn't been ill for years. Not that he didn't occasionally long for an attack of influenza which would, at least if only for a few days, or a week at most, free him from the struggle to find his way in life, without the usual feelings of guilt. What he wouldn't do for a period like that occasionally when he could stay in bed, doze, day-dream, or simply feel sorry for himself. Other people had them regularly so why should he always be passed over? Probably he was being saved for something much more grave later on: a multiple heart bypass operation, cancer, or Parkinson's disease perhaps. Just thinking about what he might get made him anxious.

One thing was certain: before the end he would have to get something – everybody did. Perhaps one of those diseases was already growing inside him at that very moment. How long would it be before it came out into the open and he really would have to be hospitalised. He'd only ever been in hospital once and although he was only six or so at the time, memories of it still came back to him. The traumatic feeling of being abandoned when his father left him there. Bernard remembered asking him to wait and that he wouldn't be long but he didn't see him again until they came to collect him two weeks later. That stay in hospital was also to give him his first experience of injustice when the nuns distributed his liquorice allsorts round the ward (he wouldn't have minded so much but they wouldn't even listen when he told them that they belonged to him and had been sent by his grandfather). And then every morning, there was the ordeal of crossing the Styx of grey porridge, to reach the familiar landfall of a slice of bread and jam, that lay, half submerged and soggy, in the middle of the bowl.

Yes, illness, old age and death were all drawing closer now that he had crossed over the border of middle age. People said that thirty-five was far too young to feel middle aged, but he felt it nevertheless. Gone were the endless slow summers of childhood. You looked out of the window now and another few minutes you weren't going to get again had rushed past. It wasn't old age that he minded so much though. In a strange sort of way, he'd always rather looked forward to it; or perhaps the real truth was he'd always felt old. He'd practically always preferred to look back on his life rather than live it. There could be no other explanation why he was always making jokes about having opted for early retirement, or why he repeatedly had the fantasy of being admitted into Sam's private old people's home by the time he was forty. He even knew how he would reply should anyone question his right to be there. He would just point to the picture of the founder in the dining room and in a conspiratorial whisper utter the word – *'Protectsia!'* There was no doubt about it, he really did look forward to the time when he would be able, with complete justification, to shuffle along the pavement leaning on a silver topped cane, totally without any sense of purpose whatsoever. If only he'd had the sense to purchase that old Russian one he'd seen in Venice a few years before, with the bird engraved on the handle in anelo silver, singing its heart out on a branch. But then he was always regretting not having bought something or other. One thing was certain: old age wasn't going to take him by surprise. He'd been preparing for it for years. Anyway, what could be more relaxing than to watch yourself going slowly downhill with all the struggles and failures of life behind you.

But death, that was an entirely different matter. He simply didn't agree with it. And if one really did have to die, he just couldn't see why it had to happen so soon. Perhaps seventy or eighty years was sufficient if you'd managed to get the hang of life by the age of thirty, and were already on course for a full and contented existence. But if, like him, you were still completely lost at thirty-five, that wasn't nearly enough time. If some species of turtles could live as long as they did, and Abraham was said to be well over a hundred when God sent the chariot for him, there must have been a mistake in the planning somewhere. Yes, a hundred, or even a hundred and fifty years would be more like it. But the truth was he'd never be ready to die even then. How could he when the chances were that it would still be years yet before he discovered how to live. And when his turn did eventually come, he certainly didn't want one of those slow agonising deaths from cancer like his father had. He'd never find the inner resources to cope with it the way he did, unless the stoicism and humour comes automatically with the affliction. Bernard couldn't imagine himself being able to say 'that it was perfectly okay to die if you had your family round you,' as his father had only days before the end. How would he ever be able to cope, when the mere idea of having to go to the doctor practically threw him into an anxiety state. But the probability was he would also die from cancer. Why else had his doctor given him that knowing look when he'd mentioned in passing that almost all of his relatives had died of it. But whatever happened, one thing was certain – he wasn't going to a hospice. The very idea of being surrounded by whispering nuns as the end approached was absolutely unbearable (as if death had anything to do with a hearing disability anyway). No, dying of cancer was hardly the ideal way to go. His idea of a good death would be in a taxi from a heart attack with the meter still running, although he'd always imagined that when the time came he'd die holding Olivia's hand, whilst making a final attempt to explain to her what he thought life was all about. He knew that would never happen now. When Bernard at last found a shop that sold the sweets his Uncle wanted, the old fashioned sweet jars on the dusty shelves high up above his head seemed as far away as his childhood.

It wasn't long after he got back to Uncle Jo's room that they left the hospital but Bernard's troubles that afternoon were by no means over. He still had to endure one of his mother's usual diatribes about the old man, that were set off, Bernard suspected, by the fact that as he got older he was beginning to look more and more like him. But Uncle Jo's suggestion that he come and live with her as soon as he was discharged from the hospital could also hardly have helped to improve her state of mind much either. Somehow, when his mother was in this mood, she always seemed to imply that the way her life had worked out was all his fault. It was always the same old story. If only he'd agreed to go with her when she wanted to leave his father and emigrate to California to become a housekeeper, everything could have been different. If she'd only done that she would have avoided having to endure the rest of her married life – the best part of which she'd lately taken to insisting was her widowhood. She would have missed his infidelities and having to nurse him through his last illness, as she had her favourite brother Lou, an experience she was determined not to repeat with Jo whom she claimed never to have liked much anyway. If she hadn't been there she would never have had to share all his suffering, when he was haemorrhaging nearly every day, or had those terrible nightmares in which she always seemed to be carrying suitcases full of blood.

What she invariably chose to forget, was that at the time she asked him who he wanted to be with, he was only seven or eight years old. No wonder he had become such a virtuoso at anxiety in his so called maturity, it was they who had given him his first lessons. His father wasn't much better. Bernard couldn't have been more than ten years old before he started to share his money worries with him, during their long walks up and down the beach in Allassio on the Italian Riviera. Often during those holidays he would lie awake in bed at night anxiously wondering if they would stay together, as he listened to them arguing in the room next door. Perhaps it was experiences like that which explained why he had been such an accomplished bed-wetter and head-banger, or why he had ridden miles and miles on his rocking horse in the middle of the night. It was a pity he no longer had that rocking horse – he certainly wasn't much less anxious now than he was then.

That afternoon had been a real ordeal, and Bernard was very relieved when he finally got home and could throw himself down on the chaise longue. It hadn't made any real difference to how he felt, because he could hardly have felt worse. He hadn't the vaguest idea what to do next. The very real sense that Olivia would never come back to him now made him feel unbelievably bleak. Even that gorilla with whom, a few weeks before at the zoo, Bernard had experienced a moment of poignant communion, when he had peered at him with his big dark mournful eyes, had had the good fortune to die shortly after his mate was taken away from him. And anyway, being an animal, it had never had to endure all the guilt and anguish Bernard had been through. Perhaps he would have been better off if he'd shared the same fate. Sometimes he thought about suicide, but it never went any further than that. He didn't collect pills, or consider different ways of doing it. It wasn't just that he couldn't make up his mind, but that however attractive not suffering any longer might be, he didn't believe in death sufficiently to volunteer early for it. There never seemed to him any reason to believe that what happened after death was necessarily any better. No one had ever been able to prove that it really was the eternal snooze that some people liked to think. Anyway, even if he went ahead and jumped off a building, it was quite likely that being as indecisive as he was, he'd change his mind half way down. Or how would it be if fate decreed that his life was due to take a turn for the better the very day after he terminated it. No, he would never kill himself, even if the thought of doing so sometimes gave him a curious feeling of relief, as if the burden of living, for that moment at least, had been lifted from his shoulders. He would just have to carry on putting one foot in front of the other, however unbearable life felt at times like these.

2

Just as Bernard was beginning to think he was going to have to continue in this state for the rest of his life, something occurred which, once he made up his mind what to do about it, seemed to offer the solution to all his problems, well to most of them anyway. Quite suddenly Sam, who for years had resisted Bernard's frequent hints that some useful role could be found for him in the office (that magic place where Olivia as a child believed Sam grew a money tree) suddenly offered him a position in the firm. Bernard realised almost immediately, that what had made Sam change his mind was not the sudden revelation that there was some vitally important task that only Bernard was capable of performing, or that the very survival of the business depended on his participation in crucial decisions on a daily basis and he was absolutely right. The main reason for Sam's decision was simply that his cousin Max had just died and since he'd hardly done a stroke in all the years he'd worked for him, Sam had come to the conclusion that Bernard would undoubtedly make his ideal successor. It was inconceivable that he could contribute less to the success of the business than Max had done, and it was even remotely possible that, since he'd always believed Bernard had a good business brain, he might, in the fullness of time, even do a little better.

When Sam first told him what he had in mind Bernard wasn't entirely surprised. He'd sensed that something like this might happen when Max died. It was at Max's house after the funeral, as he was leaning against one of the mock Doric columns that divided the dining room from the lounge, trying to join in the sham of praising God for what had happened to poor old Max (although why God always got praised on these occasions was a mystery to Bernard – whatever happened it was always supposed to be his will), and it had suddenly occurred to him that now Max had gone Sam might well see his way clear at last to taking him into the business. He desperately needed to be taken in somewhere. Almost immediately he'd felt tremendously ashamed and guilty. How could he possibly be so vulgar and self-seeking as to think about profiting from Max's death and just a few hours after his funeral? Not that Max would have minded, he knew that for sure, he probably would have liked the idea of Bernard becoming his successor. Max had always been very fond of him. On family occasions it had always been Max who'd rushed across the room and greeted him so effusively that anyone would have thought they hadn't seen each other for years. Not that after Max had asked him in that funny way of his – 'How are you keeping Bernard?' – did they ever have very much to say to each other. But that didn't matter, because what Max responded to was that Bernard was so obviously fond of him and didn't at all look down on him for being inept, or foolish, or think him inadequate because he was unable to make a living on his own. It was common knowledge that Max did virtually nothing at the office, though it didn't prevent him going around boasting that he was a big man in the world of high finance. But then why should Bernard look down on Max for that? He hadn't proven himself to be a great bread winner either. It had always seemed to him that he was every bit as foolish as Max, the only difference being that Max was clearly blissfully unaware of his own inadequacies and Bernard wasn't. Far from looking down on Max he'd always felt that whatever their apparent differences they were really two of a kind – a pair of dopes. Bernard was also very fond of him because he had been the most sympathetic of nearly everyone he knew when he heard that Olivia had left him. But then of course he had been through all that himself, having years before been thrown out by his own wife, who had only been prevailed upon to take him back when it became clear he couldn't cope on his own. Unlike Bernard's Uncle Stanley who had never managed to get himself readmitted to the family home when the same thing had happened to him and in consequence had wandered around looking sad and sorry for himself for the rest of his life. Given how he felt about Max it wasn't surprising that he had gone so often to see him in hospital during his last illness. That illness had the strangest effect on him. Perhaps it was the imminence of death that did it, but in just a few weeks he changed from being someone who didn't appear to have an opinion about anything (Bernard had always thought of him as someone who occupied the upper circle in life, quite incapable of recognising what went on down on the stage) to a man who was intensely preoccupied with the fate of the world. It was as if he'd suddenly become convinced that the world wasn't going to be able to get along without him. 'What's going to happen to the world Bernard,' he would intone over and over, sitting on the edge of the bed, his legs dangling over the side like a child's. And Bernard had to try and reassure him that everything was going to be alright, because often Max would become anxious and tearful, although Bernard himself hadn't the vaguest idea whether it would or it wouldn't.

When Sam first asked him how he felt about taking over Max's old job, the knowledge that Max would have approved if he accepted, didn't make it any easier. Instead of being overjoyed, as he'd always imagined he would be (wasn't it after all one of his wildest dreams, but then perhaps our wildest dreams, if they look like becoming reality, are not always as attractive as we thought), Bernard suddenly found himself paralysed with doubts and anxieties. What if he discovered after taking the job that he simply couldn't do it and was even less competent than Max had been? He hadn't shown himself to be even remotely adequate as a businessman but then neither had Max. But wasn't he, if anything, even more impractical? Sometimes, when he had to do the simplest thing he could literally hear the penny drop. The only real skill he possessed, and that had taken years to perfect, was a particular kind of painful introspection but that was hardly of much use in an office. What if when it came to it he failed to be able to carry out what was required of him, like adding up, or taking messages? The only time he'd ever worked in an office before it had been a complete disaster which had ended with him getting the sack. What if the same thing happened again? It wasn't impossible that once Sam discovered just how hopeless he really was, he too would ask him to leave.

In the end he decided to accept the offer. He didn't have much choice, because he didn't know what else to do. And he was also undoubtedly influenced by Dr Lear who, predictably enough, turned out to be very enthusiastic about the idea. In his opinion it offered Bernard a marvellous opportunity to overcome his phobia about real life, increase his self esteem and make a living all at the same time. There was something else in its favour as well; Sam's office was only a few minutes walk from Bernard's flat, so what could be the harm in strolling down there every morning, even if it did mean having to have his coffee a little earlier than usual. Of course, being obliged to go to the office would mean that he would have much less time for ruminating about life, and Bernard wasn't at all sure that he wanted to spend the whole day there. After all, he never usually spent the whole day anywhere. Unfortunately, it was inconceivable that Sam would agree to him just coming in for a couple of hours in the afternoon, although it did occur to him to suggest it. Still, at least there was the compensation that from then on he would know what he was going to do with himself as every new day dawned, well at least as every weekday dawned. And it could be that working for Sam might in the end turn out to be the final solution to all his problems.

Fortunately he didn't feel at all apprehensive about suddenly having to spend his time somewhere totally new. Almost since he'd first met Sam he'd been going to his office to pick him up for lunch, or to go on somewhere for dinner. He had even occasionally dropped in there for tea, when Sam, as often as not, would produce from the wall safe a nearly perfect apple strüdel, as if the real function of that safe was to serve as a sort of humidor for cakes. There had also been occasions when he had allowed himself to be persuaded to stay on after lunch for one of Sam's business meetings, of which, when it came to it, he had understood rather less than had it been one of Socrates' afternoon philosophical discussions about the nature of love, beauty or truth.

Not that the first visit Bernard had ever paid to Sam's office had been all that easy to get through, but then they barely knew each other at the time and Sam was still intent on sizing him up. After the heavy soundproof double doors had closed behind him (the very same doors that Bernard later had to pass through to enter Dr Du Maurier's office), he had to sit facing Sam across an enormous partner's desk laden with telephones and the latest electronic business machines, while Sam proceeded to interrogate him about how much he earned, what his prospects were, how serious he was about Olivia, and what his aim in life was. The sort of questions (apart from the one about Olivia which he could answer without any hesitation) that Bernard was constantly asking himself at all hours of the day and night. That morning he felt as if Sam could see right through him, just as it always seemed to him that Olivia's grandmother and the family dachshund, who always growled whenever he came to the house, knew how worthless he really was. Wasn't it what her grandmother had really intended to convey, when at Olivia's birthday party, she had declared in a very loud voice that the handmade chocolates he'd bought Olivia were stale. No, nothing would convince her that he was *Mr. Vonderful*. Bernard had felt so ill at ease in Sam's office that morning, sitting there trying to sound convincing, that the only way he managed to prevent himself from falling off the chair on to the floor was to concentrate very hard on the fake Canaletto on the wall above Sam's desk. Of course, what caused this enormous feeling of discomfort was that he really didn't know the answer to most of those questions.

But that happened long ago and ever since he'd always looked forward to visiting Sam at his office. No doubt this was partly because it always meant he would have a much better lunch than usual, but also because it inevitably led to him receiving yet another dose of advice – advice which Sam delivered with such conviction and intensity that it often left Bernard feeling drunk and elated for hours afterwards, although this didn't mean that he ever managed to take much of it in. Yes, Bernard had certainly enjoyed every one of the meals they'd had together, right from the first one when they'd gone to an old fashioned Jewish restaurant and he'd been astonished to see Sam order chicken soup with double kreplach even before they'd sat down. A double whiskey or brandy was one thing, but a double kreplach soup! That was also the first occasion he'd ever seen Sam become tremendously anxious when the thought suddenly occurred to him that Olivia might not be wearing her gloves, although it wasn't even winter at the time.

From that day on Sam seemed to treat him as a sort of standby lunch guest, and would often phone up in the late morning to suggest they went to a new Hungarian, French, or Italian restaurant he'd heard about, because some tycoon or other had had to cancel at the last moment. But it wasn't just for the sake of the lunches, or the advice, that made Bernard enjoy visiting the office so much. Nor was it because it was situated in a very beautiful eighteenth century house, with elegantly proportioned rooms, high ceilings and tall windows, but that once you crossed the threshold practically anything could happen. How often had Bernard come into Sam's office to find him sitting on the floor in his underwear doing his yoga exercises, or chanting his latest Mantra. Or he might run into Max, in his shirtsleeves with elastics round his arms that made him look more like a professional gambler than a businessman, scurrying across the hall with an intensely preoccupied look on his face, as if he had ten phones on the go at once; whereas in fact, since he rarely did anything, he was probably on his way to pass the morning gossiping with Lieberman in the basement. Lieberman was a Lithuanian refugee who years before Sam had given a room to, ostensibly because they were engaged in some business venture together (Bernard thought it had something to do with the buying or selling of the throne room carpet of the Romanian Monarchy but he was never sure), but in reality it was because he liked to have someone around with whom he could speak Yiddish when he felt in the mood. Anyway, Lieberman never did anything in that room, since he preferred to do business in the more anonymous surroundings of the foyers of grand hotels. He was an extraordinary character who, although short and quite ugly, was a tremendous dandy. Whenever Bernard saw him he was almost always wearing a pale blue or pink ruffled shirt, a monocle, and shoes that had a narrow band of gold around the toes. Lieberman was also a renowned womaniser, who although by then nearly eighty, was still able to pick up women in the street by simply standing in a nearby square and asking any woman who passed by where exactly he was. His activities probably accounted for the pained and worn expression that Bernard noticed on his wife's face whenever he saw her. Obviously she had been suffering from his infidelities for years.

In the past Bernard was sometimes summoned to the office to participate in the prayers for one or other of Sam's dead relatives (apparently even an atheist like him wasn't disqualified from making up the necessary number of men required). These rituals meant a great deal to Sam, who Bernard always thought got more out of religion than God himself. Certainly, he practised his Judaism so assiduously it could only be assumed that he was trying to become perfect at it. Once everyone had arrived they would assemble in the boardroom and, after the usual squabble about in which direction the East was (the prayers presumably had to be directed towards the Middle East, since that was God's last known address), they would deliver their prayers facing Sam's portrait. A portrait which, with its severely sceptical and judgemental expression, would have made an excellent icon for the Jewish God had not the use of graven images been banned more or less right from the beginning. It was to that room also that Bernard would occasionally wander through the cloud of smoke that emanated from the receptionist's cigarettes, when he was tired of examining the bland prints of Sam's office buildings (all of which looked remarkably alike). There he'd stare at that face with its wonderful expression of doubt and disbelief, which he always imagined saying such things as: 'Do you think what you're doing is really worthwhile?' or 'Is that really a serious business proposition?', while he waited for the real Sam to come down the stairs from his office on the first floor and take him out for lunch.

No, it wasn't all that difficult, once he'd got over his initial feelings of anxiety and apprehension, to imagine himself whiling away his days in Sam's office, listening to Lieberman's stories, or going out with Harry Goldman – Sam's rather manic personal assistant, whose toupée had a tendency to slide forward when he became over-excited – to various business meetings, if only to keep him company. After all, what could be so unpleasant about having to stay on at the office between meals.

Life at the office turned out to be neither unpleasant, nor excessively arduous. For the first few weeks or so, apart from having to appear promptly at nine in a business suit and tie, Bernard carried on more or less as if he were at home. He looked out of the window of his office. He day-dreamed. He thought about life and raked over his weaknesses just as before. In the afternoons, during which he usually had a siesta, he would sometimes wake up imagining that he had finally achieved the sleeping partnership of his dreams. During all those weeks no one ever asked him what he was doing, or suggested what he should do, perhaps because they imagined that he was somehow learning the ropes, or playing himself in gradually, or that he was even using his initiative. They couldn't have been more wrong, especially as far as the latter was concerned, because he simply didn't have any. Bernard had always been the sort of man who, had he arrived in New York as an immigrant in nineteen thirty-nine with five dollars in his pocket, would have had precisely the same amount of money twenty years later. It was the identical fault in his character which had resulted in his being sacked from the ice-cream factory all those years ago. Then too no one had told him what to do, with the result that he had done absolutely nothing but wander around aimlessly in and out of the misty gloom of those enormous fridges, quizically observing the frantic activity of the other employees.

Gradually, he was given various tasks to carry out, but they were never very taxing and consisted largely in the writing of routine letters and making phone calls, all of which he executed, much to his surprise, rather efficiently, with the result that he soon began to think of himself as a real executive. In time he also took over Max's old job of going to post the letters, although at first Sam had to be convinced of Bernard's ability to perform such an important task properly – a lack of trust which offended Bernard deeply at the time, because he had always derived great satisfaction from posting letters and had over the years developed what he believed to be an incomparable technique. He just couldn't imagine that there was anyone who could match the artistry with which he first approached a pillar box (almost as if stalking it) and then, with a perfect flip of the wrist, sent the letters hurtling down into the darkness within: the satisfaction this gave him was almost orgasmic. It was a performance that was almost equal in delicacy and finesse to a busker he'd once observed outside a cinema who, after first placing a matchbox from which a feather protruded on to the pavement, retreated a few yards and then ran slowly and gracefully forward and jumped over it. Sam of course wasn't remotely interested in his technique but was simply anxious that once out of the office Bernard would forget what he'd gone for altogether. But when, in due course, he managed to convince him that he really could be relied on to do it efficiently, he was also given another of Max's old jobs, that of going to the bank once or twice a week. But this was much more nerve racking, because the moment he stepped out of the office with his bundle of cheques and cash, he couldn't help but imagine that at any moment he was going to be mugged, or that no sooner than he arrived at the bank then it would be held up. Apart from the things that he actually did, Bernard soon began to feel that his very presence in the office every day was a contribution in itself, since just by being there he was by definition assisting in looking after the business, which as Sam had always insisted, was a vital part of a businessman's duties.

As the months passed Bernard found his new life increasingly satisfying. In addition to solving the problem of what to do with himself everyday, it also began to give him a sense of purpose, even if, as he knew perfectly well, it was really somebody else's. His presence in the office also inevitably meant that Sam's invitations to lunch became much more frequent than before, as did the volume of advice he now received. Another advantage that followed naturally from being there every day was that it provided Bernard with an opportunity to witness a side of Sam that he had never seen before and to observe at first-hand what it was that had enabled him to accumulate such a vast fortune. Aside from the sympathetic and philanthropic Sam who always seemed to be surrounded by people like Bernard who couldn't cope with life (sometimes Bernard thought that Sam actually went looking for them), Bernard now saw more clearly than ever that there was also another Sam, a master of reality who was amazingly energetic, full of drive, decisive and, unlike Bernard, totally lacking in self-doubt. From the moment he arrived in the office in the morning he was like a curled spring ready to unfurl. If anything had to be done it always had to be done right away. 'Do it now, this morning,' he would often say, even if it was by then already the afternoon. On the telephone Sam was an absolute virtuoso. Never for a moment did he lose the initiative, speak for a minute longer than he wanted to, or say what he didn't mean to. How different in that respect he was from Bernard, who was forever being caught in endless phone conversations, during which he often found himself agreeing to do things he had no wish to do and then finding himself forced to phone back and wriggle out of them – a predicament it was impossible to imagine Sam ever finding himself in. Sam was equally skilled at dealing with the constant stream of visitors who came to see him. Once their allocated time was up they would find themselves being shown out but in such a diplomatic way that although they might feel rushed, they never felt treated discourteously, largely because their departure was always accompanied by innumerable expressions of affection and esteem. But it was in business meetings that Sam really showed what he was made of. Business was conducted as if it was his last day on earth and the man with the scythe was already knocking on the door. Anyone making an even slightly long-winded contribution to a discussion of policy, or tactics, would suddenly find themselves cut short with an ironic or scathing remark. And when it came to negotiating a deal, Sam organised his campaign like a general. He meticulously planned all his moves, decided on what he could and could not accept, his mind never for a moment deviating from his objective, which was always to win. Yes, when he was in his office, Sam was like a prize-fighter who was constantly in training for his next bout against the world.

 In almost every way working at the office was ideal for Bernard. After all, what could be more perfect for a person like him than to have been given a sinecure. True, it was perhaps not quite as satisfactory as inheriting a vast fortune, or as fulfilling as his fantasy of being employed to evaluate the expressions on the faces of Teddy Bears in a toy factory, but who was he to complain; especially since he was aware that after only a few months his self-esteem had definitely begun to rise considerably, just as Dr Lear had predicted it would. What's more Sam seemed to be pleased with his efforts and even said that since business had been no better or worse since he'd joined the firm he'd obviously been right in thinking that Bernard would make a perfect replacement for Max. It wasn't long after he'd said it, that Sam told him that in view of the progress he'd made he'd decided to include him in the company pension plan. Unfortunately, Bernard nearly messed up that offer when he reacted to the news by throwing himself down on the reclining chair in Sam's office and declaring that if that was the case he thought he'd take early retirement right away. Almost immediately Bernard realised that he had said the wrong thing, because Sam looked deeply shocked. Perhaps this time he really had gone too far. After all, Sam never spared himself, so why should he tolerate a sloth like Bernard working for him, even if he hadn't expected all that much from him when he took him on. But he needn't have worried, because a few seconds later Sam just laughed and said that he thought that perhaps it would be a good idea if Bernard did some work first before contemplating retirement. No, there really hadn't been anything to feel anxious about, not now that he had equalled and even possibly surpassed Max's contribution to the business. All he had to do was to keep it up, but even if he wasn't quite able to, he knew for certain that now Sam had got used to his presence, it was more than likely that he would be able to tolerate him for at least as long as he had Max, if not longer. For his part Bernard felt he'd at last found his true vocation, and would be perfectly content to remain at his post for the rest of his life.

3

Working at Sam's office had a profound effect on Bernard. There was something about doing nearly nothing all day, accompanied of course by a sense of purpose that really agreed with him, and it wasn't long before he began to go about with an aura of incredible self-confidence and well-being. One curious consequence of this was that, for perhaps the first time in his life, he started to become extraordinarily successful with women, at least in the sense that large numbers of them suddenly appeared to find him overwhelmingly attractive. Whereas in the months before he started work he hardly ever seemed to meet any women he didn't already know, or, if he did, it invariably came to nothing (particularly if he engaged in his characteristic habit of singing Olivia's praises on the slightest pretext), suddenly all that changed, and far from being scarce as before he began to feel he was being besieged by them. There could be no doubt that this must have had a great deal to do with his new persona. The fact that now he wasn't nearly so desperate for female company they were all over him, made Bernard think that an old idea of his that women often behave like banks – the more you need them the less likely they are to give you anything – might have some truth in it after all.

This abundance of new amorous experience also made him wonder if, as well as beginning to look like his father, he might not be becoming like him as well. Could it really be possible that after years of being a romantic monogamist he was now on the verge of turning into a philanderer and ladies' man like his father was reputed to have been? According to his mother the old man had always chased women; had an affair with his so called secretary that lasted for years; and on one occasion (believing that Bernard's mother had taken her sleeping pills) was discovered in bed with the maid. No, it was unlikely that he would ever be able to achieve such heights himself, but he was certainly giving the impression that he was capable of it. He was meeting so many different women in the Polish tea room at that time that one afternoon the middle aged blonde cashier, who always used a long amber cigarette holder, came over and asked him if he was what was known as a womaniser, without perhaps realising that this was an expression of disapprobation and simply couldn't be put as a question to a man you thought might be one.

Even women who had long ago given him up as a hopeless case now began to see Bernard in an entirely new way. Racquella, who he'd started to see again from time to time, showed every sign of wanting to resume their relationship. She had nothing but praise for him and acted as if he'd miraculously acquired all the qualities which previously she had been so insistent that he lacked. It was as if he had become her ideal man and now she always seemed to be phoning up to suggest they went to a film together, or that she come round and cook dinner for him. One evening, as they were lying on the bed watching the late night film on television, she came out with the astonishing remark that of all the men she'd ever known Bernard was the only one who knew how to touch her, which was hardly what she used to say and, if it was true, he could only imagine he'd stumbled on the right approach by pure chance. He couldn't see how the way he touched her that evening could be so very different from the way he had before. He was aware that working at the office had changed him, but he could hardly see how it could have changed his technique as a lover as well. She also told him that he could have anything he wanted from her. But it was too late. He was no longer seriously interested in having what she called a meaningful relationship; he wasn't even entirely certain that he was interested in having a meaningless one with her. One evening, when he had failed to appear for supper at her flat, she sent him an incredibly aggressive letter (Racquella was never a woman to give one the benefit of the doubt; after all, he could just have got the day wrong). Receiving that letter was only further proof that, although he might have changed, she hadn't, and was far from being the easy going sweet thing she liked to pretend she'd become.

Racquella wasn't the only woman from Bernard's past who suddenly started to show a renewed interest in him. There was also Anne, who years before had left him to marry a famous saxophonist (an instrument she didn't even care for very much) because she couldn't resist the world weary expression on the face of his borzoi, Leopold. What agony that had caused him. He had been in Rome when it happened and everyday he experienced the crucifixion of going to the post office to look for letters from her, which of course were never there because she hadn't sent any. Now she too started to phone him up all the time and when they finally decided to meet for dinner he became quite convinced that she was going to say that she'd always regretted leaving him and she'd now decided, even if if it was ten years later, that she wanted to come back. She didn't go as far as that but what she said and the way she looked at him all evening suggested that she might well have. All of which only confirmed a vain thought that Bernard had sometimes had in the past: that sooner or later every woman who'd ever left him would come to regret it.

It wasn't just women from his past who seemed to be pursuing him.

Practically every week a new romantic opportunity presented itself. Not that most of them really ever came to anything. Often he would find himself falling in love for ten minutes, or embarking on a relationship that would begin to flounder after only a week. Or he would enter a relationship full of romantic fantasies only to discover that it amounted to little more than an exchange of ambiguous postcards. This was almost precisely what happened with Margaret Bloodstone, an up and coming young novelist who after picking him up in the park almost immediately refused to see him again until he had read her novel (a task that nearly defeated him, despite the fact that he had the greatest incentive a reader could ever have to finish a book – the possibility of sleeping with its author). Even after he'd finally read it, she would only grant him an audience for half an evening (although she did give him the choice of which half), because by then she was deeply immersed in writing her second one. Of course nothing came of that romance. How could it, when during the half evening he spent in her claustrophobic semi-basement flat, which felt like a bunker and was full of narcissistic photographs of herself looking poetic and intense in an ethnic dress and heavy silver jewellery, Margaret wouldn't allow him to smoke a single cigarette. And in answer to her questions about his reaction to her book he wasn't able to think of a single intelligent thing to say. But what did it really matter if none of these adventures came to anything because they definitely helped to make him feel he'd come back to life again, and perhaps he wasn't open to anything more substantial yet anyway.

It really was quite miraculous the frequency with which women started to appear in Bernard's life. It wasn't long after his bizarre half an evening with Margaret that he got to know Adriana. The way they met was so extraordinary that for a time he seriously wondered, atheist though he was, if there wasn't behind it the hand of divine providence. Was it possible that for some reason God, if there was such a being, had suddenly decided to view his case in a more favourable light? Or perhaps he'd simply chosen to send him all these women just to stop him moaning for a while. After all, he could so easily not have had the opportunity of meeting her. It was true that he had been captivated by her beauty from almost the first moment he saw her in the street and immediately had experienced an enormous desire to approach her and say: 'tell me where can I meet a woman who is as beautiful as you are', words which had rushed unbidden and spontaneously into his mind. But he still didn't have the self confidence to do anything as bold as that. Instead, he had simply followed her at a safe distance, until she paused to look in a newsagent's window, which made him wonder if she hadn't perhaps sensed that he was following her. Then, once again feeling too self-conscious to speak to her, and since he couldn't very well just stand there looking over her shoulder, he had gone into the shop and bought a packet of cigarettes. When he came out she had vanished. Well, that's that he'd thought to himself and though feeling a little downhearted he carried on walking. As he went past he looked in Café Sorrento (one of his favourite haunts) in the vain hope that she might have gone there, but since she hadn't, he decided to give up and go home. But a minute or so later, for some reason he changed his mind and went back. Then the miracle happened. She was sitting right at the back near the kitchen, and what's more the only seat vacant in the whole place was the one opposite hers. All he had to do, apart from avoiding pouring coffee over her in his excitement, was to captivate her with his charm, a mere bagatelle compared to that vacant seat. Surely that was no accident, something or somebody must have intended they should meet that afternoon.

But after the enchantment of their first meeting, Bernard soon discovered that for all her beauty Adriana wasn't at all easy to get along with and their relationship only lasted a few weeks. She was a very unusual women. She might have been the most independent woman Bernard had ever met. Even the boiler suits she often wore seemed to emphasise it. It would be hard to imagine anyone else responding with the acerbic remark 'that's your problem not mine', after they had made love one evening, and he had said that he could easily imagine himself falling in love with her. Still, at least with Adriana, there was always the consolation of looking at her dark eyes and olive skin and dreaming about the Mediterranean, which in turn sometimes led ineluctably to his thinking about his favourite Italian dishes. Just looking at her almost made his mouth water. But it wasn't long before he discovered that of all the Italian women he'd ever known she was easily the most ascetic: she barely ate, never touched wine and was totally incapable of cooking. She didn't even know how much ravioli you needed to buy for two people. But even if their relationship came to nothing, Bernard felt he would never forget the wonderful way they'd first met.

The most extraordinary thing of all was that one of the women who were attracted to Bernard at that time actually wanted to marry him. He first met Estelle Kornbloom at one of those receptions that Sam often held in his house for some charity or other. It might even have been the one where Bernard had shaken Lord Sieff's averagely warm hand, and had only just managed to resist the temptation of complimenting him on the quality of the Swiss black cherry jam sold in his shops. For many years, Bernard had been in the habit of swopping the jam for the socks his mother used to buy him for Christmas. What a faux pas that would have been! The moment she said who she was he realised that she must be the daughter of the well-known tycoon Kornbloom, he had heard so much about from Sam, a few years previously in a taxi on their way to lunch. Bernard remembered how shocked he'd felt at the time when Sam referred to him as a real tycoon, as if implying that he himself wasn't. Pretty soon it occurred to him that Sam might well have invited Estelle that evening specifically so he could meet her. He always said that one obvious solution to Bernard's problems was for him to marry a rich woman. Bernard was never really sure whether Estelle's presence that evening had altogether been a matter of chance. But what was certain was that almost as soon as they'd met she began to pursue him remorselessly, a task she went about with the same tenacity that her father must have brought to making his vast fortune.

It wasn't long before Estelle began to phone up all the time to invite him over for dinner and, unlike Racquella or Adriana, she really could cook, having, in a not entirely successful attempt to find an aim in life, recently completed a cordon bleu cookery course. She also knew, as his sisters most certainly did, that the way to get him to come over was to recite the menu for dinner that evening down the telephone. Just the mention of certain dishes, such as turbot with hollandaise sauce, roast duck, or beef en daube, was enough to make him put on his jacket and rush out of the door straightaway. Then there were the presents: the silk shirts, cashmere pullovers and gold cigarette lighters that she was always giving him. But not once, unfortunately, did she ever appear with handmade cigarettes, like the Imperial Russians he enjoyed so much, which at that time were still just about obtainable from certain exclusive tobacconists. Had she done so he may well have succumbed to her overtures. The poignancy of being wooed by a woman in precisely the same way as his father had been, forty or more years previously, would have proven irresistible.

It wasn't unusual for her to put one or two of his favourite dishes into the boot of her car, together with a bottle of Chateauneuf du Pape, or Côte de Beaune and bring the food to him. Bernard was very flattered, if not somewhat amazed by all the attention she paid him (she even made a pretence of liking his poems, which even his relatives had trouble taking seriously). He simply couldn't understand why, a not entirely unattractive, extremely rich, thirty year old woman with a sweet and loving nature, should find him, an ex-depressive with a patchy inchoate past, quite so attractive. Alright, she was plump and the firmness of her bosom left something to be desired, and perhaps her ankles were a little thick, although who cared about that particular flaw anymore apart from him. The only thing he could think of was that Estelle, like the others, must have been totally overwhelmed by the impression he now gave of being a completely self-confident and mature man, someone who not only knew what life was all about but how to live it as well. She might also have been impressed that he was further advanced with his therapy than she was. Whatever it was, something about him must have had a profound effect on her, because little more than a fortnight after they'd first met, while they were having dinner one evening in a fashionable restaurant she'd insisted on taking him to, she suddenly made the astonishing statement, that if Bernard married her all her problems would be over. He realised that she didn't mean it literally but even so it was amazing. Not only because for the first time in his life had he more or less been proposed to, but because the idea that he, Bernard Steinway of all people, who in the past had brought to women nothing but more problems, had it in his power to solve all of someone's pre-existing ones, was just incredible.

It wasn't only Estelle who was so keen on him but her father as well. If anything he was even more determined than she that their relationship should be a success. Oscar Kornbloom was one of those men who Bernard was always drawn to (no doubt largely because he was his opposite). A completely self-made man, Oscar had arrived from Romania shortly after the end of the war completely penniless. In just a few years he had managed to accumulate a vast fortune. Beginning in scrap metal, he had gone on to create a huge property empire and an internationally renowned bank: Oscar Kornbloom and Son. He didn't have a son but nevertheless had chosen the name because, despite his thick accent, he liked to give the impression his family had been in the country for generations and that the firm was an old established one. Even if that wasn't completely convincing at least he did have a title. Only a few years before, the Pope had made him a knight commander of the Order of St. Gregory the Great for helping the Papal Bank recover from the effects of a financial scandal (it wasn't for promoting Christianity that was for sure). Since then Oscar, who was inclined to make mistakes in such matters, or simply because he had an eccentric streak, had taken to wearing his ceremonial uniform consisting of a dark blue tail coat with gold sash, sword and cocked hat almost every day when he went to his office. Oscar wasn't just a tycoon, he was also a great philanthropist, though, unlike Sam, he wasn't a remotely self-effacing one. When Oscar opened a newspaper his greatest pleasure was to see a photograph of himself opening an old peoples' home or some kind of charitable foundation, or better still receiving an award for his philanthropic work. Right from the start he had set out to become as well-known as possible and all manner of colleges, institutes and hospital wings were named after him, or at the very least after his father, Mennaseh Kornbloom, a one-time street musician and furrier from Bucharest. Presumably, what lay behind all this self-promotion was a not all that secret desire to add a peerage to his somewhat exotic knighthood.

Oscar lived in great splendour in a white Spanish style hacienda that he designed and built for himself out in the suburbs. Inside there was every conceivable luxury. His seventeenth and eighteenth century antique furniture was so rare that no one would ever have imagined that it hadn't been in the family for generations. Bernard was so moved by the exquisiteness of the eighteenth century walnut Venetian secretaire in the study, that he more than once felt like falling to his knees in front of it. Every bedroom had its own sunken bath with gold taps and a jacussi and there was a huge indoor swimming pool surrounded by palm trees, in which glass fibre mermaids floated towards you with salacious and tempting expressions on their faces, whilst on their backs, depending on the time of day, there was champagne and caviar, or tea and smoked salmon bridge rolls. Oscar, a widower, was looked after by a Lithuanian couple called Boris and Olga and a beautiful Chinese masseuse, whose job it was to keep his body in good condition and his mind clear and calm at all times. Whenever Bernard happened to drop in unannounced, Oscar always seemed to be upstairs in the midst of what Olga and Boris referred to, rather mysteriously, as one of his 'treatments'. One evening, arriving for dinner, Bernard thought he was going to die of envy on seeing the beautiful Miss Thong, wearing one of those Oriental silk dresses with slits up the thighs, in the process of massaging one of Oscar's thumbs. For a few minutes he contemplated faking an injury in the hope of being offered a sample of the treatment himself. But it didn't come to that because Oscar, noticing how he felt, instructed Miss Thong to take him into the study and give him a good going over. What followed turned out to be one of the most deeply sensual experiences of his whole life. What Oscar loved most about his house were its enormous grounds in which there was not only a maze and peacocks imported from a famous pet shop in Paris, but also a huge pond, at least as big as Monet's at Giverny, where he was endeavouring to breed coy gefilte fish for the Japanese market.

 Naturally enough for a man in his position Oscar also had several other homes. For the summer there was a villa on Capri that had once belonged to Maxim Gorky and he had apartments in New York and Paris as well. He even had a flat in the Vatican – also a gift of the Pope – which was the only one not occupied by a member of the church hierarchy, a fact which gave Oscar special pleasure. He told Bernard that from his window there was a particularly good view of the balcony where the Pope used to appear to greet the crowds. Apparently, if he ever noticed Oscar looking out he would always without fail give him a special little wave.

Outwardly Oscar appeared to have everything a man could want – power, money, influence. Bernard often thought of him as one of the most fully realised people he'd ever met. But this wasn't true at all. There was one thing missing: Oscar was desperate to have grandchildren. He was sixty-five, and Estelle was his only child. As far as he was concerned it was absolutely imperative to get things moving as soon as possible if the name of Kornbloom wasn't going to die out altogether (there was no doubt in Bernard's mind that had he agreed to marry Estelle before very long he would have come under considerable pressure to adopt the name of Kornbloom himself). It was years since Kornbloom had established the necessary trusts to avoid taxation. But what good was that if there were still no grandchildren to take advantage of them and the last thing he wanted was to have to rescind all those arrangements now – not that Oscar had any illusions about Bernard. He was aware almost from the first moment they met that he was a nogoodnick, a man who quite clearly was unable to make a living unaided. But what did it matter if he had to give him even a dozen directorships or thousands of pounds a year, if it meant he would get the grandchildren he longed for in return. At least he was absolutely sure that Bernard wasn't a crook because if that had been the case he would have been only too keen to marry Estelle without any persuasion from him. It also occurred to him that if she married Bernard it might in the end save him money. As it was she was spending a fortune every year on her analyst, not to mention her couturier clothes and the crackpot things she was always getting involved in, in an attempt to find herself. Yes, if she married Bernard at least he'd always know where she was and who she was with. Everything considered, he was more than willing to welcome Bernard into the bosom of his bank account, as well as, of course, into the bosom of his family. Estelle and her father were so keen on Bernard marrying her that one evening, after they'd dined together, they both more or less proposed to him simultaneously, to which he'd experienced the greatest difficulty in avoiding shouting out 'snap' in response.

The only two who didn't find the idea of this marriage so overwhelmingly attractive were Bernard himself and Estelle's octogenarian analyst, Dr Freida Weiss. Dr Weiss was, as it happened, one of the last analysts alive to have been trained by the great Siggy himself, and had arrived here on the same train from Vienna as he did. It was her professional opinion that if the marriage was allowed to take place it would inevitably end in complete disaster. She didn't even feel the slightest need to see Bernard in person to arrive at this judgement, because, as she put it: 'How vos it possible for a man who vos still married to form a lasting and meaningful relationship vis a anozer voman anyvey?' She was also not convinced at all by his apparent stability, especially since almost everything Estelle had told her about him indicated to her that he had all the signs of the long-term depressive personality. That she took this line was very convenient to say the least as far as Bernard was concerned. While he thought he had finally arrived at the point where he was ready to embark on a long-term relationship with a woman, he wasn't anywhere near ready to get a divorce from Olivia. The idea of all those directorships was more than a little appealing, and had he married Estelle and received them it could well have signified his final symbiosis with the Reality Principle, but since he was absolutely sure that he didn't love her, it seemed to him that had he married her, he would not only have been a bigamist but would have ended up in a far bigger mist than he was in already. Even if he had loved her, he couldn't see how – since providing Oscar with his longed for grandchildren was the main purpose of their proposed marriage – he could possibly have agreed to do it, as he'd long ago come to the conclusion that he hadn't the slightest desire to procreate, a decision which hardly seemed to matter much anyway, as there didn't appear to be any shortage of people in the world.

Naturally, once he told Estelle what he'd decided, they gradually began to see less and less of each other. A few months later he heard she'd married a man who had made a fortune in the whole-food business. The last he heard they were living in a Gothic mansion somewhere in California, that had once belonged to the Hollywood starlet, Gloria Ronson, and spent all their time growing organic vegetables, meditating and listening to tapes of their favourite guru (or rather his favourite guru, since it was her husband, Vidal Gold, who was obsessed with the Wisdom of the East, not her). From time to time over the next few months, especially if he was worried about money,

Bernard would wonder what his life would have been like if he'd never had to worry about money again (a phrase Oscar had used that night they'd both proposed to him in the restaurant). Was that also something he was going to have to regret in the future?

It wasn't only women who were attracted to Bernard. All kinds of people, many of them perfect strangers, sometimes after catching a mere glimpse of him, seemed to imagine that he was someone famous, at the very least a television personality or a well-known actor. It all began one afternoon when two small boys came up to him in a department store, just as he was in the middle of the difficult and delicate process of choosing a new bow tie, and insisted he was somebody they'd seen on television. That he denied it made no difference whatsoever, because a little while later when he passed them on his way out, he distinctly heard one say to the other, 'I'm sure he is you know.' And then, it could only have been a week or so later when he was having dinner in Goody's restaurant, as he did most Friday evenings, that the Polish waitress, the one who tinted her hair green (he'd always assumed because she had a lawn fixation, or an overwhelming desire to be at one with nature) after years of avoiding the admiring glances he'd always given her, seemed to want to engage him in conversation. Was he a film director she enquired, as if after all these years she'd suddenly decided she wanted to throw herself on to his casting couch. An even more bizarre experience was that occasion when a fishmonger, to whose shop he had never in his life been before, started to tell him that he definitely knew him from somewhere. For a moment he was obviously struggling to think where that could be, then, with a look on his face as if he'd just had a revelation he said, 'Yes, that's it I've seen you on television.' He became quite aggressive when Bernard insisted that that simply wasn't true because he'd never been on television. Of course he was aware that if you didn't look like everyone else people tended to have all kinds of fantasies about you; that you were on television or in show business were amongst the most obvious ones. Even so, it was an amazing development.

But perhaps all these experiences weren't so strange after all. Apart from the obvious effect working for Sam had on his demeanour, he had always tended, although quite unintentionally, to give the impression of being something he wasn't. People were forever imagining that he must be either rich, aristocratic, or distinguished in some way. He had a bank manager who'd once remarked – when he was especially short of money – 'It must be terribly hard for someone like you Mr Steinway to find yourself in this position,' as if Bernard had been suffering from a case of genteel poverty, instead of mere financial ineptitude, which of course was the real situation. To listen to him anyone would have thought that Bernard had once been the possessor of a great fortune which he had somehow contrived to lose. Even so, suddenly finding himself the object of so much attention, did make Bernard wonder if his real achievement in life wasn't in the end going to be that he happened to look distinguished, rather than it being a consequence of anything he might actually do.

Even more significant than the fantasies he evoked in the minds of people who didn't know him, was that people who really knew him quite well had also begun to come to him for all kinds of advice and help. It was as if they had suddenly reached the conclusion that he knew something they didn't, or by some miracle had become the possessor of great wisdom and profound insight into life's mysteries. This happened so frequently that he soon began to believe that he really was turning into the sage-monger someone once, inaccurately it had seemed then, accused him of being. What was even more astonishing, was that some people began to ask him for business advice, although they must have known that no greater failure as a businessman probably ever existed.

After this had been going on for some time Bernard had the brilliant idea (at least he thought it was brilliant), that if so many people now thought of him as a kind of guiding light, perhaps the thing to do was to set up an ashram of his own. If Baksheesh could do it why shouldn't he? After all it wasn't as if he didn't have any experience of that kind of thing. He'd learnt something about how those places were run from all the time he'd spent at the School for Higher Awareness and Traditional Wisdom and as a follower of Gotsky. All you needed was to know a little more than your customers, plus the usual gobbledegook: a generous supply of incense, a few black and white photographs of holy men in loin clothes, a painting of the elephant lady and off you went. If it was a success he might even end up rich the way the founders of Scientology and Este had. And what lost soul, or seeker after truth, would want to go all the way to the East once he'd discovered that the Y-Shlep Ashram could offer him all the enlightenment he could ever possibly need here at home, for less than the price of the return air fare to India. Not to mention the guarantee that after successfully completing a course at the Ashram he could look forward to success in whatever walk of life he might choose, including, of course, business. Bernard also had the rather innovative idea of awarding enlightenment certificates that would state precisely the degree of enlightenment the holder had achieved during their stay at the Y-Shlep, something that he was absolutely certain didn't exist in any other ashram in the world and which he believed would turn out to be an irresistible selling point.

Naturally he had hoped to get Sam interested in the project. He wasn't at all certain that without him he could really make a go of it. Sam would have made the perfect titular head of the organisation (Bernard envisaged a role for him not unlike that of God: all seeing but invisible) although a photograph of him in flowing robes, with that expression on his face full of insight and scepticism that Bernard admired so much in his portrait, would have made the perfect icon for the Ashram. Unfortunately, although Bernard had imagined that his idea, and especially the entrepreneurial spirit that lay behind it, would have appealed to Sam enormously, he was completely mistaken. Sam had long since peaked as a tycoon and on none of the several occasions Bernard had managed to raise the subject with him, did he seem even remotely interested. And without his advice, encouragement, not to mention his energy, of which he had so much that when he sometimes took Bernard's arm when they went for a walk together, he seemed to be vibrating with it, Bernard knew for certain that he would never be able to overcome his innate lethargy sufficiently to get the project off the ground. How could a man who was easily capable of letting hours (or even days) go by, before he bothered to bend down and pick up a piece of paper that had fallen on the floor by his desk, ever summon up enough energy to start an ashram all on his own. If only he had even ten per cent of the energy of a Sam or an Oscar, who knows what he might have achieved in life!

That such a good idea should have come to nothing was a great pity, especially since he was firmly convinced that there were customers for what he had to offer and it could easily have worked. He certainly did feel he had something to offer. Even Dr Lear once remarked – albeit during one of Bernard's better periods – that he had the makings of a therapeutic personality and could easily see him making a living as a therapist if all else failed. Yes, it really was a great shame, particularly since soon after he had the idea, he began during the afternoons at the office to write a handbook for his future clients in secret, with the provisional title *A New Guide for the Perplexed*. But it was no use being sorry, because it was inevitable, that once Sam had shown so clearly he wasn't interested, it would come to nothing. It was always the same story. Every now and then he'd have a bright idea, become excited about it and then, because of lack of energy, or initiative, he'd do absolutely nothing about it. Wasn't this precisely what happened with his plan to produce videos that, for the first time in history, would enable the dead to speak at their own funerals.

But having to confront yet again his inability to start a business on his own, didn't in the end seem to upset him all that much and a few days later he practically forgot all about it. He still had his sinecure at the office and the sense of purpose that went with it to fall back on. If he wasn't going to bring light into the darkness of the multitude, was it really all that important? Fortunately, unlike Christ, he didn't have God the father, breathing down his neck all the time telling him to get out and save souls. It was one thing to try and help people who happened to come your way but did he actually want to go out looking for them? One thing was certain: he would never have had that extraordinary experience at Uncle Jo's funeral a couple of weeks later, had he not felt just as good about life as before the idea of founding an ashram had ever occurred to him.

On the day of the funeral Bernard was late as usual, so late that he was full of anxiety in case he missed it altogether. When it's a cremation the one thing not to be is unpunctual. A few minutes late and the dear departed can quite literally have departed by the time you arrive. This had very nearly happened at his cousin's funeral a few months before. What a sad business that was. Poor Naomi, despite being a pioneer health fanatic, long before it became fashionable, had been allocated cancer and died a few days before her forty-eighth birthday. On the day of her funeral Bernard arrived so late that there was virtually nothing left for him to do but become incensed by the Rabbi's funeral oration. He couldn't have known her very well, but surely he could have found more to say about her than that she had been a good sister-in-law! She had to have deserved more than that. If they said that about her, what would they say about him? The truth maybe – that he had been profoundly lethargic and one of the greatest worriers the world had ever known. It was the anger Bernard felt that day which had given him the idea of producing videos to enable the dead to have the last word at their own funeral. Not that any amount of editorial advice (an important part of the service Bernard had intended offering) would have helped Uncle Jo very much, because he'd never had anything to say for himself when he was alive anyway.

Fortunately, he wasn't quite as late for Uncle Jo's funeral as he had been for Naomi's but even so, by the time he'd found a seat and began to concentrate on what was going on, his heart was pounding away so ferociously that he thought for a few minutes he might be about to have a heart attack and die, barely a few feet away from where poor old Jo was lying in his coffin. He didn't only feel anxious because he was late, but also because, as he got older, he was becoming increasingly aware that death wasn't only something that happened to other people. Another few years and he'd be lying in one of those coffins himself, and when that day came it wouldn't make any difference that he didn't believe in death, because it was a fate from which no one was ever exempted.

No sooner had he calmed down and become absorbed in listening to the reading of Psalm 23, particularly that part which goes – 'Yea though I walk through the valley of the shadow of death, I will fear no evil, for thou art with me, thy rod and thy staff comfort me,' which Bernard had always found deeply moving (no doubt because he felt he'd at least skirted that valley more than once in his life himself), than he suddenly became absolutely convinced that the man sitting in front of him, whom he had at first thought – since he didn't recognise him – must be one of Uncle Jo's cronies from his days in the sweet trade, or someone from the guest house where he had been living for the past few years, was none other than God himself. What was even stranger, especially for someone with his atheistic inclinations, was the joy he felt that at last he was going to have the opportunity to thank him in person as it were for the way his life had improved so dramatically lately, although how exactly you went about thanking God wasn't immediately clear to him. Should he merely shake his hand and express his gratitude, or perhaps it would be more appropriate to prostrate himself, or even kiss the hem of his garment (he seemed to remember reading that that was the sort of thing they did in the Old Testament). He had to get it right. The last thing he wanted to do was to cause God any embarrassment, especially since he was probably travelling incognito. But if that was the case, why he should have appeared looking so much like God, or at least like everybody's idea of what God looked like, was rather mysterious. If he really didn't want to be recognised: the long biblical beard; those monumental features, which looked as if they had been carved out of marble; that face that expressed not only humour and melancholy but also seemingly depthless wisdom as well, was hardly a good disguise.

But if he was God, literally what on earth was he doing here! Was it possible that Uncle Jo, unbeknown to everyone (including quite obviously the Rabbi who at that point in his funeral oration was saying how he had been kind and generous to everyone he knew, which showed conclusively that he couldn't possibly have met Uncle Jo when he was still amongst the living), had in fact been a deeply pious and religious man. Bernard would have found it amazing had that been true, because he'd always thought that Jo's idea of being Jewish amounted to little more than hating Germans and eating as much Jewish food as possible at every available opportunity. But even if it was true, that in itself wouldn't explain God's presence. Unless God was in the habit of putting in an appearance at the funerals of his favourite followers from time to time (who consisted perhaps mainly of those who had practised their Judaism so assiduously in their lifetimes that they had become perfect at it by the time of their deaths); and even on occasion chose to lead the delegation that came to welcome them to the after-life in person. Perhaps he even considered this to be his sacred duty as chief Heavenly Host?

Once the service had ended and Bernard went over to where God was standing surrounded by a small group of people (not that he had decided yet what he was going to say or do when he finally came face to face with him), he realised almost immediately that he had made a big mistake, and the whole thing was just another one of his crazy fantasies. No, however much that man might look the way one would have expected God to look, it couldn't possibly be him. It wasn't just the extraordinarily loud hounds-tooth jacket he was wearing that convinced him of this, although one would have expected God to have dressed in a much more conservative way (a three-piece navy blue suit with a gold watch chain strung across his middle would have been more like it – since who could be more conservative than God), but his accent was the real give away. It just wasn't credible that God, who after all apparently came from the Mediterranean, would appear amongst us and speak in a Scottish accent. An Israeli or Arab accent would have seemed the most appropriate, an Italian, Spanish, or even a Greek or Turkish one, might have been believable, but a Scottish brogue was just out of the question. Nor was it likely that God would have been able to resist such a good opportunity as a visit to earth to deliver his new and revised edition of the ten commandments in person, including no doubt number eleven: Thou Shalt Not Moan. It certainly wasn't possible that they hadn't been revised in all this time. Hard as he looked Bernard couldn't see any sign: no bulge under his jacket; no package wrapped up in ancient newspaper; and there were definitely no stone tablets anywhere to be seen, although he wouldn't have expected that anyway, since there had to have been progress, even in heaven. Everything considered, whoever this man turned out to be, he wasn't God and however grateful Bernard might feel for the new life he had been given, it looked as if he was just going to have to keep his gratitude to himself.

One thing puzzled him though – how was it possible for an atheist like him to suddenly find himself in the grip of a fantasy like this in the first place?

4

Bernard had changed a great deal since he first went to work for Sam. It wasn't just that he felt better, or that he seemed to exercise a peculiar fascination over other people, but that he had begun to feel freer and much more self-assertive than ever before. The well behaved quiet boy his mother used to boast about, and who he had continued to be until long after his childhood had ended, seemed to have gone for ever. Perhaps he had never been really good at all, only repressed. One evening he even came close to telling his mother to shut up when she started yet again to tell him what an awful man his father had been and what a terrible life she'd had with him, although when it came to it he couldn't bring himself to but instead adopted his usual tactic which was to withdraw into himself and wait patiently for her to finish. After all, he thought, if he had put up with listening to her bitter reminiscences for all these years, surely it was far too late now, when she was nearly eighty years old, not to carry on doing so to the end. But with others he wasn't nearly as inclined to be so forbearing and had recently developed such a reputation for candour that people hesitated to invite him over for dinner, for fear of what he might say to the other guests. They weren't wrong either. He hadn't behaved very well when he'd gone one Friday evening to have dinner with a born-again Jewish vegetarian couple. Admittedly, it had been very annoying to have to sit there in the fading light in the dining room (naturally, with their new found beliefs they couldn't very well turn the light on) while trying to appear to be enjoying the egg-free chola, the locshen and carrots in what appeared to be aspic jelly and the caffeine-free Japanese bonzai tea, amongst the other delicacies that they put in front of him. And if that wasn't enough to put up with, sitting opposite him was a deeply unattractive woman in her late thirties (the kind of woman who if his father, great chauvinist that he was, had ever seen he would have said 'shouldn't be allowed out'). She wore a broach on her breast in the shape of a key (which Bernard, rather unkindly concluded, no one in her whole life had ever wanted to turn) and had clearly been invited for his benefit. Even so, it was rather extreme to have got up even before the meal had ended, told them that he couldn't bear to listen to them talk all that rubbish about religion any longer, and walked out of the house – a way of behaving that he would have found inconceivable even a few months previously.

As he went about his ordinary everyday life Bernard noticed that he had begun to act in ways he hardly recognised. Now, when he paid his weekly visit to Greens, to purchase his favourite childhood foods and to get his regular dose of aromatherapy, by leaning over the delicatessen counter and inhaling the mingled aromas of the pickled herrings, fried fish, chopped liver and the viennas and salamis decked out in their gay, bright red, synthetic skins, he was no longer intimidated by the aggressive young businessmen clamouring to be served, or by the aging Viennese widows who always assumed – wherever their place in the queue really was – that they must be ahead of him. When his turn came there was no question of holding back, he simply demanded to be served.

One Sunday morning he was even bold enough to tell Mcpherson, a diminutive, choleric Glaswegian, who in the past Bernard had found positively frightening, and who lorded it over the sides of smoked salmon (it was in his power to decide whether one received the finest or merely the best smoked salmon, a decision based on the generosity of the tip he received), that by slicing the salmon from the tail up towards the head he was doing it the wrong way. Bernard knew he was right, because his uncle Lou had devoted his whole life to slicing salmon. Mcpherson was furious and said that Bernard should clear out of the shop and never come back. He probably would have assaulted him had not some of the other assistants restrained him. But Bernard didn't in the least regret what he'd said (although it meant he wouldn't be able to show his face in there ever again), if only because he felt that Uncle Lou would have felt that his whole life had been in vain if he'd witnessed the abominations carried out on those poor dead fish.

But it was how he reacted when he saw Olivia and Christopher walking hand in hand in the park one afternoon, which finally led him to conclude that something really fundamental must have changed in his whole personality. He'd seen them together before, apart from that first time when he arrived at the hospital to find Christopher sitting at Olivia's bedside, and sensed almost instantly something between them.

It had happened several times subsequently. There was that terrible evening when he'd seen them embracing on a street corner as he drove past, an experience which, naturally enough, had given him several sleepless nights. But although every time it happened he'd felt like punching Christopher on the nose, or knocking him down with the car, or at the very least, as his mother would say, giving him what for, he had always acted completely in character and done absolutely nothing; although he invariably told Olivia that he was going to do one of those things the very next time he saw them together, which of course she didn't believe for one minute. He'd always avoided confrontations, partly because he was aware that he lacked the necessary aggressiveness but also out of a feeling of apprehension that when it came to it, instead of punching whoever it was at the time on the nose, he would end up being sympathetic and friendly, which was precisely what had happened years ago when his girlfriend ran off with a close friend of his. He had rushed round there almost as soon as she told him but then, instead of punching Jerry on the nose, or at the very least, telling him what he thought of him, they had ended up having a completely civilised conversation about what had happened, after which he found himself beginning to feel sympathetic for what Jerry must have been was going through. It was to ensure that nothing like that ever happened again that Bernard had tended to avoid confrontations ever since. The last thing he would have wanted was for something similar to have happened with Christopher and so he reserved the expression of his real feelings for when he was alone at home. Then would he allow himself to make a fist and take a swing at that much hated nose, and when that wasn't sufficiently satisfying he would, on occasion, give the chaise longue a really good kick.

On that particular afternoon when he saw them coming towards him in the distance, he didn't even attempt to suggest to Issidore Popoff, his old teacher from the university, with whom he'd just had lunch, that they should wait for a few minutes behind some nearby trees until they'd gone past, or better still, avoid them altogether by going in another direction. Instead, Bernard found himself rushing towards them and before he'd even thought what he was going to do, he had given Christopher a great shove in the chest, with the result that he fell into a puddle. By the look on Olivia's face she was clearly astonished by his behaviour, which was hardly surprising since she'd never seen him do anything remotely like that ever before. She became quite hysterical and started to shout at him to stop; although by then Bernard wasn't doing anything at all, except looking down at where Christopher was still lying in the mud and trying to resist the temptation to offer him a hand up. He was practically as astonished at what he'd done as she was. But most of all he was absolutely delighted that at last he'd been able to express what he'd always felt about their liaison and so skillfully as well. He couldn't have done it better had he been one of those experts in the martial arts who use the strength of their opponent to overwhelm them. It was also a relief that he hadn't ended up doing anything as undignified as rolling in the mud, or as painful as breaking his fingers because he still didn't really know how to make a fist properly. But of course that wasn't entirely unrelated to the fact that Christopher (he wasn't called Christ Bearer for nothing) as a one-time follower of Gotsky, obviously still adhered to the injunction not to engage in any acts of violence, even in self-defence. Something which Bernard must have been dimly aware of somewhere in the back of his mind, though naturally he would have objected most strongly to any suggestion that it had made the slightest difference to how he'd acted.

Nothing could diminish his pleasure at what had happened, especially since it had taken place in the presence of Olivia whom he felt, once she recovered from the shock, couldn't fail to be impressed that he had at last behaved like a real man. It was also deeply satisfying that Popoff happened to be there, not only because Popoff was very sympathetic, having already devoted many hours of his life to listening to him go on and on about his feelings for Olivia, while he lay on the old, red-leather couch in the study (Popoff not having the theoretical objections to Bernard lying down when misery overwhelmed him, that Dr Lear did), but also because Popoff had developed over the years into yet another of Bernard's father figures, who he constantly found himself trying to impress with his achievements in life. In that respect, he made an ideal stand-in for Bernard's father; it being unfortunately impossible to bring back the dead for the great occasions in our lives, when, more than anything, we would like them to witness our triumphs. And if this wasn't a great occasion, at least it was a deeply significant one. Bernard couldn't remember having asserted himself in such a clear and unambiguous way since he was a small boy. Not since that day at primary school when he had steeled himself to push over an older boy who had been persistently bullying him for weeks, either because Bernard's long trousers were too short, or because he didn't like the look of his face. It couldn't but be significant that now, nearly thirty years later, he had done the almost identical thing again. Could this possibly mean that out of the wreckage of the grown man's life, a new, almost child-like, aggressive and self-assertive Bernard was rising to the surface at last? A man who would no longer be prepared to put up with slights or insults and who would always be able to express what he felt and – most importantly – at the precise moment he felt it? Was this the final proof then that he was at last becoming a free and unrepressed human being? If he carried on like this, he would soon resemble his late Russian grandfather, who had had no hesitation in losing his temper and storming out of the room when he realised that he hadn't been left all the money in his son's will. Perhaps now complete self-fulfilment itself was just round the corner? But even if that was too much to hope for he had acted with far more freedom than ever before in his whole life.

Bernard's personality wasn't quite as transformed as he liked to think, but what happened in the park that day convinced him, more than anything else, that he must be cured at last. After all, if being able to assert himself like that didn't mean that he had finally achieved the greater degree of freedom which Dr Lear had always insisted was the real purpose of his therapy, then what did? He felt his treatment had been going on for far too long, although it was only two years since he'd first sat in that old armchair opposite Dr Lear and commenced going over his past, in an attempt to try and discover how he had managed to arrive at the position which he sometimes summed up as: Life ten, Steinway nil.

There was no doubt that he felt much better than that now, which could only mean that the time had come for him to take responsibility for his own life once again, and give up running to Dr Lear every week. Dr Lear had never really given him any answers anyway. Instead of at least pointing him in the right direction, all he ever did with his long silences, preposterous suggestions (like the time he tried to suggest that the woman in one of Bernard's dreams was really a man) and irritating habit of answering a question with a question, was to throw Bernard back on his – at the time – nearly non-existent inner resources. The occasion Bernard had gone to see him complaining of being unable to sleep all night, after having listened to two Beethoven piano sonatas consecutively was typical. Surely he could have thought of something more helpful to say other than, 'The real question you have to ask yourself Bernard is why you did it in the first place.' Yes, a fine Virgil he'd turned out to be! It was things like that which sometimes made him wonder if his therapy hadn't been a complete waste of time, and that the only reason he felt as he did was simply because time had passed, or because of the beneficial effect working for Sam had on him.

But he knew that this wasn't entirely true. He couldn't imagine having been able to deal with Christopher the way he had without first having undergone all that therapy. Whatever the real truth was, it was absolutely obvious from what had been happening, or rather not happening, during his recent sessions with Dr Lear, that his therapy was drawing to a close all by itself. More and more often lately they just seemed to be going over the same old ground. Frequently, he couldn't think of anything new to say at all and instead would jokingly suggest that perhaps they should play last week's tape over again, though in reality there was no tape. All of which led him inevitably to the conclusion that, if he now had so little to say it had to mean that all his troubles were over, and that having finally got everything off his chest at last, his therapy must be at an end.

If only that had turned out to be really true. It didn't and it wasn't long after leaving his analyst that Bernard once again found himself slipping back into one of those familiar depressive states. Not only did his old symptoms begin to re-appear – as if sensing that the coast was now clear – but new ones seemed to be developing as well. Worst of all, he soon realised that far from being cured of his obsession with Olivia, now that he no longer had the opportunity to talk about her freely every week, he was more pre-occupied with her than ever. After a longish period in which they had hardly communicated at all, he began to telephone her all the time, and when he wasn't talking to her on the phone, he often caught himself holding imaginary conversations with her in his head. He also started to dream about her and one night woke up in a cold sweat after having dreamt that he had attended her funeral.

Bernard tried to persuade himself that things weren't nearly as bad as they felt, or that what he was experiencing was what anyone would have to go through when they gave up their therapy. It was probably temporary and the best course of action was to be stoical and simply wait for it to pass. The last thing he wanted was to have to go running back to Dr Lear because he couldn't cope; especially after he had so confidently told him that he couldn't imagine anything ever happening which would make him want to come back, although admittedly he had felt rather anxious a few moments after he'd said it.

What finally convinced him that how he felt wasn't transitory and that he had been deluding himself in thinking he was cured, was what happened one morning on the way to work. He must have passed the window of that medical bookshop hundreds of times before without paying any particular attention to it, but that morning those books on the revolving perspex stand, which purported to offer ways of coping with among other things: anxiety, depression, insomnia, panic attacks, claustrophobia, agoraphobia, anti-success patterns, phobic life styles, chronic procrastination, performance anxiety and post-natal depression, made an enormous impact on him. With the exception of post natal depression (even he had his limits), he was aware that he suffered from all of those conditions; and moreover, it was beginning to look as if he would continue to suffer from one or other of them, until he finally ended up like the skeleton that was propped up on the other side of the window, and which, at that moment, seemed to be laughing at him, as if it was aware of everything that was passing through his head. If that shop had been open he would have gone in and bought every one of the books that even remotely applied to him. Now he understood why Dr Lear had been so sceptical when he had appeared that day and with complete confidence declared he was cured. He remembered him saying, 'Oh, have it your way if you like Bernard, but it's all a lot of nonsense. No one is ever really cured you know, least of all someone with a depressive personality like yours. The symptoms might come and go but there's no real cure.' Could it have been possible that he'd known even then that his apparent stability and feeling of well-being was nothing more than another one of his periods of remission, and that it wouldn't be long before he collapsed back into his usual state of anxiety and depression once more?

As Bernard walked home that evening he began to wonder yet again whether, since he still seemed to have so many psychological problems, he had gained anything at all from having therapy. Was it possible that all that energy he'd spent excavating his past had been a complete waste of time? On the positive side, he had been able to show Olivia's boyfriend exactly what he thought of him at last, and he was clearly more aware of what went on inside him than ever before. But what good was that if, instead of making life easier, it was now even more difficult than ever? Wasn't the world full of people who didn't have the vaguest idea about their inner life and yet nevertheless managed to function perfectly well? It seemed to Bernard that he was now so acutely aware of how he felt about everything that even doing the simplest thing, like going to the dentist, had become practically impossible. It might be true that the unexamined life isn't worth living, but was an examined one really livable? Perhaps he would have been better off if he'd left his inner life where it belonged – on the inside. But maybe he'd got it all wrong, and that what had happened was that having brought everything to the surface, instead of reaching the end of his treatment, as he'd thought, he had only arrived at the beginning. If so, there was only one thing to do – to go back to Dr Lear and begin his treatment all over again. Only this time he would have to be prepared to take it to a much deeper level and carry on until absolutely every one of his problems was completely resolved, even if it meant going every day, and ending up being quite unable to recognise himself. After all, with his position at the office, it wasn't as if he couldn't now afford it. The question was though: could he really face going through all that?

The Beginning of the End

When Bernard woke up again a couple of hours later he felt awful. But then how else could he expect to feel when, instead of the deep refreshing sleep he had longed for when he'd gone to bed especially early the night before (he had hoped to sleep not just like a log but like a whole forest), he had hardly slept at all. True, he had dozed off from time to time, but what he had really been engaged in most of the night, when, that is, he wasn't being devoured by nightmares about Olivia, was reviewing his past life. Hardly an activity conducive to waking up feeling calm and refreshed. It wasn't even as if he could any longer get through it all in the space of one night's insomnia. No, there was far too much of it now for that to be possible, not that it would have mattered all that much if he had been able to, because these nocturnal enquiries could hardly be called fruitful. He never reached any lasting conclusions about his life which altered anything very much. But that wasn't surprising since, instead of thinking clearly, what he'd been doing all night was worrying, an activity at which he was becoming – if that was at all possible – more and more accomplished as he grew older, so accomplished in fact that he sometimes contemplated offering to do other peoples' worrying for them.

The terrible thing was that the nights he couldn't sleep were becoming almost as frequent as those in which he could; proof, if any was really needed, that he was still deeply troubled by many things in his life, including of course his unresolved feelings for Olivia. Recently though, he had finally reached the conclusion that they would never be resolved, and that the pain he felt would be there like a dark shadow round his heart until the very end. Perhaps, after all, he should have resumed his treatment with Dr Lear. But even if he'd gone there every day he doubted if that would have been enough to have made any significant difference. It was nights like these which made him feel that what he needed was not just a few hours of therapy a week, but the constant companionship of a psychiatrist day and night. Someone who, rather in the manner of the private tutors of aristocratic families in the nineteenth century, would take up residence in his flat and devote himself exclusively to Bernard's well-being. A person who would be in a perfect position to keep his mental state under constant observation, and to advise him on any course of action he was contemplating before he decided whether or not to take it. Yes, that would be the last word in luxury, and was certainly far superior to employing the kind of decrepit and unreliable retainer he had often read about with such pleasure in Russian novels. A valet, after all, could hardly be expected to do more than advise you which coat to put on, or see to it that you always left the house respectably dressed, even if his presence ensured that you were spared the worst vicissitudes of the solitary life, and that you never had to prepare your own meals or pour a drink for yourself ever again. But this was just another one of his fantasies and perhaps what he ought to do now was to consider the more realistic alternative of attempting to become one of Olivia's patients. A few months previously, Olivia had finally, at least partially, forsaken the spiritual path to become a holistic therapist specialising in re-birthing techniques, or was it some sort of mind clearing therapy? He was never quite sure. Not that it mattered much, since the idea of going back to the beginning and starting all over again was just as appealing as having his mind vacuumed and all his worries swept away. And having Olivia as his therapist would also have the advantage of enabling him to see her once or twice a week.

But still, if he had his troubles (and who didn't!) at least he didn't get deeply depressed the way he used to. Or, to be precise, when he got depressed he somehow contrived not to take it personally, which was quite an achievement for someone who, according to Dr Lear, had a depressed man inside him who was constantly looking for an opportunity to break out and take over altogether. Perhaps after thirty-six years he had finally found a way of getting along with himself. He used to think that this had a lot to do with working for Sam, and there was little doubt it had helped to improve his self-esteem. But this change in him could just as easily be a consequence of age. Time seemed to rush past so quickly now, he sometimes wondered if the perforations in the hour glass of his life hadn't become bigger. It was certainly clear to him now that he simply no longer had the time to devote weeks, or even months, of his life to being depressed, the way he had when he was younger. Perhaps at last he'd understood the true significance of his friend Maurice's observation, 'that depression was just a waste of time', although when he first heard him say it he remembered feeling that he was just being unsympathetic and simply trying to shut him up.

Bernard stopped staring up at the ceiling, turned on his right side, lit a cigarette and looked at one of the many clocks on the bedside table. There were so many of them because every few months he became immune to the alarm of the current one and had to go out and replace it. The present one was supposed to be the loudest on the market, and sounded as if it was designed to announce the onset of a nuclear bombardment, rather than to drive a nearly middle-aged neurotic like himself from sleep. Not that a clock had ever been made which didn't make him feel uneasy. He only had to look at one to imagine that the hands were just about to lift up off the face and point accusingly at him, as if to say: 'Are you going to waste the next hour the way you wasted the last one?' But then hadn't he often thought that anxiety was in reality only the acute perception of time. Still, for the time being he could go on lying there, since there was nearly an hour before he really would have to drag himself out of bed. God knows he hated getting up in the morning. But why did he always use that expression when he didn't even believe in God? As far as he was concerned the day could just as easily begin after lunch, thus getting rid of the necessity of having mornings altogether, as if they were the pages of a tedious book that you skipped because you couldn't be bothered to read them. The difficulty he experienced getting up was yet another way Bernard resembled his father. Bernard never remembered him ever getting up before eleven a.m., but then he had often been out most of the night carousing, or had stayed awake late, reading and smoking huge Havana cigars in bed. Recently, Bernard had begun to think that his father had been depressed for years, from the time when he'd been forced to come home just before the war, and had to abandon his elegant way of life in that villa near Lake Como. What had he been like as a young man?

Bernard had no idea, but then large areas of our parents' lives always remain a mystery. Yes, he must have inherited his melancholy disposition from him. He was slow like he had been too. He'd noticed that after the yoga classes he'd started to attend lately, he was always the last out of the changing room, no matter how many clothes he was wearing. Observing himself getting dressed reminded Bernard of the slow, meticulous way his father used to trim his moustache in the morning. But it wasn't just mornings Bernard hated: he hated all beginnings. In that respect death would probably not be all that bad after all. At least it always came at the end.

But he couldn't do what he liked any longer, not while he worked for Sam at any rate. Sam was obsessed by punctuality, and was much more concerned with his arriving at the office on time, than about anything he might do when he was there. Fortunately, when Bernard glanced at the clock, he saw that, although, as is its nature, more time had passed since he last looked, there was nearly half an hour still left to put the finishing touches to his worries before he really would have to get up and face the day, or risk yet another dressing down for being late again.

Once Bernard had finally managed to drag himself out of bed and had drunk a couple of espressos, he began to feel better. Being in the vertical seemed to encourage the anguish he had been going through all night to descend to his feet. But the coffee helped a great deal too. There had been a time when he'd almost believed that several cups of strong black coffee, taken after about half a litre of chicken soup was a cure for depression, or at least a way of alleviating the worst symptoms of it. Certainly, having the two together was very stimulating. He'd thought, on occasion in the past, that he felt low because he was suffering from caffeine deprivation, but since he'd bought that espresso machine (a mammoth relic of the 1960s made out of chrome and cream plastic) that couldn't any longer possibly be the case. Perhaps this wasn't such a mad idea anyway. After all, it was no secret that coffee gives you a lift, and depression, whatever else it might be, was definitely a descent. Sometimes, when he felt it coming on, he could almost hear a voice in his head – rather like one of those old-fashioned lift attendants in a department store – shouting out 'going down'. Yes, that was something he'd done a lot of in his life.

Bernard got up from the table where he'd been sitting and went over and looked out of the window. It was a cold grey day. Down below him in the park the trees were almost bare. There wasn't much to see, just the usual people hurrying to work, or walking their dogs, and the inevitable joggers; about whom, Bernard had long ago reached the conclusion that they weren't so much trying to keep fit, as expressing a desire to run away. Looking out of the window only made him feel bleak, so after a few minutes he made another coffee, turned on the radio and sat down again. He'd never thought he'd end up like this. Once he'd thought the world was at his feet, now it often seemed as if it was on his head. He remembered how the night before he got married he felt so happy and excited he had gone out and walked the streets for hours. Maybe he'd been too happy then. Now he had no desire to be happy. The most he hoped for was a little of everything: a little contentment, a little anguish, a little sadness, and occasional periods – days, hours, or even just moments of happiness. The last thing he wanted was to be marooned in any one of those states.

Perhaps it was his fate to end up on his own. Maybe he really was a lone wolf like his mother always said. He'd never been very successful with women. The idea of sustaining a relationship with someone for a lifetime seemed to him one of the most ambitious of all human endeavours, and one that often failed, though some men nevertheless managed it. He couldn't any longer imagine it ever happening to him. Sometimes, he thought that intimacy itself brought out the worst in him. He'd always found it difficult to be consistently open to someone else, consistently on call. Sometimes he was and sometimes he wasn't. If he was woken up in the middle of the night because the woman he was sleeping with felt unwell, he wasn't always able to be as sympathetic as he imagined most men could be. He'd never entirely recovered from the sense of failure he'd felt when Olivia had that serious attack of food poisoning in a cheap hotel in Agrigento, and all he'd wanted to do was to pretend it wasn't happening and go back to sleep. Admittedly, that had occurred in one of his most depressed periods but even so there was no excuse for the way he'd behaved.

Perhaps he was hopeless at love altogether. Recently he'd begun to think of love as just a kind of disease. Not an entirely unreasonable way of looking at it, when you think that one of the major characteristics of being in love is a sudden distaste for your own company. If love meant anything at all to him, it was as an extreme form of friendship, but it was friendship in its milder forms that had always been been his real forte. It had never been difficult for him to give himself unreservedly to other people, at least for a short while. Total intimacy with someone else had intrusion built into it. With an intimate relationship the loved one feels entitled to judge and criticise. If they feel you are not giving them enough, or in the right way, they don't hesitate to point it out. It was this that Bernard always found so hard to tolerate. Why should he even bother to contemplate the possibility of living with someone else when he managed quite well on his own? Most of the time he didn't mind sleeping on his own. He often felt it was a real necessity to be able to withdraw into himself for those few minutes before descending into the dark solitude of sleep. Anyway, he had never really liked being cuddled much, which could just as easily make him feel claustrophobic as comforted. Maybe he just wasn't suited for a life on the pillow.

For years people had said that he had a strong feminine side, and it was true. He was very good at looking after himself. He cooked well; he was a discriminating buyer of food. He knew exactly when and where to go to obtain the delicacies he liked so much. He enjoyed buying and arranging flowers. He sometimes wondered, since he was so bad at relationships and had such a developed feminine side, if he shouldn't perhaps add to his aims in life, that of becoming his own Jewish mother; so that his feminine side could look after his masculine side even more successfully than he, or rather she, had done in the past.

Bernard had known for some time that the most important relationship he had to sustain in life was with himself. Perhaps in this respect, the loneliness he often experienced was a small price to pay for the solitude he seemed to need so much. Being alone might also have a positive side. If he really was able to carry on like this, when the time came to have his final illness, at least he wouldn't inflict on anyone else the anguish of watching him die, and the grief they would experience after it was over. So even choosing to be alone, which was so often considered selfish, could in the end become a form of altruism, but he wasn't convinced that he was going to be be able to keep it up much longer. Too often lately the pleasures of solitude had a way of turning into loneliness. Last night he'd felt so lonely and restless that he had wandered from room to room not knowing what to do with himself. It only took a week of having breakfast with the radio to make him realise that he wouldn't be able to carry on this way much longer. He must have been deceiving himself when he'd told his niece a few weeks before, that he wouldn't in the least mind ending up a lonely old man. The truth was that more and more often lately the idea of having to go all the way to the terminus by himself filled him with anxiety and a sense of foreboding.

No, although he had a strong inclination towards the bachelor life, and was probably able to cope much better than most men with living alone, it wasn't the whole story. He had lapses. There were times when he wished he were in love, times when he longed to put a dent in the infinity of loneliness we all feel from time to time. It was then that he realised that there was no escaping the universal truth: that man is born of woman and it is his fate to have to spend the rest of his life trying to keep on good terms with them. If he was honest with himself, he really didn't feel all that different from that day when a student of his at Dullworth had so charmingly and naively asked him, where she could go to fall in love, and he had responded without thinking for a second that if he knew that he'd go there himself. There was no doubt about it, he needed a woman in his life. But the question was: how far in?

Still, the first thing he had to do was to find one. Not that he thought that would be very difficult. The world was full of women. Apart from the obvious fact that everyone who wasn't a man was one, marriages were failing so frequently now that the supply of available women was growing all the time. It was also the case, that as time passed Bernard was beginning to find himself a victim of that old injustice – that an older man invariably finds it easier to find a companion than does an older woman. At his age he could play the whole field, from the fading divorcee to women in their twenties, for whom he was old enough to offer the stabilising delights of the older man experience. Mrs Gestetner, the elderly widow who lived downstairs, who was forever going on at him about his solitary way of life, and whose knowledge of the widow and divorcee market was without equal, was always telling him that he could find a woman without any trouble at all. She suggested once that he might consider marrying for money. According to her a man of his obvious charm ought to be worth at least three or four hundred thousand pounds. It was Mrs Gestetner also, who had wanted to introduce him to an apparently charming thirty year old Romanian widow. That she was so young made him oddly apprehensive. He couldn't help worrying about the reason for her being such a young widow. Far better to find a woman for himself, even if it meant advertising, or pounding the streets wearily with a sandwich-board. At least now he knew exactly the kind of woman he was looking for – someone who was beautiful, wealthy, very intelligent, independent, sensual, selfless, generous, giving, a wonderful lover and an excellent cook. He was convinced that all he had to do was place an advertisement in the papers and he would be besieged by applicants. It wasn't as if he had nothing to offer. He might not be the greatest of breadwinners, but at least he was relatively stable, amusing and about as mature as he was ever going to be. Only the week before his old teacher, Professor Popoff, had volunteered the opinion that Bernard was easily the most contented man he knew, and how that would inevitably make him very attractive to women (although if he was right Bernard couldn't help wondering what sort of a terrible state the other men he knew were in). Even Olivia had recently said that anyone would want to be with him, anyone that is but her he supposed.

Taking everything into account: his age, his improved mental state, the favourable condition of the market, he shouldn't have any difficulty in finding exactly the sort of relationship he wanted, which, it was becoming increasingly clear to him, given the peculiarities of his personality, could only be a part-time one. What he needed was a relationship with some incomparably beautiful woman for holidays, weekends and the occasional weekday afternoon or evening, which was as satisfying as it was uncommitted. She had to be beautiful because, since he found all women so difficult to deal with, it was definitely preferable to have one who was at least lovely to look at. So perhaps the answer to the question – as to how far he should allow a woman into his life – was perfectly simple: not too far.

The face that stared at Bernard from the bathroom mirror as he shaved, looked old and haggard. Was it possible that he'd aged overnight? Could that be white hair in his beard, Bernard wondered, bending over the wash-basin and splashing water on his face, which removed the shaving soap but only revealed the white hair even more clearly than before. It was another sign that he was getting older, as was the hair that had lately started to sprout from his ears, which made him feel that any day now he would turn into a Orang-utan. The anxious expression on his face was also worrying. His only hope was that other people wouldn't notice it. Olivia had once remarked, when she had been standing beside him in the bathroom, that the way he looked in the mirror wasn't how he really looked. An observation he found tremendously disconcerting at the time. If that wasn't how he looked then what did he look like? How could he possibly feel secure about himself if the inner man had only a vague idea of how the outer man appeared to the world. Of one thing he was certain: he didn't have one of those faces which perfectly conceal how you are feeling. Anyone could tell what sort of a state he was in just by looking at him for a moment or two. But whatever the precise truth about his looks was, it seemed to Bernard that they were bad enough to make it imperative he set about finding a woman, before he lost them altogether.

If only he'd had just one wholly successful relationship with a woman to look back on. Instead of which, probably the best one he'd ever had (apart from the first years of his relationship with his mother of course) was with Dahlia, his dental hygienist, whom he had been visiting every three months or so for the past five or six years. His relationship with her was perfect. He'd never been in love with her, or even for a moment considered attempting to make love to her. On the one occasion they'd met by chance outside the surgery, and had coffee together, it soon became obvious to both of them that they had almost nothing in common. All that ever happened during all those half hours they spent together, was that he lay down in the chair while she bent over him and cleaned his teeth until they became quite unnaturally white. True, he did sometimes feel as if he was in her arms – and there were times when he quite consciously flirted with her by looking deeply into her beautiful blue eyes. At this she barely responded and simply continued to concentrate on his teeth as if nothing unusual had happened. Admittedly, she did sometimes give him little presents to take home – a tube of toothpaste or a packet of dental floss – but by far the most intimate thing that ever happened between them was that he always kissed her on the cheek before leaving and, on those days when she wasn't in a rush to see her next patient, he might also linger for a few minutes and flirt with her, but only in the mildest possible way. The truly wonderful thing about their relationship was that in all the time he'd been seeing her, they'd never once had a single row, or even a moment's misunderstanding. It was a relationship which worked perfectly. Yes, Bernard thought, moving closer to the mirror, and looking carefully at his discoloured teeth, it would soon be time to telephone for another appointment.